INNOCENT LIES

ROBIN PATCHEN

JDO PUBLISHING

For Jacob.

From baby to back-flipper to skateboarder to social media star. I can't wait to see what God has in store for you next.

I know it'll be good.

ALSO BY ROBIN PATCHEN

Chasing Amanda

Finding Amanda

A Package Deal (part of the Matched Online anthology)

Hidden Truth series

Convenient Lies

Twisted Lies

Generous Lies

Innocent Lies

ACKNOWLEDGMENTS

There are so many people involved in creating a story like this.

First, thank you to Amy Byers from the New Hampshire Department of Health and Human Services for your expertise in foster care and abandoned children.

Thank you, Quid Pro Quills—Kara Hunt, Jericha Kingston, Candice Sue Patterson, and Pegg Thomas. Also, thanks to Sharon Srock and Terri Weldon. Your critiques make me a better writer, and I'm proud to call each of you friend.

Thank you to my line editor, Normandie Fischer, for not being afraid to tell me the truth about bad scenes.

Thank you, Ray Rhamey, for your insightful edits.

Thank you, Lacy Williams and Misty Beller, for your marketing brilliance.

Thank you to my family, and a special thanks to Jacob, the inspiration for Daniel.

And, of course, thank you to my Lord Jesus Christ for the grace that made this story possible.

ONE

"My name is Daniel Anderson. My mama's name is Carrie. I don't have a daddy. I am eight years old."

Daniel repeated the words over and over, holding onto them the same way he was gripping the skinny tree in the forest.

Mama had told him to walk to the white house and knock. Not that there were any other houses around here, deep in these woods. Seemed easy when Mama was standing beside him. With her gone, the house seemed far away, and he had to get through all the trees and bushes and stuff.

He shivered, and his teeth chattered. He couldn't make them stop. He let go of the tree and stuck his hands under his armpits. Didn't help. Nothing was warm. Not even his toes. He wriggled them but couldn't feel anything. They should have been toasty in his new boots.

It hadn't been snowing when they first got here. Now, Mama was gone, and snowflakes were falling everywhere, sort of hiding the house.

And it was getting dark. What would happen if the sun went all the way down before he got up his nerve?

There was nothing between here and the back door but woods and trees and probably bears. Except bears hibernated in the winter. He'd learned that in school. He probably wasn't gonna get eaten by a bear.

He'd just freeze like a snowman.

What if the man there wasn't as nice as Mama said? Just 'cause he was a police officer didn't mean he was nice, right? Except Daniel had only ever met nice ones. If only he could get up the nerve to go like she told him to.

"My name is Daniel Anderson. My mama's name is Carrie. I don't have a daddy. I am eight years old."

The words were mostly true.

Daniel took a few steps toward the house and tried not to cry. 'Cause he was too old to cry, and anyway, Mama told him he had to be strong. He wished she was with him. He'd hang on tight and beg her not to leave him, no matter what she said. It made no sense to him. If it was okay for Daniel to talk to the police officer, why couldn't Mama?

He turned and stared at the forest behind him. Maybe she'd change her mind. Maybe she'd come back for him. If he went to the house and found the police officer, then Mama wouldn't come back, not right away. Maybe not ever, even though she promised she would. She'd never broken a promise before. But she'd never left him in the woods before, either. He stared behind him as far as he could see. If he went that way, he might get lost and never get found again. Except by the bears. They were sleeping, weren't they?

And anyway, he'd promised to go to the house.

She shouldn't have made him promise. That wasn't fair. Mama was usually fair, but not this time.

A noise came from the house. Daniel turned, saw the back door open.

A big yellow dog came outside, a man right behind him. The man was wearing jeans and a sweater, but no coat or hat. He probably just wanted to make sure the dog did his business, as Caleb's mama would say. "Make sure he does his business before you let that mangy mutt back in the house."

Daniel always laughed at that, because the mangy mutt, Peanut, was little and cute. Caleb's mama practically treated it like another son.

Daniel missed Caleb. He missed Caleb's mama and Peanut and everybody from back home. Mostly, he missed his own mama, and she'd only been gone a little while.

The dog stepped down onto the snow and sniffed the air. This was no cute little dog. It was a big dog. Its head came up, and it stared into the forest, right at Daniel.

Then it bounded across the yard, straight toward him.

The man hollered after it. "Magic!"

But the dog kept running. Daniel told himself to run, to get away from that crazy dog, but his feet might as well have been stuck to the ground.

He knew that dog was gonna take a big bite out of him. He fell on the ground and covered his head. Wasn't until he was like that that he remembered the food in his backpack. The dog would probably attack his back to get at the beef jerky and granola bars Mama had left him.

Mama. Why? Why did she leave him? How would she feel when she found out the nice policeman's mean dog had eaten him for supper?

Bushes shimmied, snow plopped. The dog's huffing breaths came closer and closer. It nuzzled his ear, his hat, his backpack, too, probably, but Daniel didn't dare look.

"Magic, come." The man's voice was closer.

The dog barked three times.

Twigs snapped. The dog panted into the near silence.

"What'd you find, girl?" The man's voice was deep and kind, even though the dog disobeyed him. Maybe he was a nice man like Mama said.

The dog kept sniffing Daniel, found his ear and licked him, which tickled, but it wasn't funny, not one bit. Daniel wanted to run, to get away and find Mama. But he was too scared to look up, scared the dog would bite his face off.

Instead of running, he prayed the man would get the dog before the dog decided to eat him. Or his beef jerky.

"Magic, come."

Daniel peeked to see the dog join a pair of legs just a few feet away.

"Sit," the man said.

The dog sat. It wasn't as big as Daniel had thought, and it looked like it was smiling.

The man stepped a little closer. "Well, hi there."

Daniel hid his face again.

"You're okay, son." He stepped closer, crouched down, and rested his hand on Daniel's shoulder. "My dog won't hurt you. She might lick you, but if you're not afraid of a little dog slobber, you can sit up."

Daniel sat back on his heels and looked at the man, who was studying him just as closely.

"What are you doing way out here?"

He shrugged. Everything he was supposed to say had been chased away by the dog, who was still sitting like his master told him, smiling at him as if he'd found a new friend.

Daniel smiled back. That dog wasn't scary at all.

"I'm Eric Nolan." The man snapped his fingers, and the dog joined them. "This is Magic."

Daniel stuck out his hand and let the dog sniff his mitten. "Funny name for a dog."

The man nodded like he agreed. "I found her wandering down the highway. Her tag told me her name but nothing else."

"You rescued her?"

"I guess." He ran his hand down the dog's back. "Maybe we rescued each other. I really needed a friend, and there she was."

"What kind of a dog is she?"

The man shrugged. "A mutt. The vet thinks she has some shepherd in her."

Daniel could imagine that, the pointy shape of its face, the dark fur on its snout.

The man said, "But her legs are shaped a little like a pit bull's."

Daniel pulled his hand back. "They're mean."

"Oh, I think most dogs are like people," the man said. "If you're nice to them, they'll be nice back. And Magic's as sweet as they come." He ruffled the dog's head. "Aren't you, girl?"

The dog kept smiling at Daniel.

He didn't know what to say. He knew his jeans were soaked from kneeling in the snow, and his legs were about to freeze right off. A giant shiver jerked his whole body.

The man stood and brushed snow off his jeans. He didn't even have on a coat, much less mittens and a hat like Daniel wore.

"Where are your parents?"

Daniel shrugged again.

"You live around here?"

Daniel shook his head.

The man looked into the woods for a moment, then looked back down at Daniel. "Is your family around here somewhere? Did you wander off?"

The words came back to him. His teeth chattered so badly he could hardly force them out. "M-my name is Daniel Anderson. My mama's name is Carrie. I d-don't have a daddy. I'm eight years old."

The man frowned. Kept his mouth closed for a minute. Then he held out his hand. "Come on, Daniel Anderson. Let's get you warmed up."

TWO

Eric Nolan led the boy back to his house while Magic bounded around them, kicking up snow, sniffing everything in sight, and generally acting like a kid on Christmas morning.

"Magic likes company," Eric said.

"She's funny."

Magic circled them at top speed, sometimes running, sometimes doing that funny kangaroo hop thing she did when she was so excited she couldn't get her front legs to catch up with her back ones.

"She's a goofball," Eric said. "And she's been cooped up in the house all day. She needs to burn some energy. When the weather's warmer, I leave her outside." They stepped out of the woods and into his backyard. He pointed to the dog run, which spanned the length of it. "But it was too cold today."

He glanced at the boy, who shivered at the mention of the cold. How long had he been out there? And where had he come from? Eric's house sat on the edge of the woods. His property extended into the woods a couple hundred feet. Behind that sat thick forest that went on for miles, empty except for a few old logging roads. Great for hunting, but there was nothing to hunt in February. And, aside from the fact that he was too young, the boy wasn't dressed for it.

They reached the back porch, and Eric led the way up the stairs, pulled open the storm door, and held it open.

"Come on in."

The boy stared up at him, didn't move.

"It's okay. We just need to warm up. Then we'll figure out what to do next."

The boy stepped inside and stopped right inside the threshold.

Eric managed to slide in behind him, and Magic squeezed between them both. The dog stayed near Daniel, who seemed to lean toward her as if she would protect him. Funny how fast Magic had won him over. Eric hoped he could do the same.

Eric passed his small kitchen table and headed for the fireplace in the living room. "I was just about to light a fire." Not entirely true. He'd been contemplating it because his house was freezing and heating oil was danged expensive. But many evenings after work, Eric just plugged in the space heater and made do. No sense heating the whole house for only him.

"Why don't you take off those wet things and leave them there by the door?"

The kid stared at him.

"Go ahead. Off with the wet stuff—and those boots." They looked like an eight-dollar Walmart special. Hardly warm enough on a chilly day like today. "And then you can wrap up in a blanket while I light the fire. Okay?"

Daniel pulled off his hat and mittens, then shrugged out of his jacket and dropped everything where he stood like only an eight-year-old could do. He stepped out of his boots. The floor was wet from the melting snow, so Eric snatched him up and carried him to the couch.

The boy weighed hardly anything. He had too-long brown

hair and thick round glasses that made his blue eyes look bigger than they were.

Eric set him on the couch and covered him with the blanket. Daniel snuggled in deeply. For good measure, Eric grabbed his parka from the front closet and laid that over the boy, too. That should do until the fire got going. Stupid to light it—he was obviously going to have to go right back out. But he thought a fire might help the kid relax. It always worked for Eric.

"That'll keep you warm for now. I'll get this fire going and then we'll talk."

He felt the boy's eyes on him as he tore newspaper into strips, stacked the kindling, and added a few smaller pieces of wood. After opening the flue, he set the paper ablaze and turned toward the boy. The kid was staring at the flames. Better than staring at Eric. He wasn't used to being watched in his own home. Of course, when had anyone but himself and his dog been here? Probably the last time his parents had visited. Too long ago.

"That should warm us up right quick," Eric said. "You hungry?"

Eric took the boy's shrug for a yes. Leaving Magic in the house during the day meant he had to rush home to let her out instead of staying in town for dinner. In warmer weather, he ate out a lot. Ate alone, but at least there were other people around. And sometimes friends would see him and take pity and ask him to join them. But in the winter with the temperatures in the twenties, he spent most evenings here with just Magic for company.

This was not the life he'd envisioned for himself a decade ago.

And what foolishness had brought that thought on?

Eric checked the fire, then put the screen in front of it to keep embers from popping out.

"How about something warm to drink?"

Daniel shrugged again.

Quite the conversationalist, this one.

Eric stepped into the kitchen, where he could keep an eye on the fire and the boy across the counter's peninsula, and opened his cabinet. And there it was, an unopened can of instant hot chocolate, a gift from his mother, who figured he must be freezing all the time, living up north, as if New Hampshire was akin to the Arctic Circle. Mom also seemed to figure Eric was still a child who wanted hot chocolate for every snowstorm. He was glad now he hadn't tossed it out or given it away. He filled two mugs with water and set them in the microwave, then peered into his fridge. He'd been planning to cook a burger, but he figured he'd probably better get Daniel into town sooner rather than later. Maybe they'd grab food on the way.

Right now, he needed a snack. And he needed to warm the kid up—literally and figuratively—if he wanted to find out where he belonged.

He sliced a hunk of cheddar and grabbed a sleeve of crackers. He set the snack on the coffee table.

"Help yourself," he said.

"Thank you, sir."

Sir. Hmm. The accent. Sounded Southern, not too different from his own, though there was a bit more twang to it. Add to that the fact that he'd called him sir—Daniel was not a local boy, that was for sure.

Eric fixed the hot chocolate and returned to the living room with two steaming mugs. He set one in front of Daniel and sat in the chair beside the fire.

Daniel reached for the cup.

"Careful. It's hot. But while it cools, it'll warm your hands."

The boy cupped his hands around the cup for a moment, then set it back down. He glanced at the cheese and crackers.

Eric took a cracker, covered it with a slice of cheese, and added another cracker on top.

Daniel watched him eat it, then he did the same.

They ate and sipped their drinks in silence while the fire warmed the small living area. Eric added another log. "Tell me, Daniel. How did you happen to be in my woods today?"

The boy sipped his hot chocolate, didn't meet Eric's eyes.

Hmm.

Eric settled back on the couch. "Were you with your folks?"

"I don't have a daddy."

Right. He'd said that. A funny thing to add to his introduction.

"Were you with your mother?"

"She had to go."

"Where did she go?"

Another shrug.

"Do you and your mother live around here?"

He shook his head.

"Where are you from?"

After a shrug, he took another piece of cheese and a cracker.

"Do you know your mother's phone number?"

Daniel nodded and rattled off a number that began with four-oh-five.

Eric crossed the room and snatched his phone off the kitchen counter. He dialed the number. It went straight to voicemail, and it was an automated message. No voice. No name. He left a brief message with his phone number and hung up. Somehow, he didn't feel any closer to finding the woman than he had before.

"What's your mother's name?"

"Carrie Anderson."

"Where do you live?" Based on the accent, the use of the word sir, and the four-oh-five area code, which was not from

New Hampshire or any of the surrounding states, he'd guess they didn't live anywhere nearby. But maybe they'd recently relocated.

"We don't live nowhere."

Huh. Transients? In Eric's experience, homeless people weren't this well dressed—not that the clothes were appropriate for outdoor living in February, but they were new, and they matched, and they looked like they fit him well enough. This boy looked cared for. Clean, shiny brown hair, bright white teeth, a healthy complexion, nice glasses. Certainly didn't look homeless to Eric.

"What do you mean?" Eric asked.

Again with the shrug.

"Before you didn't live anywhere, where did you live?"

"Oklahoma."

That answer came fast. Eric was tempted to grab his computer and start searching, but he didn't want to make the kid nervous.

"How'd you end up in New Hampshire?"

"Mama brought me."

"Why here?"

"She never said."

"You guys move around a lot?"

"We left Oklahoma after Christmas. We been on the road since then."

On the road. "What kind of car does your mother drive?"

"Old van, but it died a while back. Then we just rode on busses."

"Okay. But how'd you get out here. No busses come this way."

"Mama borrowed a car. She drove us."

"Borrowed? From who?"

Daniel shrugged.

"What kind of a car?"

"A black one."

"How many doors?"

"Uh...four. And the trunk. Does that count?"

A black sedan. That narrowed the search to just about every third car on the road. "Did she borrow it in New Hampshire?"

"I guess. Not too far from here."

"A city? Maybe Manchester?"

"Maybe."

Eric stifled a sigh. That was hardly helpful. "Besides your mother, do you have any other family? Grandparents? Aunts? Uncles?"

"Don't have any of those."

"No family at all?"

"Just Mama."

Eric stared into the flames, frustrated. He didn't want to have the boy thrown into the system, but what choice did he have? "Well, kiddo, unfortunately you can't stay here. I'm going to have to take you to town. Maybe we can find your mother."

The boy set his mug down. He looked...disappointed. "Okay."

"Unless you can think of a way to get in touch with her."

Daniel shrugged. "She said she'd come back for me when she could."

"Did she leave you in the woods?"

"She had to do something."

"Okay. But...do you think she'll look for you where she left you?"

Daniel snuggled beneath Eric's parka and stared at the fire. His voice was small when he answered. "No, sir. She's not coming back that soon."

By the time Eric and Daniel settled into Eric's Jeep, the sun had set and the snow was falling harder. Magic had planted herself between them, her rump on the seat with Daniel, her front paws on the console between them. Eric glanced at the clock. Five-thirty. Winter was tough in New Hampshire, especially for a Texan like himself. He didn't mind the cold. He didn't mind the snow. He didn't mind the frequent rain, which made the world green and lush. But the short winter days got to him. The long dark nights, all alone in his little house in the woods, made for some melancholy thinking. Thank God for Magic, whose doggie smile and crazy antics often raised his spirits. And having a warm body—albeit a furry one—on the other side of the bed helped him sleep at night.

Beside him, Daniel patted the dog but remained silent. Stoically so. How could an eight-year-old boy abandoned in the woods not be more emotional? It was weird. Not that he knew a lot about kids, but he'd have guessed most kids in that situation would be crying, begging for their mamas. But Daniel seemed to accept this as normal. Poor kid. What would it be like to grow up without a stable home life? Eric had been blessed more than most. He knew that. But to have a mother who abandoned you in the woods in the middle of winter? Had the woman wanted him to freeze to death?

Daniel smiled at Magic. The kid's attitude was far too casual for this situation. Which made Eric wonder—had his mother done this to him before? Maybe he'd already been in the foster system somewhere. If so, a social worker should be able to figure out where he came from, maybe find some family. If nothing else, they could start looking for the kid's mom.

Eric slowed the Jeep automatically as he approached the rickety bridge that separated his home from Nutfield. The state had plans to replace it the following summer, but until then, Eric would proceed with caution. He had no fear of bridges, but he wasn't an idiot, either, and this thing was nothing but old boards and rotting timber.

They crossed slowly. The bub-a-dum, bub-a-dum beneath the tires was loud enough to interrupt conversation. Not that they'd been talking. Daniel was still petting the dog, and Magic was lapping up the attention.

Maybe Daniel's mother was one more victim of the opioid epidemic plaguing the state. Or maybe she was suffering from a mental illness. Either way, Eric thanked God the kid had been abandoned near his house. There were plenty of folks who wouldn't be rushing the kid into town right now. Eric had a file at the station filled with names and information about a few of the men in town who Eric suspected might be involved in some unsavory things. He had no real evidence against any of them. Some were registered sex offenders, and Eric always kept a close eye on them. He'd seen one guy from his file in the Nuthouse, the local hangout for teens. A grown man, alone, leering at teenage girls. But as his chief had told him, there's no law against leering. Another guy he'd stopped in a routine traffic stop. Grown man with a fifteen-year-old girl who'd looked... Eric hadn't been able to put his finger on the expression on her face. Frightened, defeated. Eric had been sure that guy had been up to no good. But they'd called the girl's mother and it turned out the girl was his niece. Eric kept his name in the file anyway.

Eric still suspected that guy was up to no good, but he had no evidence.

Wait. Maybe there was a connection from the mother to one of the men on his list.

"Did y'all meet anybody while you were up here?" Eric asked. "Friends, maybe?"

"You talk like home," Daniel said. "Folks up here don't say y'all."

Eric chuckled. "It's always 'you guys.' Even if you're talking to a bunch of women."

"Weird," Daniel said. "Where're you from?"

Eric considered the question, not because it was a tough one but because the kid seemed pretty mature for an eight-year-old. Another clue he'd been well cared for. "Plano, Texas, a little north of Dallas."

"How'd you end up here?"

Eric adjusted the heat and glanced at the boy's curious face. "Now that, kiddo, is a very long story."

"I think it's too cold."

"Winter doesn't last forever, and it can be great fun. Sledding and skiing and ice skating. You don't get to do those things much in Oklahoma."

"No, sir. Sure don't."

The boy seemed willing to talk when Eric wasn't questioning him about his past. "So...did you and your mother meet anybody when you got to New Hampshire?"

"Nope."

"Did you meet anybody along the way, maybe friends of hers?"

"Nope. Mama doesn't know anybody 'round here."

Fine. Maybe Eric was just paranoid.

"Where we goin'?" Daniel asked.

"I'm taking you to the police station where I work."

"Okay."

"I'm a police officer," he said, though the kid hadn't asked. "Actually, I'm a detective now. I investigate crimes."

"Like what?"

"Nutfield's a little town, so I investigate all different kinds of crimes. Burglaries, robberies, drugs." He snuck a peek at Daniel, but the kid didn't flinch at the word. Maybe his mother wasn't an addict. Or maybe she just hid it well. "Vandalism. Stuff like that."

"What's that...vanderism?"

Eric smiled. "Vandalism. When people ruin other people's property. Like when people paint on the sides of buildings."

"Or write on bathroom walls. Sometimes people don't write very nice stuff on walls in bathrooms."

"Very true."

"Cool job."

Eric did like his job. He'd known since he was Daniel's age that he wanted to be a cop someday. Though he'd always pictured himself in a big city, not a place like this.

"What do you like to do?" Eric asked.

"Skateboard. When the car broke, Mama said we had to leave my skateboard with it, because we couldn't carry it in our backpacks. But she's gonna buy me another one when we get settled."

Sure she was. Eric suspected the woman would never return for Daniel. What kind of mother must she be? He searched for a normal question to ask the kid. "What grade are you in?"

A moment's hesitation. Then, "Second. But I haven't gone back since Christmas."

The boy needed to be in school. He needed stability. Eric prayed the county social workers would be able to give him that, at least that.

"What else do you like to do, besides skateboard?"

He shrugged. "I like to draw. I like to make videos with Mama's cell phone. She won't let me post them yet, 'cause I'm too young. But she lets me watch other people skateboarding on YouTube. You should see some of the cool stuff they can do. I'm gonna learn how to do all that stuff."

"I used to love to skateboard," Eric said. "But I wasn't very good."

"I'm good. There's a skate park in the city that Mama took me to a few times. It was so fun."

"What city was that?"

He shrugged and looked out the far window.

"You don't remember the name of it?"

Silence.

"Was it Oklahoma City?"

More silence.

"Tulsa?"

Nothing.

Very strange.

They reached the Nutfield PD. He parked, went around, and opened the door for Daniel. Magic bounded out, but after Eric's sharp command, the dog hopped back inside, her doggie grin gone. "Don't look at me like that." Eric patted the dog's head. "I'd take you if I could, but there are rules."

He shut the door on his pouting dog and took Daniel's mittened hand. "You ready?"

The boy shrugged, and they walked inside.

THREE

It was all Kelsey could do to put one foot in front of the other. She'd been trudging through the woods for hours, parallel to the roads but not on them, terrified somebody would see her and stop to help, and maybe remember her face. Terrified the car would be discovered and she would be the best suspect in its theft. She stayed just far enough in the woods that she was forced to push between bushes and fight low-hanging branches, leaving footprints in the too-deep snow, which had stuck to her jeans and slipped into her boots and frozen her toes.

She always chose older cars to steal. Old cars usually didn't have alarm systems. They were easier to break into, easier to hot-wire. They were perfect, except for the fact that they were old and thus, unreliable.

The stupid thing had broken down.

She was miles from everywhere, and she couldn't very well call a taxi out here, a stranded woman right next to a stolen car.

But, she'd thought, like the fool she was, that it was only three miles to the lake. Only. Like that was nothing.

How could it take this long to walk it? Hard enough with

the cold and snow, but twigs and branches kept getting caught on her pack, yanking her back like the hand of God.

Warm tears collected on her eyelashes and blurred her vision, ran down her face, and froze on her cheeks. What kind of world was so cold a person's tears froze? There was a metaphor in that, but she was too tired to figure out what it was. She kept telling herself to stop crying, but the words didn't help. Knowing she'd had no other choice didn't help. And crying sure didn't help.

She swiped at the tears with her thin gloves for the millionth time and trudged forward. A light up ahead told her maybe, just maybe, she was getting close.

It was nearly dark by the time she reached the turnoff. She'd been here before, had driven by just that day. She took the turn, keeping to the woods, and within a few minutes saw the first of many summer cabins. The sight of Clearwater Lake, frozen, surrounded by bare trees and abandoned houses, nearly started her tears again. And wasn't that the perfect metaphor for her life. What had begun full of promise was no more than an icy hell today.

She ought not to let her thoughts drift to such dark places. She'd fallen into those dark places before, and it was hard to climb back out. Too hard. And she had a job to do. Only problem was, she had no idea how to do it. She didn't even know where to start. And now she'd abandoned the one person who made life worth living.

No. She couldn't think about Daniel. Not until she was somewhere she could break down. Otherwise, she might just lean up against one of these trees and let the cold take her home.

She kept walking, still in the woods, following the road. She studied the cabins, which were all on the opposite, lake-side of the street, searching for one that looked well-insulated but not fancy enough to have an alarm. The first few cabins' exterior walls seemed barely thicker than her cheap jacket. She wanted something empty but winterized.

It was nearly dark now. She stopped and tugged her flashlight out of her backpack and used it to illuminate her path. She was glad she had, too, when she came to the stream. It was frozen, though how thick the ice was, she couldn't tell. She wasn't dumb enough to step on it and see.

How did people live like this? Growing up, she'd thought it criminal when the weather dipped into the thirties, which it very rarely did. She'd gotten more accustomed to cold in Oklahoma, but this...this was different. Not just cold, but damp-cold. Snow falling like an attack from above. And now that the sun was down, she feared she might just freeze solid where she stood. She might never be warm again.

She pointed the flashlight at the ground beyond the stream. Not a long jump, but her legs were tired, and with the heavy backpack... She aimed the beam upstream and down, looking for a better place to cross. The terrain looked about the same everywhere. She ought to walk down to the road, just twenty or so feet from where she stood. She could see the stream eventually funneled into a tube that'd take it beneath the road and onto the lake. Problem was, she sure didn't want to risk being seen now, not after all she'd done to stay out of sight. And no doubt if somebody saw her walking out here, they'd stop to check on her.

Which left her no other choice. She shined the light again to see what she was aiming for, then put her flashlight in her pocket. She took a deep breath, shot up a quick prayer, and jumped across the stream.

Her foot landed, slipped a bit, but she fell forward and kept herself from sliding into the icy water. Phew. That was close as a cat's whisker, as PawPaw would say. She stood, brushed the snow from her jeans, and stepped forward.

Her foot plunged through snow into a hidden hole. Pain

wrenched her left ankle, and she went down hard, crying out until her gloved hands hit the wet bracken.

She pulled her foot out and sat on the snowy ground. Her ankle screamed in pain.

No, no, no. This was the one thing she could not do. Words her mama had forbidden her to say filled her mind, but she remained silent.

Think. She had to think.

Using a nearby tree, she wrenched herself to standing, cursing the backpack that weighed her down. Where a minute before she'd only been cold and tired, now she was also wet and injured. Nice going, girl. Way to make a terrible situation worse.

She had all her weight on her right foot. She set the left one down, but as soon as it hit the snowy ground, pain shot up her leg and sent fresh tears to her eyes.

Tired as she felt, it was all she could do to stay upright with all her weight on one leg. She had to figure a way out of these woods or she'd freeze to death right here, twenty feet from the road.

Wouldn't it be fortuitous if a downed tree rested nearby? If there were a walking stick of just the perfect length? If she were in a movie instead of living this ridiculous life she'd fallen into, there'd be one. But all she saw was snow. And trees. Everywhere, trees.

Okay, she'd use the trees.

She turned and peered at the road, then at the cabin that sat beyond it. Wood-sided and rustic, it was probably freezing inside. And not nearly far enough from the main road for her liking. She didn't have much choice now, did she?

Pulling her focus closer, she found a tree between herself and her final destination. Just a few feet away.

She did a one-legged hop across the space and wrapped her arms around the skinny birch trunk. Her right leg shook with exhaustion, her left throbbed with pain. She needed to get ice on that sprain and quick.

Ice. She was an imbecile.

She sat on the cold ground, ignoring the wet that seeped through her jeans, and shoved snow into her left boot. The pain was excruciating, but she didn't stop until she'd packed her ankle. Maybe that would keep the swelling down until she reached the cabin.

Teeth chattering now, she spied another tree, made it her goal, and hopped to it. She did that again and again until she reached the road.

No trees to help her now. She leaned against her latest crutch, a pine, and listened. The forest was silent. Nothing but the rustle of the breeze in the treetops.

She was alone out here. Good thing.

She took a deep breath and hopped to the road. She'd barely made it to the gravely pavement before she pitched forward and landed on her hands. She'd managed to keep her ankle off the ground. She crawled across the road, her knees feeling the jabs of every pebble beneath the snow. If she hadn't feared she might collapse from pain and exhaustion, she might have laughed at herself. She must look a total fool. All that work to stay hidden, and if a car came now, the driver wouldn't stop to help her until after he'd felt her thump beneath his tires.

Finally, she reached the far side of the road. She didn't have the energy to stand, so she crawled until she was far enough into the yard that nobody would see her unless they were looking. She studied the little house. Old, but cozy. Wood siding and a fireplace sticking up from the back. Not that she could light it. At least inside would be warmer than out here. She crawled around to the back and up four steps to the deck. A wall of windows looked out over the frozen lake. She rested and took in the view. She could imagine what it would look like in the summertime, but she decided not to. Those memories would be the end of her.

When she caught her breath, she crawled across the deck to the back door and levered herself up by hanging onto the knob. It was locked, of course. She'd try the windows if she could walk. But they were probably locked, too. Not that she was an expert, but she'd learned to pick locks a long time ago. It had become a basic survival skill.

She took off her backpack, propped herself against the door, and unzipped the biggest compartment. A moment later, she pulled out her lock-picking kit, a fifteen-dollar online special. Her fingers were freezing, but she took off her thin gloves and managed to unzip the canvas case and select the right tools.

She warmed her fingers with her breath until she could move them, then stuck the flashlight in her mouth to illuminate the lock and got to work. It took less than two minutes before the lock clicked. She swung the door open.

And waited.

No alarm. At least not one she could hear. She hopped inside the rustic living area. It was chilly, but fifties was better than freezing. She'd take it. The cabin smelled stale, abandoned. An old leather couch and matching La-Z-Boy faced the brick fireplace. She longed to throw herself on that couch and sleep. Not yet. A flat-screen TV rested on a stand in the corner. Kelsey swung the flashlight through the door on her left and saw a galley kitchen. Using furniture and walls, she hobbled in there. She found a glass and turned on the tap. Nothing.

Of course not. That'd be too easy.

She opened the fridge, and the light came on. Power in the house—good to know. Not that she would use it. Two bottles of water and a half-full gallon of expired apple juice. She grabbed both bottles of water, opened one, and downed the whole thing.

She didn't feel thirsty, but she knew she needed to hydrate after that walk.

She stuck the second bottle of water in the inside pocket of her jacket and hopped through another door to the eating area, which was open to the cabin's front door. Across from it were stairs leading to the second floor. She should walk up there, make sure she was alone. Grab some blankets. No way she could do it.

There was a door beneath the stairs. She opened it and nearly cried with relief. On the shelf just above her head lay a pillow, folded blankets, and sheets. She pulled them down, dropped the pillow and sheet, and squeezed the blanket beneath her armpit. She hobbled back to the living room, where she tossed it on the couch.

She sat on the chair and set her backpack beside her. From the front zipper pocket, she took out her handgun, a little Taurus revolver that probably wouldn't shoot straight. She'd never tested it and had no plans to do so.

Unless she ran into Carlos. She'd be happy to shoot him.

After the stupid van had died, she'd bought the gun at a pawn shop in hopes that pointing it would scare away thieves, thugs, and guys who got the wrong idea about her. After everything, she still wasn't that kind of girl.

She stuck the handgun in her pocket, then tugged out the tablet along with her wallet and phone. She stood again, heaving a sigh at the thought of hopping across the floor one more time. She gathered her strength and managed to make it back to the closet without falling.

The closet would be a good hiding place. It was close to where she was sleeping, so she could retrieve her stuff quickly—assuming her ankle healed. On the floor, she'd seen a jumble of things before she'd grabbed the blanket. She took out her flashlight and looked closer. Deflated inner tubes, foam floats, a couple of Frisbees, a football, and a volleyball net propped against the wall. On the other side, a pile of beach towels. Perfect. She shoved her things in the back corner beneath everything else and hoped she was just being paranoid.

Paranoia was another life skill she'd picked up along the way.

She grabbed a towel, lifted the pillow and sheets from the floor, closed the closet door, and hopped back to the living room, where she dropped the pillow and sheet on the sofa before she collapsed on the La-Z-Boy. After a few minutes to rest, she slipped the boot from her good foot. Then, after a prayer for strength, she pulled off the other one.

The muttered, "Ow-ow-ow-ow-ow" didn't help, nor did the sight of the swollen ankle.

That done, she stripped to her bra and underwear, teeth chattering in the chilly air. She dried her wet feet with the beach towel, very careful of that aching joint, then wiped the floor where she'd dripped. She slipped on her fleece pajamas and dry socks, grabbed her jacket, and hopped to the couch. She covered the cushions with the sheet, a thin layer against the cold leather, put the pillow on the far end, then sat against the armrest. She lifted her foot onto the pillow, gritting her teeth against the pain. Then she stretched the blanket over her and reached for her jacket.

Out of breath, she rested a minute. Then she emptied the jacket's pockets. Water, flashlight, gun. She set them on the coffee table beside her and laid the wet jacket over her freezing feet.

She should be safe here tonight. Tomorrow night, she'd move on. Assuming she could walk.

She closed her eyes, and images of her beautiful, perfect son filled her mind. Her sobs filled the silence until, finally, she drifted off to sleep.

FOUR

Vanessa Bakočević had been at the high-end Miami salon earlier that day preparing for this charity ball, and she'd overheard a conversation between a hairdresser and a client about that feeling a woman gets when a man rests his hand on the small of her back. Possessive, the client had called it.

The hairdresser had nodded and smiled as if it were a good thing to feel possessed. Obviously, neither woman had any idea what it meant to be possessed by a man.

As Carlos and Vanessa had walked into the party that night, a black-tie affair for which Carlos had allowed Vanessa to purchase a new dress—skin-tight, floor-length, plunging neckline—Carlos's hand on her back had felt kind. It felt loving. It felt far from possessive.

Those women were *lud*, as Mama used to say. Crazy. Maybe just stupid, because possessive was never gentle.

Possessive was a grip on the wrist. Possessive was fingers pressed into the soft flesh of an arm. Possessive was a huge hand squeezing the neck. Cutting off oxygen. Making you dizzy with fear.

That gentle hand on the back. That was only tenderness.

Vanessa could live her life in happiness if only Carlos would keep his hand right there, inches above her bottom.

Of course, the hand wouldn't stay there.

Clearly, normal women would never understand.

Vanessa had been a possession almost as long as she could remember. There were snatches of her childhood, memories of a small apartment in Belgrade, her mama and *tata* in the kitchen, arguing about money. About sanctions, which she hadn't understood. Still didn't. Her life hadn't left a lot of room for history lessons, for any lessons apart from how to survive. From her childhood, she remembered there was always fighting somewhere. Inside, outside. She'd understood very little. But she'd felt cherished by her parents, her grandparents, and her aunt. And of course her younger brothers and sisters, who all adored her. She'd been their caretaker, helping entertain the little ones while the adults argued and worried and cried. She'd changed diapers and fed them meals and loved them. They'd loved her, too, their big sister who wasn't all that big at eight, nine, ten years old.

Even then, she'd been a possession, though too young to understand. How could she not have been? If Tata had sold her, then he must have owned her, too.

She could remember her mother holding her tight, screaming her protest. "Vojislava, my baby."

Tata had pulled her away. "Better to lose one than to watch them all starve."

Vojislava became Vanessa. Property to be loaned, rented, and sold.

But Carlos's hand on her back had said something else. That hand had said she was more than a possession. Perhaps it meant she could belong somewhere. She could be loved as she'd thought she'd been loved as a child.

Was it so much to ask?

Now Vanessa posed beside Carlos, sipped champagne, and smiled at the women gathered there. She felt their husbands' stares, their desire. She knew how to stand, how to move, how to speak to get their attention. She had a decade of experience now. People called her young, as if a person could be judged by her years. Vanessa had lived a thousand lifetimes since she'd been wrenched from Mama's arms at ten years old. How did the men not see her scars?

Mateo Ruiz joined their group. Tonight, he wore a tuxedo, a far cry from the jeans and T-shirts he preferred. His gray hair was freshly cut in the very short style he liked. He looked for all the world like a fit-and-trim grandpa. He shook the other men's hands, smiled at the women, nodded kindly to Vanessa. But she wasn't fooled. Mateo resented her for the place she'd taken in Carlos's life. He feared how close they'd become. Mateo's frustration gave her courage. If Mateo thought Vanessa was a threat, then she must have been more than just a bedmate to Carlos.

After polite conversation—Mateo was always polite—he apologized to Vanessa and pulled Carlos away, leaving her to talk to the strangers.

She made conversation about clothes and hair and shoes, then her accent, all the while watching Carlos and Mateo out of the corner of her eye. Carlos didn't look upset or worried, and Vanessa allowed herself to relax. His temper was terrifying, though he'd never unleashed it on her. She knew better than to believe he never would.

He glanced at her across the gilded ballroom, and in his gaze she saw something more. Not just desire, but that new thing she'd noticed lately. She'd seen hate in men's faces. She'd seen scorn. She'd seen murder. She'd seen fear. She'd even seen kindness, at times, born out of pity. But this was new.

She smiled at him, not the seductive look she'd learned after hours of practice. This was an affectionate smile, like the smiles normal women gave their normal men.

He excused himself and returned to her side.

She barely kept herself from looking at Mateo. She knew he'd see triumph in her eyes, and she didn't need to make more of an enemy of Carlos's right-hand man than she already had.

Carlos reached her and whispered in her ear, "You look lovely, my darling."

My darling.

Her granite heart thumped. She hardly dared to hope. Could it be that Carlos truly cared for her? He treated her as if he did. He told her he did.

Was it possible that Vanessa could someday be like normal women? Could she be loved?

Did it matter if she didn't deserve love? Ha. What mattered, this *deserve*? People deserved what they fought for. And she would fight for this.

Carlos would want her, not just as his bedmate and helper. He would want her as his wife. As a wife, Vanessa would be free. She'd already started putting her plan into place to make sure of it. And God help anybody who stood in her way.

FIVE

"But I want to stay with you."

The boy might as well have wrenched Eric's heart right out of his chest. He crouched beside Daniel's chair in the conference room of the police station. The air still carried the scent of the fried chicken and potato wedges someone had picked up for them at KFC. "I wish you could, son."

Daniel had been stoic before, but now his bottom lip trembled and tears filled his eyes. "I won't cause you any trouble. I can feed Magic and take her for walks. I'm a good cook, too. Mama taught me how to cook frozen french fries and pizza, and I can even make a grilled cheese sandwich with ham. I won't be any trouble, I promise."

Eric barely knew this kid, but somehow, his arms opened as if he'd been comforting eight-year-old boys all his life. Daniel slipped off the chair and into his hug. Eric held him close, rubbed his tiny back, and cursed the woman who'd abandoned such a special kid. "The state has rules about these things, and I'm not allowed to keep you. You'll have to go to a foster family."

Daniel slid his skinny arms around Eric's neck and rested his face against Eric's chest. Warm tears soaked Eric's sweatshirt and seeped into his heart. He lifted Daniel up, sat in a chair, and settled him in his lap. The boy was probably too old and too big to be held like this, but Daniel wasn't complaining, and Eric sure didn't mind. He'd longed for this, just this, most of his adult life. Well, not just this. He'd like a mama to go with his son, and not one like the heartless monster who'd thrown this boy away like last week's leftovers.

They sat like that until a knock sounded on the open door. Eric looked up to see a gray-haired woman step inside. She approached them and held out her hand. "Marcia Lamont."

He shook it. "Eric Nolan."

"And who is this young man?"

Daniel squeezed Eric's neck tighter. He didn't look.

"Daniel, introduce yourself to Ms. Lamont, please."

The boy shook his head.

Eric took hold of Daniel's little arms and gently separated them so he could lean back and face the boy. "Fighting it won't make it easier."

"Will you come see me?"

His answer came fast. "Of course. I'll bring Magic."

Little Daniel's grip lessened a little.

"Mr. Nolan," the woman said.

Eric met her eyes over Daniel's head. "It's Detective Nolan."

A quick nod. "Detective, don't make promises you can't keep. Daniel, come along, honey. There's a nice family waiting for you."

Daniel flung his arms around Eric again.

"It's okay, son. I always keep my promises."

The woman huffed like a dragon. "Detective, Daniel will need to become accustomed to his foster family, and having you make promises won't help."

Eric stood, and Daniel wrapped his arms around his neck and held on tight. "Nobody's ever been harmed because too many people cared, Ms. Lamont." He snatched his wallet from his back pocket and managed to open it and extract a card without dropping the boy. Not that Daniel would have fallen, the way he was latched on. He set Daniel on the floor and held out the card.

"You hang onto this. When you get settled, ask your foster parents if you can use the phone and give me a call. Okay?"

He could see the woman shaking her head and feared she'd take the card away.

He returned his gaze to Daniel. "If you lose my card, that's no problem. Just call the Nutfield Police Department. They'll know where to find me."

Daniel took the card and stuffed it in his jeans' pocket. Then he glanced at the woman.

"Where are you taking him?" Eric asked.

"I can't tell you that."

"Why not?"

"There are rules about these things. He's a minor. You're not family."

"That's all right," Eric said. "I'll figure it out." He looked down at Daniel, whose face had lost all its color. "I promise to come see you, make sure you're doing okay."

"Can you try to find Mama? I'm worried about her."

Eric forced a kind expression, though the woman who'd done this deserved no kindness. "I'll do my very best."

Daniel crossed the room, and Ms. Lamont held out her hand for him to take. He did, then peered over his shoulder one last time. Eric nodded at him, trying to convince him it would all be all right. It had better be. He'd be checking up on that boy to make sure he was being well cared for. If he wasn't, those foster folks would have to answer to him.

Eric stood at the window and watched through the darkness as Ms. Lamont settled Daniel in her car—back seat, and was that a booster? Safety Nazi.

Eric tried to shake off his anger. The woman was only doing her job, and she knew better than he did how to manage an abandoned child. She certainly knew better how to care for one. It was ridiculous there were policies in place to handle this situation. How could such an unnatural, aberrant thing as a mother abandoning her kid be so common that there needed to be a procedure?

The world was one seriously messed-up place.

"Good thing there are no pigeons in here."

Eric turned to find Brady Thomas behind him.

The chief said, "You'd be covered in pigeon poop, standing there like that."

Eric tried to think of something funny to say, but he came up empty. He settled for, "Thought you went home for the day."

"Thought you did, too. Donny called to let me know about the child."

Eric gazed out the window again, but of course Daniel was long gone.

"You okay?" Brady asked.

"I'm fine." A lie, but there was no way to explain the connection he'd felt to the boy, the way his heart seemed to be cracking in two.

"Let's go to my office."

Eric followed his boss to the only office with a door in the small police department and sat. As always, the desk was tidy. A picture of Reagan, Brady's wife, and Johnny, their son, rested on the corner. They looked...complete.

"So, what happened?" Brady asked. "You went home, and the kid was there?"

"Not exactly." He recounted the events automatically, trying not to get riled again at the thought of the mother.

"You think she hiked through the woods with him, then just left him there?" Brady asked.

Eric shrugged. "Daniel wouldn't say much about how he got there. Just that his mother had brought him, and then she'd left."

"Did you search the woods?"

"Probably should have, but I was more concerned with getting Daniel taken care of. And if there'd been anybody nearby, Magic would have sensed it. I'm fairly sure the boy was alone."

"I bet the mother calls here frantically looking for him. They'll be reunited by tomorrow."

"You really think so?"

Brady shrugged. "Can't hurt to hope, right?"

But it could. He knew too well how much it hurt to hope.

"I gave him my card, told him to call me."

Brady lifted one eyebrow, and Eric shrugged. "Kid needs a friend." He thought again about the strange events of the day. "Thing is, why there? Why the woods behind my house? It makes no sense."

"True." Brady looked beyond Eric, nodded slowly. "There anything back in those woods?"

"Not that I've ever found. Maybe I should investigate further."

"What are you thinking?"

Eric shrugged. "Maybe a meth lab."

"Possible," Brady said.

"Maybe..." He shouldn't voice this. He knew what Brady would say. But if there was any possibility... "I was thinking... You know, I have that file of sex offenders and possible—"

"Don't start jumping to conclusions."

"But if I'm right, it's worth checking out." Eric was obsessed. His obsession had done no good and probably never would.

"What is it about human trafficking?" Brady studied him until Eric wanted to look away. He forced his gaze to remain on the chief's face. "You have a...fixation on those particular crimes."

"Maybe we should all be more fixated," Eric said. "Sex trafficking happens everywhere. The fact that we're not seeing it doesn't mean it's not here."

"You're sure about that?" Brady's eyebrows lifted. "Nutfield's a pretty small town."

"You're right. I know that." He met Brady's eyes again. "But if it is in Nutfield, I'll find it."

"You still haven't told me why you're obsessed."

"Nobody should..." Eric struggled to voice his opinions without letting the truth escape. "It's the worst torture, the most degrading..." He couldn't make his mouth form the words that went with the images in his mind. "How can you not be disgusted by it?"

Brady's eyes narrowed. "That's a heck of an assumption."

He looked at the floor, blew out a breath. "I don't mean it like that."

"You lost somebody, didn't you?"

Eric's gaze snapped up.

"Who was it?" Brady asked.

He swallowed. Hadn't talked about this...ever. "A friend. A good friend."

"Where is she now?"

Eric licked his suddenly dry lips. Swallowed again. "They say she's dead."

"Do you think someone in Nutfield—?"

"No. No. She was... It happened a long time ago. In Miami.

I was in college. This isn't about her. It's just that... It's awful. All of them need to be stopped."

"I agree," Brady said. "And if we get any whiff that anything like that is happening in town, we'll stomp on it like a cockroach. But until then, you need to focus on your job and the crimes we know are happening here."

"Yes, sir."

Brady smiled. "There's that Southern country boy."

Eric couldn't help but chuckle. "I've told you a million times, I'm not a country boy. Plano is about as country as Manchester. There're more folks in the Dallas-Fort Worth area than there are in the whole state of New Hampshire."

"You sound like a country boy." Brady appraised Eric from head to toe. "You look like a country boy."

"You look like that quarterback, but I've seen you throw a ball."

Brady's laugh filled the room. "So much for the Southern gentleman."

Eric stood. "I left Magic in the car. I'd better get us home."

Brady walked with him to the door. "We'll find that kid's mother and figure out what her deal is."

"I hope so. Meantime, I'm going to check in on him, soon as I figure out where he is."

Brady smiled. "I may be able to help you with that. Check with me tomorrow."

SIX

Kelsey's eyes felt dry as chalk when she opened them, squinting at bright sunshine coming through the back door. Morning again. Wednesday?

She sat up, swung her feet to the freezing floor, and tested her left ankle. It still ached, but she could put weight on it. A little.

Yesterday, the first morning she'd woken up here, the ankle had been swollen to three times its normal size. Stupid. She should've kept ice on it all night, and boy, had she paid for that mistake. That day, she'd been careful to ice it all day, twenty minutes on, twenty minutes off. At some point, she'd found the water valve beneath the kitchen sink and turned the water on. That made living in this abandoned cabin slightly more tolerable. The automatic ice maker had been a godsend for her poor ankle. The storm had ended Monday night, and the sunshine the rest of the week had warmed the place a little. Maybe into the upper fifties. At least she wouldn't freeze.

She'd have to remember to shut the water off before she left. And tidy up, and leave a note of explanation. She wasn't in the habit of breaking into people's homes, lock-pick set notwithstanding.

That was for breaking out, not breaking in. And thank God, she hadn't needed to use it in a long time.

She hobbled to the foot of the stairs, then used the handrail to hoist herself to the second floor. She'd done nothing but sleep and cry since she got there. Today, she had to leave this place and finish what she'd started. If it worked, if she managed to bring Carlos down, then she could find Daniel and get him back. Then and only then would she be free. And if Carlos found her first? Well, at least it would be over. But she couldn't do any of that until she made the phone call that would ensure Daniel's safety, the one she'd planned to make on Tuesday. Stupid ankle.

She prayed Daniel would be okay. She'd been doing a lot of that—praying. A habit that had been ingrained in her since childhood, one she'd shoved aside years before. But being trapped, alone in a silent cabin for three days... There was nobody to talk to but God.

She'd given him an earful.

Not that she really believed anyone was listening. An involved, caring God was a lovely little myth, one she'd given up on the day she'd watched her sister die.

She had no time for morbid thoughts. She'd eaten her last protein bar. She'd raided the pantry the day before and forced down a bowl of rice. The only other ingredients in there were flour, sugar, and spices. She'd spent all of that day trying to figure out what she could make with flour and sugar, but without milk and eggs, she couldn't think of a thing. By dinnertime, she'd been hungry enough to try pancakes. What she'd created had been barely edible, but she'd eaten it. Then she'd turned the TV on for company and fallen asleep.

She'd woken up after dark and cursed herself. Stupid,

stupid, stupid. The light flickering through the windows could have alerted somebody she was here. She'd shut off the TV, then barely slept all night, waiting for the sound of a car door, anything that would tell her she'd been discovered. The world had remained blissfully silent. She'd survived that one foolish mistake, survived the first when she'd sprained her ankle. She doubted she'd survive a third.

Her stomach growled, and it occurred to her that today couldn't be Wednesday. It was Thursday. Had she really been here three days?

The days all bled together. But the nights...yes, there'd been three. Each night held its own exquisite pain.

She closed her eyes against the onslaught of images. Daniel. Her Daniel. Cowering in the woods. Afraid. She'd watched, far enough away that he'd been barely a speck between the trees. She'd heard the dog barking. Seen the man.

Her stomach filled with acid, churned the emptiness until she thought she'd be sick.

Nothing worse than throwing up stomach acid. She forced the images away. She'd had no choice. Neither of them would ever be truly safe until Carlos was in prison. Or dead. Preferably dead.

She started the shower, thankful beyond words when steam filled the small room. This was the only time she'd be truly warm all day. She stepped inside.

Thirty minutes later, she'd collected all her things from the upstairs bathroom and hobbled back down. She still hurt, but it didn't matter. She needed to make her phone call. She'd considered emailing the police instead of calling, but she feared somebody might be able to track that, might be able to find her or know who'd sent the email. It was absolutely imperative that she stay anonymous.

She needed a public phone. Her plan had been to take her

stolen car back to Manchester and make the call from there. The most important thing on Monday, the most important thing still today, was to make sure she wasn't seen or, even worse, arrested. She could survive just about anything but that.

The very thought of it sent terror through her veins.

No. She'd rest until dark, shut off the water, and lock the door behind her. She'd walk to the little country store on the main road, make her phone call, and then hitchhike to Manchester. From there, she'd begin her quest.

She forced herself to drink a glass of water, settled back on the sofa beneath the blankets, and ignored her rumbling stomach. Seven more hours, and she'd leave.

She allowed the images of Daniel to overtake her. Her sweet boy. Would she ever see him again?

A CAR DOOR slamming woke Kelsey from her nap.

Forgetting her ankle, she stood, then cursed when a sharp pain shot up her leg. Three days of healing ruined in one careless moment.

She hobbled to the window, saw the police car in the driveway, another car behind it.

No, no, no!

She dropped to the floor, crawled to the sofa, and pulled the blankets off. She hooked her arm through the backpack straps and backed herself and all the stuff against the wall, out of view of the front windows and the back door.

With her eyes squeezed shut, she prayed to the God who'd only ever let her down that this time, this time he would help her.

She thought of her things hidden in the closet and thanked

God at least she hadn't put those in her backpack yet. Maybe, somehow, she could come back for them.

The banging on the front door sent jolts of fear down her spine.

Anything but this. Please.

A moment later, she heard more banging, this time from the back. Not that she could have made a run for it, but the cops had cut off the possibility.

The question was, would they enter? Would they give up and leave? Surely, they didn't have keys to the cabin.

Her gun! She yanked it out of her bag, scooted to the sofa, and shoved it beneath the cushions. As she scooted back to the corner, she cursed her own stupidity.

A muffled voice, a shout, and the pounding of footsteps on the porch.

Then, the unmistakable jingle of keys. The sound had her blood running cold.

The lock turned.

The door opened.

And her last chance for escape melted like snow.

SEVEN

ERIC SPENT Thursday afternoon talking with business owners about a break-in at McNeal's. Fortunately, not much had been stolen. A couple of bucks and, oddly, a case of black olives. The robbery had taken place in the middle of the night, and, naturally, nobody had seen anything unusual. Eric had asked people to keep an eye out after dark and suggested they upgrade their security systems and consider video surveillance. Most folks just laughed.

"The great olive caper of the century," quipped the owner of a souvenir shop. "Or maybe, the great olive-caper salad of the century." She'd cackled as she'd shown him the door.

Admittedly, crime was rare this time of year. There was always the drug trade to focus on, year-round. But during tourist season, there was more to keep them busy. Nutfield's population nearly doubled in the summer when folks populated the cabins surrounding their beautiful lake and filled the rooms of the many bed-and-breakfasts and hotels that had cropped up. Autumn brought folks, too. The local apple shop had a steady stream of visitors. People loved to pick apples and pumpkins and enjoy the breathtaking foliage that surrounded the town.

Eric had to admit, chilly as Nutfield was, it was a far sight more beautiful than north Texas. He gazed at the little downtown area as he strolled the few blocks to the police station. Even in February, Nutfield was charming. The leafless trees were beautiful in their starkness. The sky was as sapphire as a field of Texas bluebonnets in spring. Icicles dripped from every roof and plinked in a melody that accompanied his footsteps. Last week's snow, piled against the sidewalks, was melting in the heat.

He chuckled at that. Heat? The sun was shining, and the temperature hovered near forty. That'd be considered downright frigid in Texas. Here, folks didn't bother with jackets when the temperature got this high in the winter.

What had possessed him to move to New Hampshire?

The question chased the lighthearted moment away. He knew why he'd taken a job here, and he knew why he stayed, even now. Even when all hope was lost. He figured he'd die keeping vigil for a woman who'd never return.

He wouldn't think about her.

He let his mind drift to Daniel. True to his word, Brady had found out where they'd taken the boy. Apparently, it hadn't been that hard. Brady's friends, Marisa and Nate, had recently been approved to be foster parents, and Daniel had been taken there Monday night. There was something to be said for small-town living.

Nate and Marisa had been delighted to hear from him when he'd called to check on Daniel on Tuesday. Apparently, Daniel had told them all about the nice police officer who'd found him in the woods. He'd already been to visit a few times that week. Marisa had gone on and on about how smart the kid was. "Daniel was helping Ana with her homework today," Marisa had said. "No idea how he ended up in foster care, but his home life couldn't have been that bad. The kid is smart, especially for an eight-year-old. He reads like a fifth grader."

Marisa would know. She'd been working as an aide at the local school. Maybe the boy had had some good teachers in his life. No way that rotten mother of his was responsible.

They'd had zero luck finding her. She was probably zoned out in some heroin haven in Manchester by now. At least Daniel was safe. Nate and Marisa were good folks with enough love to share with the boy. Marisa'd worked in an orphanage in Mexico for years, and she had a heart for abandoned kids.

If they didn't find Daniel's mother, what would happen to the kid? Maybe he'd be better off if they never found her. Except long-term foster care? Would Nate and Marisa keep him for a decade? Would Daniel thrive there?

It wasn't his problem, but he couldn't seem to keep thoughts of the boy far from his mind.

Eric pushed through the front door of the police station and passed the dispatcher with a wave. Inside the squad room, he headed for his desk. Only one desk was occupied. His friend, Donny, was booking a long-haired woman. All he could see from here was a thin parka and the woman's shoulders. Her back was to him, and long hair spilled over the wooden chair. Her hands were cuffed behind her back. Donny asked for her name, and her answer carried across the empty room.

"I can't tell you that."

Eric froze in the middle of the room.

He knew that voice, but it was pleading, afraid. He'd never heard her voice like that. He shook his head. It couldn't be her.

The woman leaned across the desk. "You have to call that number I gave you."

Donny was using his most patient voice. "How am I supposed to ask about a woman whose name I don't know?"

She leaned even further forward, almost a posture of

begging. Her voice... That voice. "When you have her on the phone—"

"Name." Donny's voice left no room for arguing, but the woman only shook her head.

"I can't. You don't understand. I can't."

It was the way she said those words. The accent. Southern, but not Texas. Deep South. Like...

"Fine." Donny stood. "Maybe a couple hours in jail will change your mind."

Eric crossed the room, his heart pounding a drumbeat, hoping, afraid to hope.

Donny pulled the woman to her feet, and she turned. Just a fraction. Just enough.

There were no words. Or maybe every word he'd ever known. Words of love, words of hate. Words of heartbreak. Too many words. Too many feelings.

She hadn't seen him. She stumbled, crumpled, and Eric stepped forward, took her arm, spoke to Donny. "Don't touch her."

Donny swiveled toward him, eyes wide.

"I..." Eric swallowed, couldn't look at her. Had to, to be sure. He took a deep breath and faced her.

Her hair was much longer, lighter than it had been. But her eyes, the color of the sky. Wide with fear. Maybe something else. Her jaw dropped. Looked like she didn't have words, either.

"Remove the cuffs."

"She's under arrest," Donny said.

Eric faced his friend, took a step closer. He was the detective here. He had rank. "I said, remove the cuffs."

Donny did as he was told and backed away.

"I'll take it from here." Eric tugged on her arm, and she

stepped beside him, then hobbled on her left foot. She was injured.

He didn't stop to think and sure wasn't going to check Donny's reaction. He scooped her up and carried her into the conference room, where he closed the door behind him with his foot. It slammed, and the noise bounced off the silence in the empty space.

He set her on a chair, then stood back. Stared.

She stared, too.

A moment passed, and then she opened her mouth. "I—"

"Don't."

She snapped her jaw closed.

He looked at her lips. Cracked and colorless. Trembling. He'd always loved her heart-shaped face. High cheekbones. Healthy and pink. But right now, sunken. Emaciated. Her usually bright eyes were dull and rimmed in red. Her pearly skin was mottled, pale.

She was injured. Looked like she hadn't eaten in days.

She was the most beautiful sight he'd ever seen.

He stepped closer, held out his hand. She took it, stood, and stepped into his embrace.

They stayed like that a long time. His arms around her. Her face against his chest. He inhaled her scent. Beyond shampoo and sadness, his Kelsey was here.

She sobbed against his shirt, and he knew exactly how she felt.

He could have stayed like that forever.

The door pushed open. Kelsey jumped like a skittish cat, but Eric held her close. He shifted, saw the chief in the door.

"Your sister?" Brady asked.

They both knew she wasn't. Eric only had brothers.

When he didn't answer, Brady said, "In-law? Mother? Cousin?"

Eric couldn't form words.

"Even if she's an old friend, Nolan, we have rules." Brady's voice trailed off as he stared at the scene. "Why don't you step back?"

Eric glanced at her, saw Kelsey was looking down, avoiding both their gazes. She was gripping him as if he were the only handhold on a high canyon wall. He was holding her just as tightly.

"Ma'am," Brady said. "Sit down."

Her fists tightened around the fabric of his shirt.

"Give me a minute," Eric said. "Please."

Brady crossed his arms. "I need to know who she is."

There was no other option. He gazed down at the top of her head as words he feared he'd never get to say filled his mouth, settled on his tongue. He considered all the chips falling and all the places they might land. Considered how, once the words were out, he could never pull them back. Brady could never un-know. Eric could never go back to being the man he'd pretended to be for a decade.

Not that he wanted to.

"Don't," she said.

Eric ignored her. She'd lost her influence a long time ago. He met Brady's steady gaze.

"She's my wife."

The unflappable Brady flapped. His jaw dropped, and his eyes widened. Then narrowed. He started to speak, stopped, seemed to see the moment differently, and nodded. "I need to see you when you're finished."

"Yes, sir."

"And Eric? She's still in custody."

Brady closed the door behind him.

Kelsey exhaled a long breath, almost a sigh. But they had a lot of territory to cover before anybody could relax.

"We should sit," he said. "You're hurt."

She didn't move. "Just a sprain."

"Even so."

She let go of his shirt and sat, and he took the chair beside her. Swiveled it to face her. Couldn't stop staring at that face.

Her gaze was unwavering. "I would never have left you."

Eric swallowed a decade of loss. "I know."

"I didn't mean for you to see me."

He knew that, too. If she'd wanted to see him, all she had to do was call. He'd kept the same Texas cell phone number just for that reason, was teased about it mercilessly by his local friends and his family back in Plano.

She'd never called. Not even a hang-up that might've hinted she was alive, hinted she was thinking of him.

"I guess there's a story," he said.

"A very long one."

"Okay."

He sat back, saw her lip trembling, wanted to pull her into his arms again. But for every ounce of love he held for this woman, he had an ounce of sadness and an ounce of worry and, though he hated to admit it, an ounce of rage.

"I can't."

"Course not." He swiveled, stood so fast, his chair rolled back and hit the wall. "If you could have explained, you'd have done it a decade ago."

"I...it's a very long story."

"So you said. I guess you've been too busy in the last thirty-six hundred days, too. Too busy to call me. Let me know you're alive. Do you know they think you're dead?"

She lifted her chin. Not surprised. Not ashamed.

"Of course you know," Eric said. "You know how they grieved you? How your mother...?" He could still picture the woman now. Two daughters, both lost tragically. "She looked like...like a walking corpse at your memorial service." Not that he'd gotten that close. He hadn't been invited to sit with the family. Hadn't been invited back to the house after. He was just the friend from school. Nobody had known. Nobody'd ever known.

Tears filled her eyes, and she looked down. He could see the racking sobs, but he couldn't comfort her. Some words needed to be spoken.

"What about you?" Her voice was small, and he'd hardly heard the words.

"What about me what?"

"You didn't grieve me?"

He laughed, a short, angry sound that probably pierced her soul. "I never believed it."

She looked up then. "You didn't? Not ever?"

"No body, no weapon? Nothing but an anonymous call. You probably made the call yourself."

"A friend did it for me."

And there it was, the admission. He'd always believed she'd staged it. Believed it, but questioned his own belief. Because his Kelsey wasn't cruel, and to let those who loved her best believe her dead? Cruel, cruel, cruel.

"I had to," she said. "And I have to stay dead."

EIGHT

THEY STARED at each other across the small space. Kelsey could see the pain she'd caused play across Eric's features. Maybe she should have just faded away and died. If not for Daniel, she might have.

Daniel had given her a reason to fight, to survive.

Would she ever get her son back now?

A knock sounded on the door. Eric crossed the room and opened it.

The man who'd been here before, the boss, she figured, stood outside. "We need her name."

"No!"

Both men turned to her, but she focused on Eric. "I know I owe you an explanation. I'll tell you everything." Almost everything. "But you can't put my name in any system. You can't." The very thought of it made her body tremble, her voice shake. "I'm begging you. Please."

The fury she'd seen on Eric's face faded. Now, she saw her own fear reflected. He turned to the other man. "She was giving Donny a phone number to call."

The man looked at her. Blew out a breath. Crossed the room and held out his hand. "Brady Thomas, Chief of Police."

She shook it, tried to smile. "The woman you need to call is Sally Bowman. She's a Miami detective. Just tell her Kelsey, okay? Tell her Kelsey from two-thousand-seven. She'll know. She should know." Kelsey prayed Detective Bowman would remember her and be able to help.

"I'm assuming the last name is Nolan," the chief said.

She glanced at Eric, then back at the chief. "Nobody knows that. Look, if she doesn't remember me, then...then I don't know what to do. I'm afraid if I give you a last name, somebody somewhere will type it into some system, and then..."

"What?" It was Eric who'd spoken. He walked closer, dipped his chin, narrowed his eyes. "What do you think will happen then?"

"He'll find me."

"Who? Who'll find you?"

She ignored Eric, looked at the chief, who nodded.

"I'll make the call myself." He turned to Eric. "You'll stay with her?"

She was certain Eric would stay. He'd question her further. He must've had a million questions.

His jaw ticked, his mouth closed in a tight line. He swallowed. "I need some air." Eric turned and walked out of the room.

The chief watched him go, then looked back at her with pity. She waited for him to say something stupid, something about how Eric would get over it, how it would all be okay. Instead, he stepped closer and gripped her arm. "I don't need to cuff you, do I?"

"No, sir."

"Okay. Come on."

She stood, stepped, and winced again. Her stupid ankle.

He shifted to stand on her left and put his hand under her upper arm. With his help, she managed to walk slowly beside him.

"You need medical attention?"

"It's just a sprain."

"There's a doctor a couple doors down. I'll see if he can take a look. Maybe it needs to be wrapped."

They crossed the big room with the desks. She could feel eyes on her, but she didn't dare look. The chief stopped at a door, waited for a low buzz, and then pushed it open. They stepped in, and the door slammed behind them.

It was a hallway. One side, wall, the other, bars.

"You're our only visitor today." He pushed open the door to the first cell—looked like there were only two—and helped her to the bed on the far side, where she sat.

He stepped back, and she thought sure he'd leave her there. Instead, he crossed his arms and studied her. She waited for all the questions she couldn't answer. But all he said was, "You hungry?"

She nearly cried with relief. "Starved."

"We got a great cafe down the street. What sounds good?"

"I have no money."

His laugh was quick. "I'm pretty sure you're the first prisoner who ever worried about paying. I'll get it if your...husband won't."

Husband. He'd tripped over the word, and she knew how he felt.

"I'm starved. I'll eat anything you bring me."

"I'll make that call now and get you some food. I'm sure Eric will..." But he didn't finish the statement.

"It's fine. I need time to process, too."

After the chief left, Kelsey scooted into the corner of the thin mattress. She pulled one knee up, careful of that stupid ankle, and hugged herself.

As prisons went, this wasn't too bad. She was alone. She was safe. She was warm. She didn't have to fear the jiggling of keys, the sound of torture and pain and humiliation.

No. It was tenderness that would torture her here. She thought of Eric's touch, thought of all that she'd lost and all she'd still lose if she didn't figure a way out of this mess. And how much more it would hurt to leave this time.

Tears filled her eyes. She couldn't think of Eric.

Daniel. What would he think of her now, his mother, locked in jail? In all his games of make-believe, he always caught the bad guys. Now, she was one of them.

She couldn't think of Daniel, either.

This cell didn't offer a lot of distractions. She'd been in worse prisons. Rooms without bars, without windows, with only locked doors and darkness. And sounds—crying girls, jiggling keys, and evil men.

As locked rooms went, this was one of the better ones she'd experienced. Except this one would signal the death of her dreams.

Hadn't she told herself, over and over, that as long as she didn't get arrested, she could make this work? Hadn't she told herself she could survive anything, anything but this?

How could she bring down Carlos from a jail cell? That was all assuming the police didn't type her name into some system that would tell Carlos she was here. Eric knew her name, married and maiden. If he shared it... Carlos would find her.

Fine.

She'd always known she'd die at his hands. But Carlos wouldn't kill her until he'd located Daniel.

Daniel. The only reason she was alive. The only thing she had to live for.

But Eric was here now. She had him, too. Her husband. Her life. Her soul.

If only she didn't have to leave him again.

NINE

Eric slammed the station doors open, nearly breaking the glass, and lunged out, bumping into the shoulder of a man in a suit on the way in. He managed to catch the man before he fell, shot a curt *sorry* his way, and kept going.

He'd longed for Kelsey to return to him. Ten empty years, he'd waited for her. And now he couldn't get away fast enough.

Of all she'd said, of the few words she'd uttered, what reverberated now was that first breathless confession.

I would never have left you.

And that was the crux of it, wasn't it? Did he believe those six words?

She'd been taken. He knew that. When she'd taken off that day, she'd planned to come right back. He knew that, too. He'd investigated enough to have an inkling of what had happened to her. He knew just enough of her story to give him nightmares for years. To keep him up at night, imagining all she'd been through. But he suspected she'd been free for a long time, ever since that bogus report that she'd been murdered. He'd waited. All these years, he'd waited for her.

She hadn't come home.

Had Kelsey had a choice? Of course she had. She could have chosen to confide in him from the beginning. She could have chosen to trust him. She could have chosen, in all these years, to reach out to him. If nothing else, she could have chosen to divorce him. At least that way, he could've moved on with his life.

At least, she could have tried. But he'd have fought that, because he'd have known.

He still knew.

His love for Kelsey wasn't the kind of thing that came around more than once in a lifetime. It was unique. It was untarnished. It was eternal.

And her love for him was no different.

Maybe he was a fool to still believe that. Well, he'd been a fool to wait for her, hadn't he? When he'd told her mother he believed Kelsey was still alive, she'd called him that. Fool.

The woman had been afraid to hope. Afraid to believe.

She'd ordered him off her stoop and told him to never return.

Kelsey's stepfather had threatened to call the police.

Her stepbrothers had stood behind their father, arms crossed, eyes glaring.

Eric had walked away. He'd never seen them again.

For years, he'd wondered if Mrs. MacKenzie had been right to accept her daughter's death. If Eric could have, maybe he'd have moved on. But the pieces never added up.

He reached the little church on the edge of the town common. The sun had dropped behind the towering pines, but the steeple reached into the sky, beyond the shadows, and reflected the last rays of evening. He stared at the steeple, waited for some flash of wisdom, of insight, until the shadows chased even that last vestige of light away.

Darkness and chill settled over him, and he turned back in

the direction he'd come. He'd begged God to bring Kelsey home, and now he had. It was time for Eric to figure out what to do next.

Two steps inside the squad room, and the chief's voice called out from his office.

"Nolan. In here."

Eric avoided Donny's gaze as he crossed the room and stepped into the office.

"Close the door and have a seat."

He did what he was told, too tired to argue, too overwhelmed to think.

"Been looking at your records." Brady peered at the computer screen on his desk. "No mention of a wife."

"Yes, sir."

"So you lied on your application?"

"Yes, sir."

"Knock it off." Brady pushed back from his desk. "We've been friends a long time. I expect more than two-word answers from you."

Eric stood, pulled his gun from the holster inside his jacket, his badge from his pocket, and set both on the desk. "Anything else?"

Brady looked at the items, looked at Eric. "Put those back where you found them and sit your butt down."

Eric sat, but he left his badge and gun between them. He wasn't sure he'd be able to pick them up again. Wasn't sure he cared.

"When did you get married?"

He hadn't told this story, ever. Now, he related the events like facts in a case. "We were in college. We met before the school year started, at freshman orientation. We married right after our sophomore year."

"That was when?"

"Almost ten years ago."

"How long were you together?"

Eric broke his friend's gaze, stared at his knees. Remembered that time, time he'd spent right here in this little town, in a cabin on the lake. Even two college students could afford the cost of an off-season rental for a week. He'd been saving all year long, able to save thanks to his scholarship and his folks' financial support. The day after exams finished, Eric and Kelsey rented a car, drove to New Hampshire. A justice of the peace married them on Hampton Beach at sunset, and they'd begun the best honeymoon two broke college students could afford.

"After we married, she stayed for three days."

Brady's eyebrows disappeared beneath his hair. He schooled his expression quickly. "Why'd she leave?"

Eric shrugged, stared back into the past. He still had the note. He'd carried it in his wallet ever since. She'd signed it, *Always and forever —Kels.*

Always and forever. Three whole days.

"Her little sister ran away. They were close. Kelsey wanted to bring her to Boston to live with us when we got settled. I never knew the whole story, but it seemed there was something going on with the stepfather or maybe the stepbrothers, something Kelsey alluded to. She never said outright." He thought about when he'd met them, how he'd wanted to blame the men in the family for all of it. But he hadn't known, hadn't ever had enough information to even make an allegation. "Maybe she thought she'd be able to find Danielle when nobody else could."

"And then?"

Eric didn't have the energy to explain the weeks after her disappearance, the months he spent searching for her. The people, the...the scum he'd met along the way. The accusations. The revelations.

The crushing grief that came with the news of her death.

The hope that had kept his heart beating for ten long years.

"And then she disappeared. A few months later, they said she was dead."

"So you thought you were a widower." Brady glanced at his computer screen. "That would explain your answer on the application."

"I never believed it."

"But if she was presumed dead..."

"She was."

"Not that I'd have fired you for it, but that does make it easier."

Like Eric cared.

"I called that number she gave us," Brady said.

He sat up straighter, leaned forward. "What'd you learn?"

"The detective, Sally Bowman? She passed away."

The cop in him voiced the next question. "Natural causes?"

"Breast cancer. Six months ago."

"Did anybody else have information about Kelsey?"

"Without more than a first name and a year? The guy who answered laughed his butt off right before he hung up on me."

"You didn't give him more information?"

"Course not." Brady sat back, shook his head. "I've been to this party before, remember? My own wife had reason to run. I didn't let her enemy find her, and I'm sure as heck not going to let anything happen to your wife."

Eric had forgotten that story. The memory of it—and the happy ending—bolstered his spirits, if only just a little.

Brady continued. "Your wife disappeared for a reason. We need to figure out what that was, and who she's afraid will find her."

Eric stood. Glanced at his gun and badge.

"Pick them up, and don't put them down again unless I tell you to."

Eric slid his gun and badge back where they belonged.

"Why don't you take a few days off?" Brady nodded toward the computer screen. "I checked your vacation time. You've got plenty. Looks like you haven't taken a vacation in more than a year."

"Took some time when my folks came to visit."

"Good thing you get more than three days a year. You're officially on vacation as of now."

Eric started to thank him, then stopped. "I might need the department's resources, after I figure out what's going on."

"Then you'll have to trust me to help."

Eric thought of his wife, thought of spending time with her regardless of what would happen next. "I'm grateful."

"Don't get mushy on me. Aren't you curious why she got arrested?"

He'd forgotten that, in the haze of the past.

"Breaking and entering," Brady said. "We found her in one of the cabins by the lake."

"Okay."

"Find Donny. He'll catch you up on what he knows. Then talk to her, see what you can learn."

ERIC FOUND Donny at his desk. His friend waited for an explanation, but Eric couldn't explain it all again. It was taking all his energy to hold in his emotions, and he'd need every ounce of strength to confront Kelsey.

"You okay, man?" Donny asked.

"You made the arrest?"

Donny's short pause held all his questions, but he kept them to himself. "We got a call this morning. One of the neighborhood watch guys at the lake thought he saw a light flickering in the window of a cabin on Lakeside last night. He didn't call it in, though. It was dusk, and he figured maybe it was a play of light. This morning, he drove by again and noticed a trail down the driveway and around back. The snow'd melted from where it had been packed down, making it easier to see."

"A trail, like..." He was trying to picture it. Places where people had stepped on snow usually melted first. He could picture that. But a trail?

"The guy thought somebody'd dragged a body." Donny chuckled. "Some people watch too much crime drama. But your...uh, friend said she'd sprained her ankle and crawled to the house. That would explain it."

Eric closed his eyes against the image of Kelsey, injured, cold... Opened them when it passed. "Go on."

Donny reached to the floor beside him, pulled up a backpack. "She was clutching this when we got there."

Eric unzipped it, found clothes, toiletries, a canvas case filled with suspicious metal tools, a flashlight, a phone charger, a flash drive, and a map of New Hampshire. "That's it?"

Donny opened his desk drawer, lifted out a revolver in a clear plastic bag, and set it between them. "This was shoved between the couch cushions."

Eric studied it. An old Taurus that needed a good cleaning. "Bullets?"

"None."

"She admit it was hers?"

"Claimed she never saw it before. Wicked coincidence, if you ask me." At Eric's look, Donny added, "Not that anybody did. Ask me, that is."

"Anything else?"

"Not that we found. We didn't search the whole place when we grabbed her. Figured she had all her stuff in the backpack."

Eric rifled through the rest of the backpack. Every small

pocket. He even searched for a tear in the lining, maybe a hiding place. All empty. "No ID, no phone, nothing personal at all."

"I thought that was weird, too. We could go back, search again."

"No." Eric left the revolver and backpack on the desk. "Just hold onto those for now. Not sure what's going to happen."

"About that. I was hoping Sam owned the cabin, but no deal. I talked to her, though, and she knows the owner. They live in Nashua. She's going to call them, see if they'll accept her story."

"What story was that?"

"That she sprained her ankle and sought shelter from the storm to keep from freezing to death."

"You believe her?" Eric asked.

Donny shrugged. "It holds up, if you don't ask too many questions. Like, how'd she get there with no car? Where'd she plan on going with no money or ID?"

"You ask her any of those questions?"

"She didn't say much of anything."

"Seems her story only holds up if you're an idiot."

"But you know Sam. She'll work her magic. And the place hadn't been damaged. Don't even know how she got in—no sign of a break-in."

Eric remembered the little canvas case. Had Kelsey picked the lock? His wife was full of surprises.

"Thanks."

"Sure. Let me know if I can do anything else."

Eric stood and headed toward the door that led to the holding cells.

TEN

VANESSA WALKED out of the Miami high-rise as if nothing had changed. As if her whole life hadn't just clicked into place.

She'd been afraid, terrified that it wouldn't stay. Afraid the years had been too hard on her body to allow such a precious thing to grow inside her. Afraid to share the news with Carlos until after those first three months had passed. But now, after months of hope, months of fear, she could almost relax.

She was carrying his child. And the child was healthy and strong. Another six weeks, and the doctor told her they'd be able to determine the child's gender.

A boy, she thought. Please, let it be a boy. She had no desire to bring a girl child into the world. She knew what happened to girls.

Not her child, though. No, her child would be doted on. Her child would be pure, innocent, cared for. Vanessa's child, boy or girl, would love her. Even when Carlos's care faded, as it was bound to do, the baby would always love her.

She resisted the urge to pat her still flat belly. Carlos's man was watching her, of course. Always, when she left the house alone, Carlos sent a man to follow her. She hadn't really earned

Carlos's trust. Maybe after the child was born, maybe then he'd trust her. Then, they could be a family.

Freedom called to her. She would wait, see if it was possible to be with Carlos and be free. Like one of those normal women, the ones with the husbands and families who didn't dream of escape every night. She would try. God help her, she would try to make a life with Carlos, because as much as she desired freedom, she was terrified to be alone.

Now, with this child, she would never have to be alone again.

She would tell Carlos tonight. He'd be as happy about their child as she was.

For this to work, he had to be.

ELEVEN

KELSEY'D BEEN so hungry she scarfed down the entire cheeseburger and almost all the fries. Now she thought she might be sick. Had it been too much food too soon after nearly starving all week? Or had the fact that she was trapped in a jail cell and would probably never see her son again contributed to the nausea?

Maybe a little of both.

Those maudlin thoughts wouldn't do her any good, and right now, she had to figure out how to get away from here. Make sure Daniel was safe. Leave town and regroup.

The thought of leaving Eric again had her brushing tears away.

The doctor had wrapped her ankle, given her Tylenol, and promised to send over crutches. He'd also suggested she get the ankle x-rayed. She'd declined. It was already a lot better now than it had been Monday. Another few days and it'd be good as new.

So now, she waited. Would Eric be back to see her? Surely he wouldn't leave her here overnight.

Remembering the anger on his face, she thought maybe he would.

But just a few minutes later, the door buzzed.

She swung her feet to the floor as Eric stepped in carrying a pair of crutches in one hand, a set of keys in the other. He stopped in front of her cell, leaned the crutches on the far wall, and turned to her. "How you holding up?"

She shrugged because the sight of him stole her voice. He was as handsome as ever. If anything, the years had only made him better looking. He'd cut his hair from the longer style he'd worn in college. Now, it was very short on the sides, longer on top, brushed back. His hazel eyes seemed gray right now, but she remembered the little flecks of green that flashed when his emotions flared. He had a five o'clock shadow that only enhanced his looks.

"What?" he said.

She'd been staring. "Just...you look good."

He gave her a once-over. "Honestly, Kels, you've looked better."

Kels. The nickname felt like a good sign. She let out a short laugh and ran her fingers through her tangled hair. "I don't doubt it."

He unlocked the cell, crossed to the bed, and sat beside her. He turned toward her, brushed her hair out of her face. The feeling tingled to her toes. "I like it long," he said.

She ducked her head to hide a blush. She'd hoped he would. With all the other things, all the fear, all the worry, in the back of her mind, she'd wondered if he liked her hair.

Stupid, but there you go.

She looked at him again. She could hardly keep her gaze away. "You still mad at me?"

His eyebrows rose. "For disappearing off the planet, for

faking your own death...? It's gonna take more than a couple hours to get over that."

"Wow. You can sure hold a grudge."

His lips quirked, and he shook his head, looked away.

She bumped his shoulder with hers. "I think you'll forgive me."

"I never was the brightest bulb in the chandelier." He turned to face her. His amusement faded. "Oh, Kels. I don't know how to feel."

"I know. Me, too."

"Except you..." He looked away again. Stared toward the ugly beige cinderblock wall across the hall, maybe at the crutches propped there. "You could have come home. You could have—"

"I couldn't."

She was sure he'd argue with her. A moment passed before he turned his gaze on her again. "Why don't you start from the beginning?"

She swallowed. She knew she needed to tell him, but here in a dingy jail cell? She hadn't imagined that. "Did Chief Thomas call Detective Bowman?"

"She a friend?"

Kelsey thought of the heavy-set woman, her frizzy hair, her salty language that would make a Green Beret blush. "Not a friend, necessarily. But she did save my life."

"Did she know you faked your death?"

"No. I wouldn't have put her in that position. I'm sure she suspected. She knew most of my story. Why, what did she say?"

"Nothing." He took her hand in his. It felt so natural, so perfect. She almost cried at the simple touch. When was the last time anybody but Daniel had held her hand? The last time anybody had cared to protect her? To know her?

Eric's gaze was tender. "Detective Sally Bowman died of breast cancer six months ago."

"Oh." The news came as such a shock, Kelsey almost couldn't process it. They hadn't been friends, but Sally was the only woman who knew the story. The only connection to that time of her life who understood and cared. And now she was gone, too.

Kelsey wasn't sure she could stand to lose anybody else.

"I'm sorry." Eric rubbed his thumb over the back of her hand. "You cared about her."

"I hardly knew her. But...she..." She couldn't explain the tears that sprang to her eyes. All the loss. This just seemed one too many. And breast cancer? A slight chuckle forced its way through her tears.

"What's funny?"

"She was the toughest woman I ever met. I can't imagine how she felt succumbing to such a...a girl disease. That probably ticked her off to no end."

"Unfortunately, cancer isn't easily intimidated."

"I'm sure it nearly met its match with Sally." The implications of Sally's death settled in her stomach heavier than the burger and fries. "There's nobody to back up my story."

"You haven't told us a story."

"I know. I thought she could help, keep y'all from thinking I'm nuts."

"You can tell me. I'll believe you."

"I have to get out of here."

"Who are you running from?"

"I'll tell you everything if you get me out of here."

He looked away, shook his head. "I don't get to decide, Kels. I'm not the boss." He turned back to face her. "Brady's a good guy. They're working on your release. A friend is calling the owner of the cabin to see if they'll buy your story."

"Buy it? If I hadn't broken in, I'd have frozen to death."

"No ID, no phone, no car, no money, and just a handful of personal items. Where were you headed when you sprained your ankle?"

She looked at her knees. She'd concocted a whole story about how she'd been hitchhiking, how the driver had tried to get fresh with her, and she insisted on being let out. And she just happened to be in Nutfield, and she wanted to see the lake, and she just happened to sprain her ankle right there... Well, at least the last part was true.

She peeked at Eric from the corner of her eye, saw him watching her. She was here, with him. Her husband. A man she'd thought of every hour of every day for a decade and more. Was she really going to lie to him?

Not lie, but not tell the truth, either. "It's a long story."

He looked at the wall again. Swallowed. Squeezed his eyes shut. When he opened them again, he didn't look at her. "You weren't going to call me."

Not a question. She didn't answer.

"How did you end up in Nutfield?"

Another tricky question she didn't want to answer. She'd planned to leave the stolen car with a full tank of gas and a note of apology. But she'd stolen it. A felony.

She couldn't tell the truth, and she wouldn't lie. Not yet. Not until she had to. She said nothing.

"You promised you'd tell me everything."

"When I'm out of here."

Finally, he turned to face her again. He still held her hand. Maybe he needed to be connected to her as much as she did to him. "Then you'll start at the beginning?"

He might as well have brought the doctor's x-ray machine in here, the way he was looking beyond her skin, behind her eyes.

He'd know if she lied, but she didn't have a choice. "I'll start at the beginning."

He leaned closer. Too close. His eyes narrowed, and she studied the fine lines at their corners. Those lines hadn't been there a decade before. Had she put them there? She inhaled the scent of his soap, felt his breath on her cheek. He never broke eye contact. "And you'll stay."

"I don't..." But she couldn't form words, not with him looking at her like that. Not with him this close. If only he'd close the last inch between them. She licked her lips, could nearly feel the kiss.

His gaze dropped to watch the action, and he inched a little more forward. Her nerve endings screamed for his touch.

"You don't want to leave me again," he said.

Leave him. What was he talking about, leave him? She would never...

But she had.

And she would again.

She leaned back just enough to give her brain room to think. "I don't want to."

He let go of her hand and stood. "But you will."

"I...I can't..."

He stepped out the door, leaned against the concrete wall, and crossed his arms. "Here's the deal, Kelsey. The only way you get out of here is if you stay in town until this mess is cleared up. You leave, and I'll put your name in the system myself."

"You wouldn't."

"Don't tempt me."

"You love me."

"With every stupid, pinheaded cell in my body, I do. But there's a very thin line between love and hate. If I were you, I wouldn't cross it."

He pulled her cell door closed and walked out.

Kelsey batted the facts of the previous ten years around in her mind until she thought she might go insane. There was the truth, some of which she could share. There were the lies she'd been telling everybody, including her own son. Her name, her history, her story. The facts all jumbled together like a tangle of discarded necklaces. How could she extract just the chains she needed without accidentally yanking them all into the open?

She couldn't. But she'd promised. She had to try. Eric deserved that.

If only she'd stayed dead. Except he'd never believed it. Which meant what? She knew he'd never remarried, but he was still young. Just thirty. She'd figured he just hadn't met the right woman yet. She'd done enough internet stalking to know Eric had been made detective a few months before. She also knew he was involved with the little church in town. She'd searched his name and discovered he volunteered with the youth group there, which just confirmed that the good guy she'd known in college had grown up to be a good man, probably a great man. Because, in New England, church wasn't expected. Folks didn't bat an eye if you didn't show up on Sundays, not like where she was from, where all the church ladies would look down their noses at the heathens who didn't dress to the nines and endure the services. Her mother'd been the perfect church lady.

But Kelsey didn't believe for a minute that her Eric was anything but sincere.

She hated herself for the way she'd hurt him. But what would she do differently if she could go back?

No, she couldn't think about all the would-have-beens. Too much pain on that trail.

At least an hour passed before the magnetic door buzzed. Eric and the chief walked in. They both stopped outside the cell. The chief spoke. "The owner of the cabin is considering not pressing charges."

"Considering it. But if he decides to?" she asked.

"Then we have to charge you with breaking and entering. The people who own the cabin have every right."

"Of course," she said. "You explained the situation?"

"They're aware."

"Okay. Did somebody shut the water back off?"

Chief Thomas's eyes narrowed, and he glanced at Eric before he responded. "I'll call their management company, be sure they take care of that. We don't want their pipes to freeze."

"Thank you," she said. "That cabin saved my life. Even if they do press charges, I wish I could thank them personally."

The chief nodded once, glanced at Eric again, and continued. "Then there's the matter of the gun."

"Oh." She didn't want to lie. She didn't say anything.

"Donny said you claimed you'd never seen it before."

"Right," she said.

"We have your fingerprints," he reminded her. "We got a good print off the gun. We could run them against each other."

"Right," she said again. Then she sighed, knew she was stuck. "I bought it at a pawn shop. I've never fired it. I don't even know if it works."

"Why'd you buy it?" Eric's voice had her meeting his eyes.

"Single woman, traveling alone. I did some hitchhiking. Stayed at some seedy places. Seemed wise to at least look like I could defend myself."

He looked like he wanted to question her further, but he kept his mouth shut. He turned to the chief, whose penetrating gaze hadn't left her face.

The silence was stickier than sweet tea.

"A gun with no bullets," the chief said, "is an invitation to get yourself killed. If you're going to have one, you need to know how to use it. Just as important, you need to be willing to use it."

"Yes, sir."

He sighed. "I can make the gun go away, but you're not getting it back."

A tiny knot of tension loosened. "Thank you."

The chief pulled keys out of his pocket and unlocked the cell door. "You haven't been charged with anything. But you need to stay in town until this is cleared up. You understand?"

She nodded.

"You have someplace to stay?"

She looked at Eric. His gaze had remained steady, his face, unreadable. She looked back at the chief. "No."

"She'll come home with me." Eric lifted his eyebrows. "If that's okay with you."

She couldn't seem to make words come out of her mouth. Home with him. But if Daniel were there... Part of her hoped he would be, but she couldn't see her son again. Not yet. "You live alone?"

"Just me and my dog."

Of course Daniel wasn't with Eric. She hadn't been able to make that phone call. Equal parts sadness and relief had her speechless. Then she thought about spending the evening with her husband. She couldn't think of anything she'd like better. It would make leaving that much harder, but right now, she didn't care.

Eric snatched the crutches off the far wall and carried them to her. "You ever used crutches before?"

"Nope."

"They're pretty simple. Stand up." She did, and he adjusted them to fit her. "There you go."

She tried them out, met her husband's eyes, and smiled. "Thank you."

He nodded at the cell door. "Let's go."

Five minutes later, she was seated beside Eric, and they were headed through town. She studied the buildings. Nutfield had changed a lot in the decade since she'd been there. Souvenir shops had cropped up, even a high-end clothing store. There were restaurants, a video arcade, and an ice cream shop. They passed a bed and breakfast in an old Victorian house, a mini-golf course, and a sporting goods store.

"The town's grown a lot," she said.

"Yup."

"I guess it's been discovered. Back then, it felt like our little secret."

He said nothing.

"Nice Jeep. It's probably good in the snow, huh?"

He adjusted the heat, turned up the fan. "You in the market for a car?"

"Just trying to make conversation."

"Stop."

"Fine."

They rode in silence. After a minute, he reached across the front seat and took her hand. She nearly cried.

He drove away from Nutfield onto the country road that led to his house. She'd wondered about his choice of a house out in the country when she'd first driven out there after she'd made her plan. Her ridiculous, doomed-to-fail plan.

They reached the dilapidated bridge that had nearly halted her progress a few days before. Only a fool would drive over a bridge like that. Looked like it had been there for centuries. Eric slowed the Jeep and proceeded cautiously. The bridge rattled loudly beneath them. She squeezed Eric's hand. He squeezed back but said nothing.

When she didn't think she could take any more tension, he turned down his long driveway. His house was far from the road and hidden by so many trees, she wasn't sure what it looked like, though she'd passed it a few days before. Now, she stared as the place came into view. It was bigger than she'd imagined, a white Cape Cod with green shutters. It had windows on either side of the front door, two dormers on the second floor, and an attached garage. Thanks to the shade provided by the surrounding trees, the lawn and bushes in front of the house were still covered in snow. In the fading afternoon light, she noticed a glow from inside.

"You left a light on."

"Always do," he said. "I hate coming home to a dark house."

All alone. She understood that.

"Besides, Magic doesn't care for the dark."

"Your dog?"

He shifted into park, turned to her. "You like dogs?"

"I've never had one."

One eyebrow quirked. "Never?"

"Mama refused to clean up after a dog."

"Been a long time since you've lived with your mother."

She didn't know how to respond to that. He didn't seem to expect her to. He opened his door, and she opened hers, started to climb out.

He jogged around the Jeep and called to her as he headed for the front door. "Stay in the car." His tone left no room for arguing.

"Yes, sir," she muttered to herself.

Eric opened the front door, then returned for her. She figured he'd grab her crutches, but instead, he pulled her door open wider and lifted her out.

Oh. She wrapped her arms around his neck instinctively. "You don't have to carry me."

"The walkway is slick." No smile.

He carried her inside and plopped her on the couch, then went back outside.

The home was beautiful. Hardwood floors, a brick fireplace, and soft brown furniture. There was a round kitchen table with four chairs in front of a sliding glass door that led to the backyard.

She turned the other direction, saw the efficient kitchen beyond a peninsula with two barstools.

A staircase stood across from the front door, and beyond that, she couldn't see. Perhaps a dining room? She wanted to hobble over there and have a look, but Eric was back before she could.

He slammed the door behind him. Then he propped her crutches against the far wall and lifted the backpack. "You want this upstairs in your room or with you?"

Your room. Not our room. She wasn't sure whether to be relieved or distraught.

"Upstairs is fine. I don't need anything out of it."

He jogged up the stairs. A few minutes passed, and then she heard the pounding of footsteps, a little metallic jiggle. A blond dog that looked about forty pounds ran down the stairs and to her side, then ran to the back door, then ran to her side again. The dog sniffed her, licked her outstretched fingers, and ran to the door again.

Eric returned to the first floor. "Don't mind my dog. She's crazy." Eric crossed the room and opened the door. "Come on, Magic."

The dog bolted out the back door, and Eric closed it behind her. "Crazy but sweet. She loves company."

"You have company a lot?"

"No."

He'd taken off his jacket and changed into jeans and a T-shirt. "I had to put sheets on the extra bed. I haven't had company since my folks visited last fall."

No company? Maybe not overnight company, but she knew he'd had a least one visitor recently. Daniel had been there. "Okay."

He seemed not to hear her as he adjusted the thermostat. "Sorry. I know it's freezing. I don't heat it much when I'm not here."

She tried not to shiver. "It's fine."

He crossed to the fireplace, where he set about building a fire.

"You don't have to do that," she said.

Again, no response.

She watched from behind. His shirt fit perfectly across his wide shoulders and trim back. She stared as he tore newspaper and stacked logs, mesmerized by the beauty of him. She'd forgotten.

How could she have forgotten?

Fire lit, he opened the back door for the dog, who came in, crossed to her side, and sat beside her. Kelsey petted her behind the ears. Magic wore a big doggie smile, and her tail thumped the floor.

This was the dog that had discovered Daniel. She bent close, whispered, "Thank you."

Magic just panted and leaned into her hand.

She looked up and realized Eric was watching. But when she caught his eye, he turned to the kitchen and opened the fridge. "Brady said you ate at the station. You need anything else?"

"I'm not hungry."

"Drink?"

"Water."

He brought her a glass but didn't hand it to her. "Why don't you take off your shoes and prop up that ankle?"

"It's fine, Eric."

He waited. Didn't say a word, just watched her.

She slipped off the boots, trying not to flinch with pain, and shifted until her feet were on the couch.

He set the water on the coffee table, grabbed a pillow from a chair behind him. She guessed it had come with the furniture. She couldn't imagine him shopping for throw pillows. He propped it under her ankle, lifted a blanket off the chair, and laid it over her. Then he handed her the glass. "Okay?"

"Thank you."

He returned to the kitchen. She sipped her water while she watched him feed the dog, then prepare a meal. He moved in and out of her view, snatching ingredients, banging pots and pans. The aroma of sautéing vegetables filled the space, then something else. Chicken, she thought. Minutes slipped away while he cooked, she watched, and neither spoke a word.

She went back to studying his house. The fire crackled, already warming the room. She studied the photographs on the mantle. His parents, his brothers. Seemed at least two of them had married in the previous decade. There were pictures of kids, too. It looked like Eric had a nephew and two nieces.

The house felt like a home. A home he'd made without her. A nicer home than any she'd had since she'd left. Would they have ended up in a place like this? During their short honeymoon, they'd talked about relocating to Nutfield. Would they have done it? Would they have picked out this warm sofa, that bland lamp? No, she'd have wanted something more unique. They might have disagreed. He'd have given in, let her decorate. And because he did, she'd have tried to find a compromise. They'd have laughed later, maybe sat on the couch and watched

TV together and fought over the remote control and kissed during the commercials.

That was the future they'd been meant to have.

Grief settled on her heavier than the blanket covering her legs. She twisted to study the other side of the room. Not much to see except a plastic sack beside the front door she hadn't noticed before. It had the logo of a store they'd passed.

"What'd you buy at the sporting goods store?" she asked.

"Gift for a boy I met the other day."

He didn't seem to catch her quiet gasp, thank heavens. Daniel. He'd bought a gift for her Daniel. *Tell me more.* Silently begging, she waited. When he said nothing else, she asked, "Where'd you meet him?"

"Long story. The kid was abandoned, left to fend for himself."

Her eyes prickled at the words. What would Eric think if he knew the truth? Would he ever be able to forgive her?

Would Daniel?

Eric continued cooking, added nothing else.

She sniffed back fresh tears. "How sad. Where is he now?"

"Foster care."

She squeezed her eyes shut, thankful Eric wasn't watching. "Good family?"

"They're a far sight better than the monster who abandoned him. If I ever get my hands on her..."

He would hate her when he learned the truth.

"How's the boy doing?" she asked.

"Fine. They got him in school. He's smart."

The best. The very, very best kid ever. She swiped away tears and forced her mind onto another subject.

Eric finished cooking, sat at the counter, his back to her, and ate his dinner.

She cleared her throat of the emotion. "What'd you make?"

"You said you weren't hungry."

"Just curious."

"Chinese stir-fry."

"Fancy."

"Frozen."

He obviously didn't want to talk. She, on the other hand, had a million questions. They would only invite him to question her, and she figured they'd get there soon enough.

She settled back on the sofa to wait. Eventually, he'd come in. He'd talk to her. And then she'd have to figure out what to say. How much to tell him. How to get out of this.

Suddenly, she wasn't in such a rush for the conversation.

TWELVE

When Vanessa returned from the doctor's office Friday evening, Carlos was out. He was involved in business ventures she knew little about. He'd only shared one aspect of his business with her, the one she'd known ever since he'd won her in a poker game in Nice. From the start, she'd set out to prove to him that she could be more than just a source of income, more than just one of *his girls*. She'd been a street hooker, then she'd been a high-priced call girl until she'd been purchased by her previous owner, a sheikh with an evil streak and a twisted mind.

Until she'd met Abbas, Vanessa had always been so focused on survival that to take her own life had never occurred to her. But as Abbas's favorite source of amusement, trapped on his yacht miles from land, she'd considered jumping, fantasized about letting the blue waters of the Mediterranean take her. But the porthole in her stateroom was too small to squeeze out of, and Abbas rarely let her leave the room. When he did, a guard was never too far away. And the guards were as twisted as their employer.

Until Abbas, a little of Vojislava had remained. Abbas and

his cruelty had destroyed any innocence Vanessa had carried with her from Serbia.

But she'd learned to play the part. And when Carlos had taken her, in those first few days before they'd flown to the States, she'd done her utmost to convince him that she could be, that she should be, reserved for only him. And miraculously, Carlos had taken her bait.

Instead of being moved into the rundown apartment building that housed his other possessions, the girls he'd stolen locally or imported from abroad, he'd brought her to his home, a glass-sided palace overlooking the sea. She'd shared his bed and her knowledge about his business. Eventually, she'd proved valuable to him. She knew how to motivate the girls. She was talented at matching just the right girl for the client's needs. She could find the jewels among the rubble, the girls who were sufficiently skilled and sufficiently broken to be more than street hookers. Vanessa had increased Carlos's income, and as she had, Carlos had trusted her with more and more.

She'd been with him for two years now. She'd proved her value to his business every day. She'd proved her value in his bed every night. She'd earned her place at Carlos's side.

Alone in her office—one of the smaller bedrooms off the south wing—she rubbed her belly. "Little one, you will change everything for me."

She sat at her computer and opened the chatroom where Carlos did much of his business. He'd taught her the system and codes and allowed her to take care of day-to-day operations, allowing him to focus on his other sources of income.

She scrolled through the messages, looking for names they'd done business with before. She made calls, made deals, and made money for the rest of the afternoon. After the sun set, she yawned, amazed at how sleepy she was. This baby was taking a lot of her energy.

She was just about to close the program when another message came in.

A request for three girls. She replied, and immediately, he replied back.

Half w/ info.

Information? This was Carlos's contact in New Hampshire, the one looking for Carlos's other child and the mother who'd escaped him. The only information that man could have would relate to Kelsey and her child.

Vanessa sat back in her chair, stared at the screen. She was close to getting everything she'd ever wanted. Could this woman steal it all away? Could her child take Carlos's devotion?

No. Carlos cared for her. He hated Kelsey. Yes, he wanted his child. If Vanessa helped him get the child back and get revenge on the mother, then she would be held in the highest regard. Carlos would love her. He would be even more devoted to her, if she could do this for him.

Maybe.

She crossed the huge house to Carlos's office. It was unlocked—more proof that he trusted her, at least a little—so she let herself in and grabbed one of the many burner phones he kept for emergencies. She activated it and searched Carlos's office for the New Hampshire contact's phone number. Finally, she found it and wrote it down. Carlos wouldn't mind—he'd want her to manage this for him. He trusted her with this job.

She returned to her office and dialed.

When the man answered, she said, "It is Vanessa. Tell me what you know."

"The deal is half."

"Yes, yes," she said. "If the information is good—"

"And I want to tell Carlos myself."

She smiled, knowing he would say that. "I don't think you do. In December, somebody called with a tip about her whereabouts. The man held onto the information, trying to squeeze more money from Carlos. By the time they made a deal, she and the child had vanished. That man won't be passing along any information, late or otherwise, again."

"You, a common whore, dare to threaten me?"

She let the word roll over her like a wave of the sea. "Carlos does not suffer fools. And he does not let people speak to me that way. You can either talk to me or you can discover those things for yourself."

A long pause followed before a huffed breath.

"I'm up here in this nothing little town a million miles from anything for one reason," he said. "To help him find her."

"And because you agreed to relocate there, you have made millions. And had a lot of fun in the process, if I'm not mistaken."

"He asked me—"

"You will get all the credit, I assure you."

"Fine. She's here, with her husband."

"You're sure?"

"Would I tell you if I wasn't sure?"

How would she know? "And the child?"

"I've seen no sign of a kid, but I'll keep watching. I'm sure she'll bring him soon enough."

Just the woman. No child. What did that mean for Vanessa? "You have proof?"

"I took a couple of photos."

"Send them."

He said nothing, but a moment later, the burner phone dinged with an incoming message. She looked at the photos—a woman and a man sat side by side in the front seat of a blue Jeep. It could be Kelsey and her husband, Eric. But these photos were certainly not conclusive.

"How did you know she was there?" Vanessa asked.

"I got lucky. I'm always on the lookout for him. When I saw him walk out of the police station with a woman, I got closer. I made it to the next block and snapped these when they drove by."

"You were on foot?"

"In my car."

"Did you follow?"

"Can't do that. He knows my car as well as I know his. And he lives way out in the country. He'd be suspicious."

Interesting that the cop knew their man. "You two friends?"

"Far from it. I did drive by his house a little while later, and his Jeep was there. She must be at the house with him."

"What were you doing in town?"

"What does that matter?"

"I'm curious." Curious to know if this was true. The deal he was asking for—half price on three girls. That was a steep discount. If he was just trying to score a good deal, she needed to know.

"I was picking up dinner at McNeal's."

"A friend?"

"A restaurant downtown. Delicious. If you guys come up here, you should try it."

As if they would be tourists. "These pictures are inconclusive. You need to get better ones, soon. Then, I'll tell him."

The man huffed another breath. "Carlos will want to know now."

"I do not want him disappointed. If it's her, we can be there in a matter of hours. Keep an eye on her, get some better pictures, and text them to this phone."

"If they're gone by the time you get here, that's on you. About the merchandise..."

Vanessa finalized the deal and hung up. Then she searched

her computer for a good private investigator in New Hampshire and made a call.

So, Kelsey had been found, but not the child. It was the worst possible scenario. Vanessa would wait until they were certain the woman was Kelsey. She'd tell Carlos as soon as she knew for sure, whether the child was with her or not.

Her news about their baby would have to wait.

THIRTEEN

Eric forced his food down. What he wanted to do was pull Kelsey into his arms and kiss her until the decade they'd lost slipped from their memories.

And then what?

He could imagine what. He'd carry her up to his bedroom, and they'd go back to being the man and wife they'd once been, the man and wife he desperately wanted them to be again.

Which was why he was staring into the kitchen, forcing food down his throat. Not that frozen stir-fry would satisfy the hunger that was gnawing deeper than his stomach.

He squeezed his eyes closed, forced himself to focus.

Answers first. Until he had answers to his questions, there could be nothing else.

When his food was gone, when the dishes were put away and the pan cleaned, when he had no more excuses, he returned to the living room. Stoked the fire. Stared into the flames.

She was here. In his home. He'd always hoped, never believed, that he'd find her someday. That she'd come back to him. But she hadn't, not voluntarily. Something had brought her to Nutfield, but it was clear from the circumstances of her arrest that she'd never intended to find him, never intended to stay. Whatever her reason for being in New Hampshire, it obviously had nothing to do with him.

He should let her go. It wasn't like he could force her to stay. And he sure didn't want a woman who didn't want him.

But she *did* want him. He was sure of it. Well, maybe not sure. But her touch, the way she looked at him... He thought she still loved him. He'd thought that before, though, hadn't he? And she'd left him, gone for a decade. If she left him again, he wouldn't wait around. He'd divorce her, move on with his life. If he were smart, he'd turn her loose right now and start proceedings. Be done with it. Be done with her.

Right. Like that was an option.

He'd been whipped since the moment he'd laid eyes on her sitting on the grass in the quad. He'd heard her voice, her accent. Seen her long legs in those short shorts, those adorable flip-flops. Stared like a fool. And she'd just smiled and waved him over.

He'd sunk like a rock in the Charles River. Classes hadn't even started yet, and he was in love.

And now that he'd found her again, was he really thinking about letting her go? Not on his life. There was a story behind her disappearance, and he needed to know it, to know who was after her, and to figure out how to keep her safe. Until he got to the bottom of all that, until he ensured her safety, Kelsey Nolan wasn't going anywhere. If that meant he had to put her back behind bars, he wouldn't hesitate. Safer in jail than on the run. For now, he had to know what he was up against. And he wasn't going to hear the story staring at his fire.

He turned to find her watching him.

"Feeling better?" she asked.

"I'm fine."

"Okay."

He sat in one of the side chairs, tried to prepare himself.

Whatever she was about to tell him, it was going to hurt. "Why don't you start from the beginning?"

Her mouth formed a little O, like she was surprised by the suggestion. Had she really thought he wouldn't ask?

She recovered fast enough. "Why don't you tell me what you know?"

"Why? So you can gauge how little you can get away with sharing?"

He waited for the flash of quick anger he remembered, but it didn't come. Her gaze remained steady and unreadable. "I don't want to waste your time."

He settled back in the chair. "I've got nothing but time."

"Fine."

But she didn't speak.

He listened to the crackling fire while she stared at him, then turned away, then looked down. "I'm just not..." she said. "I don't know if I can—"

"You promised."

"I know." She sighed, met his eyes. "Danielle ran away. I knew things were bad at home, but I didn't realize how bad."

"Bad in what way?"

She shook her head, looked at her hands. "My stepbrother, Peter. He..."

Eric waited through the long pause.

"He was a pig. He was a couple years older than I was, and sometimes he'd get fresh with me when he'd come to visit. I didn't put up with it. I told my mother, and she told my stepfather. I don't know what they said to Peter, but he backed off." She folded her hands, unfolded them, twisted them together. "I thought... I didn't realize after I left for college how often he came around. Danielle was young and sweet and more...pliable than I was."

Eric's dinner churned in his stomach. He'd met Danielle

when the family had visited Kelsey at school. She was a sweet thing, a beautiful, innocent child. Even if she'd been ugly and horrible, she'd been a child. A child should feel safe in her own home. A child should *be* safe in her own home. "Your parents should have kept him away from her."

"I don't know that they ever understood. They assumed Peter's interest in me had been romantic. We weren't blood related, after all. But with my little sister... I never told them. When she was missing didn't seem the time."

"But what if he had something to do with her disappearance?"

"He'd been in Europe on business for weeks. He was scheduled to return the weekend after she disappeared. Which is probably why she was running away." She looked beyond him a moment, then met his gaze. "So he can't have had anything to do with it."

"Did you tell them after?"

"There was no *after*. I got taken. My sister died."

When she didn't continue, he said, "And then you faked your death."

"I never had the opportunity to tell them. And I wouldn't have, anyway. Mama was broken enough."

Eric decided not to respond. Kelsey's mother had paid a steep price for her neglect.

"Danielle didn't tell me what was going on. She begged me to let her come live with me. She said she and Mama weren't getting along. Well, I know how Mama can be. She's all about keeping up appearances. That was always more important to her than us. I thought that's what was wrong. I didn't realize..."

He waited for her to go on. Finally, he said, "You couldn't have known, Kels."

She shrugged. "Maybe. Maybe I was too wrapped up in

school and in plans and...and in you to hear what my sister was saying."

"You were hundreds of miles away. Her own mother lived under the same roof and didn't know."

"My mother's not like yours, Eric. She wasn't focused on us, not ever. As long as we looked good and made excellent grades, she didn't care what else was going on in our lives. I always swore I'd be a better parent."

Kelsey's eyes filled with tears. The grief in her expression made his heart hurt. He stood, stepped toward her, but she waved him away. "If you want to hear the story, then you need to stay over there."

He took his seat.

"So Mama called me that night." Kelsey swiped away more tears, wouldn't look at him. "She'd bought me a ticket home, flying out of Boston, and begged me to come. Of course, she didn't know I wasn't in the city. That didn't seem the right time to tell her I'd eloped, and anyway, I had to help find my sister. You were sleeping peacefully, and I didn't want to wake you. I knew you'd want to come with me, but the tickets were expensive, and... Oh, it sounds stupid now. I thought I knew where she was. I thought I'd find her and be back by suppertime. I wrote you the note, took the rental car, and left."

He thought of the note he still carried in his pocket, written in a rush before she ran out the door. "That part I know."

"She wasn't where I thought she'd be. I found out she'd met a guy. Her friend told me an address Danielle had texted her. The police had already checked out the place. They said it was empty and promised they were following up on other leads. I was distraught. I couldn't leave. Not until I found her."

"Couldn't leave." Eric said. "Couldn't call, either, I guess. Couldn't let me know what was going on."

"You don't understand," she said. "This all happened that

same day. I arrived in Savannah and went to her friend's house, where I was sure she was hiding. The friend gave me the address. I made a call, found out the police had already checked it out. I went to Mama's, saw the family, everybody sitting around, doing nothing. Mama was crying, and I couldn't stand it. I couldn't stand not doing something. You have to understand, Eric. It was torture. She was thirteen."

His anger simmered. He was too familiar with the feeling Kelsey was describing. He'd felt it himself when she disappeared. Maybe Kelsey hadn't been thirteen. But she had been his bride.

He nodded for her to continue.

"I went to the address myself," she said. "It was a little house outside of Savannah in the kind of neighborhood Mama'd drive across town to avoid. There was a for-rent sign in the yard. I knocked, but there was no answer. I waited. Then I walked around and found an open window. I climbed in. The place was empty. No furniture. No food in the refrigerator or cabinets. I called out, hoping I'd hear a voice, but also, hoping I wouldn't. The place was creepy, because even though it was empty, it held the scent of sweat and cologne and I don't know what else. Like a crowd of people had just walked out." She shook her head, stared into the distance. "And then a door banged open."

Eric's insides ran cold.

"I turned, and there was a man there. He looked young, like a teenager. But maybe it was the way he dressed, because the way he carried himself—I didn't think he was as young as he wanted to seem. I thought maybe this was the man who'd seduced my sister. I asked him where she was. He smiled, but it was a terrible smile. Like a cat that cornered a mouse."

Her gaze dropped to her hands, and she continued. "He said, 'A twofer. My favorite.' And then he hit me. I woke up in the trunk of a car."

Eric clenched his fists, forced the shock and anger away until all he felt was horror. "Oh, Kels."

Her gaze was downward. Tears fell and plopped on her folded hands. He couldn't stand it any longer. He crossed the room, sat beside her on the sofa, and gathered her into his arms.

She wept against his shirt. He rubbed her back, failed to keep his own tears from falling. "It's okay. You're safe now."

She pushed against his chest, but he didn't let go.

"If you want to hear the rest..." Her voice was muffled against his shirt.

"It can wait," he said. "We're in no hurry. We have all the time in the world."

She sniffed, and in the barest whisper, said, "If only that were true."

FOURTEEN

Kelsey woke in a dark room. She bolted straight up, rubbed her wrists, checked her ankles, and hobbled to the door, where just enough light seeped beneath to show her the way. It wasn't locked.

To be sure, she pulled it open, peeked into the hallway, and closed it again.

Those old rituals should have faded years before, but some habits lingered like scars.

Disorientation had her returning to the bed. The events of the day filtered into her memory. The arrest, the jail cell, the evening spent with Eric.

Her husband.

The story she'd begun but never finished.

How many times had she gone over the day of her capture? She'd replayed it in her own mind, with detectives, even with a federal agent way back when. She'd gone over it enough that recalling it shouldn't have brought the grief any longer, but sharing the story with Eric, all those feelings had come back. The terror. The shame. The regret. Oh, the regret. Ten thousand things she should have done differently. How many lives had been destroyed because of her naivety, her arrogance, her stupidity?

When Eric had held her, those feelings had come back as if she'd just woken up in that trunk.

She'd wept onto Eric's chest. Eventually, he'd lifted her, sat on the sofa, and held her on his lap like a child. And she'd felt safe for the first time in a decade. She must have, because she'd drifted off to sleep right there in his arms. She had a vague memory of him carrying her up the stairs, laying her in bed. He'd sat beside her, stroked her hair. Those words he'd spoken—had she dreamed them?

"I love you, my sweet Kelsey."

And then he'd kissed her gently before he tucked the blankets around her and slipped out of the room.

She reached up, touched her lips, remembered that tender kiss. She squeezed her eyes shut against the painful prickling. What had she done? How could she hurt him again?

Her eyes had adjusted to the dark enough that she could make out shapes in the room. Beside the bed rested a clock, one of those old-fashioned analog types that wound up and ticked. It even had a bell on top and glow-in-the-dark numbers and hands. It was just after three a.m.

How much time since she'd first seen Eric that afternoon? Twelve hours? Not enough. Not nearly enough.

She stood, realized she was still wearing her clothes from the day before. Not the boots, though. She'd taken those off downstairs. He'd set them by the front door, and he'd draped her coat over a chair. Her backpack was in the room. She crossed to where he'd left it on top of the bureau and unzipped it. She found her toiletries then looked at the three closed doors in her room. One led to the hallway. She opened the next one and found a closet. Then she opened the third.

A bathroom. Thank heavens.

When she'd finished cleaning up, she put her things in her backpack, zipped it up, and eased open the door to the hall.

She paused, stared at the other closed doors upstairs. Which room was his? She'd give anything to peek at him one last time. But Magic was probably in there. The dog would likely wake up if she opened the door. It wasn't worth the risk.

Despite Chief Thomas's warnings, she had to leave. If she wanted her son to be safe, she had to leave. As much as it killed her, she had to leave.

When she was gone, she could make that phone call, save her son from a future in foster care, and maybe, just maybe, bring down Carlos so she could come back. But if she stayed, then Eric would be a target. And with both of them in Carlos's crosshairs, what would become of Daniel?

Maybe when she left, Eric and his boss would put her name in the system like they'd threatened. Maybe she'd be arrested the next town over. But she didn't think so. And even if the chief insisted, Eric would give her time. He knew something terrible had happened to her, and he knew she was running from someone. He'd give her time to get away before he reported her gone.

Either way, it wasn't as if she had a choice. It was her life or her son's. Though it killed her to do it, she had to sacrifice her happiness in order to ensure Daniel's safety, his future. If Eric knew, he wouldn't blame her a bit. If only she could tell him now. But that would only make leaving harder.

And once she knew Daniel was safe, she'd find a way to bring Carlos down. And if she didn't get herself killed in the process, then maybe, maybe she could come back. Maybe they'd take her back. Maybe she could have a life here. All she knew for certain was that she couldn't keep running. She wouldn't spend her life on the run, and she sure as the sun rose in the east wasn't going to make Daniel live like that.

She'd sneak out. She'd take Eric's car to the house she'd

broken into the other day and retrieve her tablet, wallet, and phone. From there, she'd go to Manchester. Leave his car at the airport. She could be there before five. Surely he'd sleep until then. From the airport, she'd take a taxi to the bus station. As soon as she was out of the state, she'd make the call that would ensure Daniel's protection. The call she'd intended to make on Tuesday.

She wouldn't return to Nutfield until she knew she could bring Carlos down. Until then, she had to get away. Let Daniel get settled.

She didn't have a choice.

She didn't.

She crept down the stairs, careful on her sore ankle, and paused at the bottom near the front door, where he'd left her boots and coat. Except they weren't there. She looked on the other side of the door, then glanced in the room she'd assumed was a dining room. No table. Just a grand piano.

The sight of it, the memories it brought, had her eyes filling with tears.

She shook off the emotions. Her coat and boots weren't there, either. Where could he have left them?

She crept to the living room.

"Looking for these?"

She gasped, swiveled, put too much weight on her ankle, and winced.

A light flipped on, and when she adjusted to the brightness, she saw Eric on the sofa. He held her boots in one hand, her coat in the other.

"Figured you might try to escape."

She opened her mouth, tried to think of something to say. Closed it again.

He set her things on the floor beside him. He'd changed into sleep pants but wore the same T-shirt he'd put on earlier. His hair was messy, and blankets and a pillow rested on the sofa. Had she woken him, or had he ever closed his eyes?

"Thing is," he said, "I can't let you go."

"I..." She swallowed. "You have to."

"I don't."

"Eric—"

"Don't."

"I don't want to go."

He crossed the room and took the backpack from her hand. He tossed it on the floor near the fireplace, where embers still glowed from the evening's fire. He turned back, lifted her before she could protest, and started for the stairs.

"Put me down."

"Nope."

She thought about struggling, but what would have been the point? Hadn't she learned years before that her strength was no match for a man's? She could fight her hardest, and she'd barely make a scratch.

He carried her and dumped her on the bed where she'd woken up.

"You can't force me to stay."

"You want to go back to jail?"

"You wouldn't dare."

He stepped back, crossed his arms, and glared at her. "You ruined my personal life a decade ago. Did you come back to ruin my career? Haven't done enough damage? Is that it?"

"What? No. I wouldn't—"

"I vouched for you. I promised Brady you'd stay in town. You're not going to make me break that promise."

"He wouldn't take it out on you. He'd..." She had no idea what his boss would do. Hadn't considered it for a moment.

"He's the chief, and he has a job. How would it look for him to have released you, a suspect in a felony, to a detective, only to have you disappear? It's more than that. He believes in me, promoted me over guys who've been there longer, because he trusts me. Brady's a good guy, but he's by the book, and letting you go today was anything but by the book."

"I didn't..." She didn't know what to say. She hadn't even considered what this might do to Eric.

"Yeah. I know. I never crossed your mind."

"No, that's not it. It's just...I have to go."

"Why?"

She could tell him everything but that. She couldn't tell him about Daniel. If she did, then he'd never let her leave. Then all three of them would be in danger. And as much as she wanted him to know... Not like this, not now.

"Tell me."

"It's the middle of the night."

"Not too late for you to go for a nice long walk, though. Or maybe you weren't going to walk. Maybe you have a friend looking for you. Somebody planning to come pick you up?"

"I don't have anybody, Eric."

"Right. Ten years you've been gone. In all that time, you've been all alone."

"What are you accusing me of?"

"Accusing you?" His face turned bright red, and his hands balled into fists. "Accusing you?" The words were roared.

She raised her arms to protect her face and head, folded her body to protect her vital organs, and curled into the fetal position.

It was happening again.

She squeezed her eyes closed, waited for the blow she knew would come.

He touched her shoulder.

A rush of red rage flooded her vision. Faces came at her, man after man after man.

The man who'd taken her.

The men who'd hurt her.

Then Carlos, always Carlos.

She opened her eyes. This man was reaching for her.

Fury flowed through her, raw power like she'd never felt before. She twisted, grabbed his shirt, and shoved him away with a strength beyond her.

He staggered back, smashed into the dresser, nearly fell.

Eric. It was Eric.

His eyes were wide, his jaw open. He lifted both hands. His voice was gentle when he said, "Kelsey. I would never hurt you."

FIFTEEN

KELSEY, his hot-tempered beauty, shriveled before his eyes.

It happened so fast, from fury to fear.

He stepped forward.

Her eyes were wide, darting all over the room. She backed to the far edge of the bed.

"Hey, it's okay."

He stepped closer still.

Her panted breaths were the only sound. She didn't move.

"Kelsey." He reached out, waited for her to push his hand away, but she didn't move. He brushed her hair back, touched her white knuckles, and ran his hand over her shoulder. He softened his voice. "I would never hurt you."

One silent sob racked her shoulders. She pulled her knees to her chest, buried her face.

He sat beside her, wrapped his arm around her, and held her. "I would never hurt you. You know that. Please tell me you know that."

She moved her head, maybe a nod. He was only making it worse. He was making everything worse.

He whispered in her ear. "If you want to leave, then you

can leave. I won't force you to stay. But sweetheart, all I want is to protect you. Maybe..." He swallowed the frustration that was trying to seep into his voice. "Maybe you could trust me. Maybe you can tell me the rest of your story like you promised, and if I can't help you, then you can go. I'll take you to...wherever. The airport. The bus station. Drive you to Boston, if that's what you want. But not until you tell me the story."

She didn't say anything.

"I have to know." He tried to temper the urgency in his voice. "I need to understand why you feel you need to leave me. If that's what you want, I won't stop you." He would not cry. He waited until that feeling passed. "I have to know the truth. I'll never be able to go on with my life if I don't."

He stood up. Stepped back. Waited.

She still didn't move.

"Will you please look at me?"

Kelsey kept her head lowered but glanced at him quickly.

He took another step back, bumped into the bureau again. "Please look at me?"

She did, finally. Fear lingered in her eyes, and shame. If this weren't his beautiful wife, he'd say she looked haunted.

He made a vow then. Even if she left him, even if he never saw her again, whoever put that look in his wife's eyes, Eric would hunt him down and kill him.

But he couldn't do that until she told him the rest of the story.

He tried a smile. "I guess I should have made you finish your story earlier. Then maybe at least I could understand."

"Maybe." But the skepticism he saw in her gaze said she doubted he'd ever understand. Well, she was probably right. Like she'd never understand what it had been like for him. Not the same, obviously, but its own kind of torture to know his wife was out there, that something terrible had happened, and that there was nothing he could do.

Sort of like how he felt right now.

"You want to tell me tonight?"

She shook her head, looked away.

"Will you tell me tomorrow?"

She shrugged. "I guess."

"And then, if you want to leave, I'll drive you myself. Okay?"

She glanced at him, shrugged again. "Okay."

Maybe he'd get some answers the next day. Or maybe she'd spend the rest of the night spinning a tale for him.

Maybe he was still a fool.

No maybe about that one.

He approached her slowly, waited for her to protest. When she didn't, he brushed her hair back, kissed her on the forehead, and tossed his heart out like a soft pitch. "I love you, my sweet."

Before she could answer, he walked out and closed the door.

SIXTEEN

Kelsey awoke to the sound of piano music filtering through the house, a mournful tune she didn't recognize. She kept her eyes closed and listened, imagining Eric's fingers on the keys, his head bowed over the instrument. How she'd loved to watch him play, to join him, adding her voice to his music.

The song shifted to something different, also unknown to her, also sad. She opened her eyes. Sunlight streamed in the window. She glanced at the clock to find it was after ten. Wow. She couldn't remember the last time she'd slept that late. Of course, the day before had been draining at best. The days at the cabin on the lake, she'd only slept fitfully, jerking awake at every sound, always alert for danger.

Here, she felt safe.

And foolish for her reaction the night before. Of course Eric would never hurt her. Seemed obvious in the light of day. But any man's rage, any man's passion, sent her scurrying for cover like a spooked rabbit. Except... last night she hadn't exactly been a rabbit, had she? Where had that fight come from? Maybe some of her strength had returned. After all those years, after fighting to survive, it seemed she'd regained at least a little.

Most people didn't see what Eric had witnessed the night before. The strange bed, the strange events of the day, the story she'd started to tell had brought out her deepest vulnerabilities and exposed her to the man she respected most.

She was such a fool.

The music had Kelsey stepping out the door and down the hall. She sat on the top step, but that wasn't close enough. Silently, she descended the stairs and sat on the bottom one, out of his view but close enough to hear every note.

The song wasn't familiar, but it was beautiful. It spoke of love and loss and regret—the song of her very soul.

And maybe Eric's too.

She had to see him. She stood, peeked around the corner. And there he was, just as she'd pictured him. But his eyes were closed. A single tear shone on his cheek and caused her own eyes to fill.

If only she could cross the room, kiss him like he'd kissed her. If only she could sit beside him like she used to in the music room in college, add her voice to his melody. They'd always made glorious music together.

He looked up, and the tune stopped. He dropped the lid over the keys, angled away, and swiped that tear off his cheek. "I hope I didn't wake you."

"It was a wonderful way to wake up."

He stood, headed through a door she hadn't seen the day before. "You hungry?"

She followed, stopped in the kitchen on the far side. "I can fix myself something."

He stared into the refrigerator. "I know." He looked at her over the door. "It'd be my pleasure to feed you."

Her cheeks warmed at the kindness. "I wouldn't want to disappoint you."

He smiled, an expression she hadn't seen in years. She smiled back. They stared at each other, trying out this new thing between them, this very old thing between them. Enjoyment. Pleasure. Comfort.

She looked away first. She couldn't let herself fall into that. She'd never be able to leave.

He cleared his throat. "I could make you an omelet, and I've gotten fairly decent at pancakes. I have English muffins. I could make a breakfast sandwich."

Normally, she'd just scarf down a piece of toast for breakfast. Single parenting didn't leave a lot of time for leisurely meals. Not that she'd ever minded. A stab of pain and longing for her son stole any words she might have formed. She endured it, waited for it to pass.

Breakfast. Right. There was no rush this morning. And it had been a long time since dinner in the jail cell. "A breakfast sandwich sounds good."

"Ham, bacon, or sausage?"

"I feel like I'm at Denny's."

He pulled eggs and cheese from the fridge and set them on the counter. "I like to eat a big breakfast. So...?"

"No meat. Just egg and cheese."

"You sure? I'm going to have ham."

"I'm sure."

He nodded to the barstools on the other side of the kitchen. "Why don't you sit over there and let the master work."

"Master, huh? This I've gotta see." She limped across the kitchen and took the seat he'd indicated.

"How's your ankle?"

"Better. Another day or two, and it'll be good as new."

"If you stay off it."

Magic was lying in front of the fire, which was burning

merrily behind a screen. The dog stood, stretched, and crossed the room. She leaned against Kelsey's leg, and Kelsey rewarded her with a scratch behind her ears.

"If she bothers you," Eric said, "just shove her away."

"I like her."

"Coffee? Or do you still prefer tea?"

"I prefer tea, but I can drink coffee."

"No need." He opened a door on the far side, next to the door leading to the piano room. Beyond his wide back, she saw a pantry filled with food. He pulled something out and set it in front of her.

It was a box of assorted teas.

"Will one of those do?"

She selected the Irish Breakfast. "I didn't know you were such a fan."

He took the little package from her and grabbed a mug. "I learned to like it. It reminds me of you."

"Oh."

After he set the steaming cup and the sugar dish in front of her, he worked on breakfast while she watched, mesmerized. The scents of toasted muffins and eggs filled the room. This... this kid she'd known in college—a teenager, gruff, goofy—had turned into a man. A handsome man with a good job, a beautiful home, and skills in the kitchen.

She hated that she hadn't witnessed it, his growing up. It was like coming in late to a movie and knowing you'd missed the best part.

Without her, he'd done what he'd always wanted. Well, perhaps not exactly. He'd dreamed of working on the police force in a good-sized city. They'd talked about where they'd live after they graduated from college. She'd already decided she didn't want to return to Georgia. Not that she didn't have good memories there, but she'd left home for a reason, and she didn't want to go back. His home state of Texas had been an option, of course, and she'd been willing. But they'd both liked Boston, too, and they'd both fallen in love with this area of New Hampshire. The few short days she'd spent in Nutfield had been the very best of her life.

He set the plate in front of her, another in front of the other bar stool. "Juice? I just have orange."

"The tea is fine."

He poured himself a glass of orange juice and sat beside her.

She lifted her sandwich, then set it down when Eric bowed his head over his meal.

That was different.

He took her hand, held it, said nothing. Then he squeezed it and let go.

"What was that?" she asked.

"Grace."

"You don't say it out loud?"

He turned and smiled. "I didn't want to make you uncomfortable, but I can next time, if you want." He lifted his breakfast sandwich and took a bite, and she did the same. It was delicious. Warm and salty and gooey.

When she'd finished a few bites, she asked, "How long have you been here?"

Eric sipped his juice. "I bought the house a couple years ago. I'd been renting a condo, but I wanted a little land and some space for Magic to run."

"Your home is lovely."

He nodded, took another bite.

"But I meant, how long have you lived in Nutfield?"

He swallowed his bite and wiped his fingers on a napkin. "I think I knew what you meant."

"Oh."

Another moment passed. Finally, he turned to face her, waited until she looked back. "I came here right after I graduated. Figured, if you ever wanted to find me..."

She looked down at her food while a flush of shame warmed her cheeks. She should have. If only she could have.

There was nothing to say. She returned to her breakfast.

"Where have you been living?"

First question about her past, and already one she couldn't answer honestly. "All over." Sort of true.

"Can you be more specific?"

She finished her last bite. "That was delicious. Just what I needed."

He ignored her comment. "I thought it might be easier for you if we started small, worked our way back. But..." He shrugged, stood, and grabbed their plates.

The dog stood at the threshold of the kitchen while Eric slid a fried egg neither had eaten, one she suspected he'd made just for the dog, onto his dirty plate. He set the plate on the floor.

Magic stood alert and quivered, but she didn't move.

"I know it's not recommended," Eric said, "but she gets a lot of people food."

"Mama always said dogs have been eating scraps for thousands of years. The folks at Purina started that foolishness."

Eric smiled, nodded. "I couldn't agree more."

The dog still hadn't moved. Finally, Eric said, "Come."

She skidded across the kitchen floor and inhaled the egg in one bite, then set about trying to lick the white off the plate.

"She likes to savor her food." Eric sent the dog back into the living room and lifted her plate before starting the dishes.

"I spent some time in Plano," she said.

He turned off the spigot and faced her. "Why there?"

She shrugged, embarrassed. "I wanted to see where you'd

grown up. First thing I saw coming into town was a giant billboard with your father's picture on it."

He chuckled. "I'd forgotten about that. His agency was doing really well. Still is. That was a few years back."

"Yeah."

"How long were you there?"

She sipped her tea. It had been torture being there, close to his folks. They'd met, of course, when they'd come to visit Eric at school. In Plano, Kelsey had steered clear of any places they might frequent. She'd been waiting tables and singing weekends at a country music bar in a nearby town. Poor Daniel had stayed with a teenager when she was at work. One day, she'd seen Eric's mother at Target. She doubted the woman had seen her, figured Mrs. Nolan wouldn't have recognized her with the lighter, longer hair. Still, it wasn't worth the risk. She'd already known she needed to move on. Being anywhere she might run into someone she'd met in the past was a mistake.

"I was there about eight months, about six years ago."

He turned back to the dishes.

"You want me to do those? Seems only fair, since you cooked."

"You need to stay off that ankle. And I don't mind." He put their plates and the pan in the dishwasher. "Where'd you go after Plano?"

"I lived near Ft. Worth for a while."

He wiped the counters, put away the toaster.

"I headed east after that. Stayed in Shreveport a few years. Got a job working as an administrative assistant, and they transferred me." And now, she had to lie. Because Daniel would have told Eric he was from Oklahoma. "So I moved to a little town outside of Kansas City." Yes, she'd be able to remember that. Oklahoma City. Kansas City. She'd learned to keep her lies simple and as close to the truth as possible. Elaborate lies were harder to keep track of.

"How long did you live there?"

"Three years." Since Daniel had started kindergarten, Oklahoma had been home. The town was small, safe, and had good schools. She'd had a decent job. Daniel'd had friends. She'd even had a few friends, women she met at work, a couple through Daniel's school. Of course, it was hard—impossible—to develop real friendships when your whole life was a lie.

She'd been fortunate, worked school hours, which was a far sight better than when she'd worked nights. But money had been tight. Very tight, and that had only been made worse when her health insurance rates had doubled. That's why Kelsey'd taken the job singing in the club on the edge of town. Daniel's friend Caleb's mom had agreed to let Daniel spend Friday nights at her house, allowing Kelsey to earn some extra money. The woman had been gracious when Kelsey'd asked, embarrassed to need the favor.

"It's a blessing to be asked," Ellie had said. "I know you'd do it for me."

She would, of course, but Ellie would never need Kelsey for anything. She had a husband at home, parents on the next block, and friends she'd known since preschool.

Kelsey had no idea what it would be like to have that kind of support system. Just having one friend to step in and help her had been a luxury she hadn't known in years.

Daniel had flourished there. He'd been like a normal kid. Begged her for a skateboard until she'd finally relented, and he and Caleb had ridden all over their little neighborhood. A year before, Caleb's father'd built a ramp for them, and they'd spent hours on that thing.

"You miss it?"

She blinked, realized Eric was watching her, and she saw no

amusement in his gaze. What emotions had played across her face since she'd last spoken?

She smiled. "I guess I do, a little. It was home."

The frown on his face told her that information hadn't made him feel better.

SEVENTEEN

THE LOOK on Kelsey's face had Eric's breakfast knotting in his stomach. He knew that look—he'd seen it in her eyes often enough. Kelsey had left somebody. Somebody she loved.

Fine.

A decade had passed. Of course she'd moved on. He ought to have moved on, too.

He poured himself a third cup of coffee he knew he wouldn't drink just to give him a moment to regroup. While he added the sugar, he said, "More tea?"

"Sure."

He grabbed another tea bag, filled her cup, and popped it in the microwave. While it warmed, he spun his wedding ring, which he'd slipped on that morning after his shower. He hadn't worn it in years, not since he'd gone to Georgia in search of Kelsey a few days after she'd left their honeymoon cabin. He'd shown up at her folks' house and realized her family had no idea who he was or what his connection to her was. He'd taken the ring off his finger then. The marriage vows hadn't been so easy to remove.

Because maybe he and Kelsey had been young, maybe they'd been crazy to elope, but he'd taken those vows seriously. Still did. Never believed for a minute she'd died, and not just because of blind hope. No body, no evidence. Nothing but an anonymous call. Only a fool would fall for that.

He'd waited.

Apparently, she hadn't.

Fine.

If she left him to go back to...to whoever, then fine. At least he'd know. He could put the ring back in the drawer where he'd been storing it for a decade. He could break the vows, move on. But not until he knew the rest of the story. Because out there, somewhere, was the person who'd destroyed his life. And with no hope of keeping Kelsey, nothing would stop him from finding that person and making him pay.

He silenced the niggling in his conscious, the one that told him revenge wasn't the answer. It sure wasn't the Christian thing to do. But there'd be no cheek-turning for Eric, not after what he'd seen the night before. Maybe revenge wouldn't make him feel better, but at least he'd be doing something. At least he'd have a plan.

The microwave beeped, and he gave Kelsey her tea, waited 'til she'd added sugar, and asked the question that would get his mind back on track.

"What made you leave Kansas City?"

"I was playing a club one night." She wrapped her hands around her cup.

"Are you cold?"

"The tea will warm me up."

"No sense sitting here shivering when there's a fire right there. Come on." He lifted her tea and offered his arm, which she took with a smile. He helped her to the sofa, though she was perfectly capable of getting there on her own. He set her tea on the coffee table. The dog had been warming herself in front of the fire as if her winter coat wasn't quite enough. But when she saw Kelsey, she padded around the table and sat at her feet. Kelsey scratched under Magic's ears.

"Why were you singing?" he asked. "Thought you'd been working as an administrative assistant."

"I just sang one night a week, to help with the bills."

He remembered how she loved to be on stage, how she'd energize a crowd. He sat on the chair catty-corner to her. "You always enjoyed performing. You must have loved it."

She frowned. "Not really. It wasn't... Things changed after..." She swallowed, looked away. "It was scary, being on stage. Knowing people were seeing me, but because of the stage lights, I couldn't see them. It was a risk every time I stepped up there. I'd search the audience for familiar faces before I went on. I played bars the locals frequented, not that there were tourists visiting where I lived. I thought I was safe."

Eric hated to think of his Kelsey as skittish. Again, the desire for revenge gnawed like hunger. "Why did you do it, then? Why take the risk?"

Her smile was shy, the smile of that girl he'd met on the quad years before. "I guess I was pretty good, because people came to see me. I made a cut of the bar's sales. I could bring home a week's wages in a couple of hours. It was worth the risk."

Nothing was worth the risk, not if the people after her wanted to hurt her. How much money did it take to support herself, anyway? How much did she need?

He was being judgmental. He didn't care. "Was it? Worth it to risk your life for a couple of bucks in your pocket?"

Her eyes flashed. "You have no idea what my life was like."

"Your choice. Not mine."

"You don't understand."

"Obviously."

She looked away, sighed like she'd been defeated, and made him feel like a jerk. "It wasn't worth it," she said. "Somebody recognized me. A girl I went to high school with. I talked to her, tried to hide my accent, pretended like I had no idea who she was. But she knew. And since I hadn't seen her until after my show, who knows who she texted? For all I knew, she took my photo and plastered it all over Facebook."

"So you ran."

"I ran."

"Smart."

"It's why I'm still alive. Every time I saw somebody, even when I wasn't sure... But it was harder this time. Kansas City had been home."

He threw his next remark out, hoping for truth. Hoping he was wrong. "You have somebody there."

"What do you mean?"

"Somebody you love."

She smiled, looked away, shook her head. "Not like you think. Just... I'd made some friends."

Nope. She was lying. About that. Maybe about more. Maybe this was all a ploy to get out of town. She'd spin her tale, then ask him to make good on his promise. And he would, too. Drop her wherever and be done.

Except it would never be done. Regardless of how she felt, he'd love her forever.

He stood, stoked the fire, and reminded himself that he'd had a life before Kelsey showed up. Maybe not the perfect life, but friends, family, and faith. He'd lived without Kelsey before. He could do it again.

He just didn't want to.

"Eric?"

He added a log then replaced the screen. He sat and folded his hands together. "So you ran."

She met his gaze, held it, seemed to be trying to convince him of something. He didn't look away, and she sighed. "I came here."

"Why here?"

"The man who"—she stared at her hands—"who took me. He has connections in Nutfield."

He repeated her words in his head. The man...in Nutfield? Too many questions left unanswered in that statement. "Tell me about this man."

Her face paled, and she reached for her tea with trembling fingers, then seemed to change her mind. She resumed petting Magic. "He... I was..." She took a deep breath. "His name is Carlos."

He remained silent, tried to will her the confidence to speak.

"Carlos Otero. I don't know if that's his real name, but it's the one he's gone by since he came to the States."

"From?"

"Venezuela."

"Is that the man you saw at the house in Savannah?"

She shook her head. "That was a lackey, the guy they hired to lure in the girls. He had a pretty face and no heart. He got into human trafficking to put himself through law school."

Human trafficking. The words were so innocuous considering what they represented. To have her speak them so casually made him want to punch someone. The man who'd done this to his wife. He let the feeling roll through him like the energy from a lightning strike, pushed the fury aside, and focused again. "How do you know that much about him?"

"My testimony put him in prison. Him and a bunch of other

guys. The highest up in the organization besides Carlos was a guy named Mateo Ruiz, Carlos's right-hand man."

Eric was still absorbing that news when she continued.

"I crippled"—she made air quotes around the word—"their operation. That's what the detective said. More like I sprained it. It healed faster than my ankle, I think. A month, maybe six weeks later, Carlos was right back at it. Apparently, there's an endless supply of greedy, heartless men who treat women like livestock."

He silenced his first response to that, flipped through a few others before settling on, "We're not all like that."

Her gaze flicked to his, then back to the fire. She didn't seem convinced.

She was getting way ahead of him. He couldn't keep up. "Let's go back to the beginning. You woke up in the trunk of a car. Then what?"

"The kid, Kyle, drove me to a little house on the outskirts of Miami. Danielle was there, along with a few other girls. I'll never forget the look in my sister's eyes when she saw me. Such hope. She had no doubt that I could rescue her."

Kelsey stared into the fire while he watched her face. He couldn't force his eyes away, though the expression he saw, that haunted look he'd seen the night before, wounded him like no words ever could. If only she'd trusted him. If only she'd asked him to go with her to find her sister, or called him before she'd gone to that house. He'd have been there for her. None of it would have happened.

By the look in her eyes, Kelsey had rehearsed those if-onlys for a decade.

She wiped a tear from her cheek, then another.

He went into the small bathroom under the stairs and grabbed a box of tissues. Back in the living room, he handed her one and set the box on the coffee table.

"Thank you."

He waited until her tears stopped falling before he said, "Then what happened?"

"Then..." But her voice trailed off. The only sound in the room was the crackling fire and the ticking clock. The dog pressed into Kelsey's leg, and she petted her, though her gaze never left the fireplace.

EIGHTEEN

THE CONTENTED DOG BESIDE HER, the dancing flames in front of her—neither was infusing her with the courage she needed to share the story with Eric.

She couldn't seem to form words.

She'd told the story many times—to police officers, detectives, lawyers. But she couldn't seem to tell her husband.

It wasn't hard to figure out why. It was quite simple, in fact. She didn't want him to know. She never wanted Eric to understand the horrors she'd been through, what had happened to her. How could she explain it to this gentle man? The truth about what happened to her in Miami would kill him.

The rest of it—how could he ever forgive her?

Those months played out in her memory until she thought of something she could share.

"Carlos seemed to think he and I were destined to be together. He had this bizarre idea that if he was just nice to me and bought me stuff, I'd forget he'd kidnapped my sister and me, forget what he'd done to us." She allowed the images those words brought to come and go before she continued. "He got to where he trusted me."

She glanced at Eric. He was still watching her, gaze intent, like he was trying to pick up every nuance of her words. She was trying just as hard to hide the truth. Not that Eric didn't know. Maybe on some level, he knew the facts. But he could never understand. And she didn't want him to.

"How'd you manage to convince him you were trustworthy?" Eric asked.

She attempted a smile. "I could have won an Academy Award for my performance."

His face only registered pain. She hated to think what he was imagining, and she wasn't about to give him more details.

She'd had to save her sister. She'd have done anything to save her sister.

She needed to keep his focus there. "I convinced him, over time, he could trust me. He got to where he let me go places by myself. Shopping, the doctor."

"Were you sick?"

She shouldn't have said that. "Nothing serious. The point is, he let me leave. So, I devised a plan. I didn't get to see Danielle very often, but when I did, I grilled her about her schedule. Once the girls had been..." She didn't know how to explain what they'd done to Danielle and the others, how they'd gotten the girls to comply. She wouldn't explain it. "They had the girls working a street corner, and Danielle told me where it was, exactly when they were there. One day when Carlos let me leave, I slipped into a McDonald's, changed clothes in the bathroom, tried to make myself look like a man—at least from far away. Then I hot-wired a car. I—"

"Wait. How'd you learn to do that?"

She shrugged. "Internet. Carlos let me use his computer sometimes."

He shook his head. "Is it harder or easier than picking a lock?"

She nearly smiled, but it faded fast. "Survival skills."

"Right."

"I planned to just drive up like a John, get Danielle in the car with me, and drive away. But when I got to the corner, Danielle wasn't there. The other girls were, and one of them approached the car. Misty. She said Carlos had picked up Danielle a few minutes before."

"Carlos picked her up himself?"

"Yeah. Which meant something was very wrong."

That moment, her plan had crumbled to dust. She'd looked in the rearview mirror, seen one of Carlos's goons approaching the car. That's when she knew, Carlos had never really trusted her. His man must have been watching the whole time—when she'd gone in the McDonald's to change, when she'd hot-wired the car. He'd called Carlos, and Carlos had taken Danielle.

"I should have gone back right then." Kelsey met Eric's eyes through a haze of tears. "But Misty knew what I'd been up to and begged me, begged me to save her. I didn't know what to do. I couldn't very well leave the girl, not now that everybody knew what I'd been planning. They'd have punished her just for talking to me." She reached toward Eric, desperate for someone to tell her she'd made the right choice. "You understand, right, that I couldn't leave her? She wasn't my sister, but she was somebody's sister, somebody's daughter. She mattered, too."

Eric sat beside her on the couch. "Of course. You couldn't leave her, not when you had the chance to save her."

"I thought I'd take Misty, we'd go to the police, and they'd find Danielle. They'd raid the place. They'd save her." She swiped the tears, angry they could still fall after all that time. "I floored it. Started beeping my horn. I had Misty call the police on the phone Carlos had given me. The goons got in their car and followed, but then, the police were there, and they took off."

She continued the story, recalling the details as she glossed over them for Eric. They'd been taken to the police station, treated like criminals, prostitutes. Kelsey had begged them to listen, and finally, Detective Bowman did. Kelsey gave her directions to the house where Danielle had been staying. Kelsey even rode with Detective Bowman when the police raided it.

The house had been empty.

The following day, Kelsey received a text message on the cell she'd gotten from Carlos. It was a video, full living color. Her sister cowering on the floor. The only other thing in the screen was a hand and a gun. Two gunshots, and Danielle was dead.

The message that accompanied it read, *you're next.*

Eric wrapped her in his arms. "I can't imagine."

"I tried." She thought of all the things she'd done to try to save her sister, all the horrible, unspeakable things she'd done. "It was my fault. She'd still be alive if not for me."

"You did all you could," Eric said. "You didn't kill her. That monster killed her."

She might as well have. Her plan had seemed flawless. Instead of saving Danielle, she'd made her a target. And she'd infuriated Carlos, who would never have killed her if he'd thought it through. Danielle was valuable only as income, but valuable nonetheless. They'd invested a lot to get Danielle.

But she knew how Carlos's mind worked. Carlos had believed Kelsey was starting to care for him. Embarrassment and shame had led to that impulsive decision—kill Danielle to hurt Kelsey.

It had worked.

Kelsey backed out of Eric's arms.

"I showed the video to Bowman, and she vowed to put them all in prison." She explained that weeks had passed while Bowman and her team put together a case. Misty and Kelsey were protected, hidden in a safe house until after the trial. Eventually almost all the men involved were arrested and charged. With the evidence Kelsey provided, most were convicted.

But not Carlos.

Eric interrupted her story. "Why not?"

"There was no evidence pointing to him. He'd been careful to make sure others were always in front. They hoped that one of his men would turn on him for a reduced sentence, but none of them did."

"But you knew," Eric said. "Why didn't they trust your word?"

"What did I know? That Carlos was in charge because the men were deferential toward him. But I never saw Carlos do anything illegal. I never saw him with the girls. I never heard him giving orders, nothing that was obviously illegal. All I knew Carlos had done was hold me against my will."

"He did other..." Eric looked away, swallowed. "He forced you—"

"Yes. He did." Her voice shook, but she made herself keep going. Keep going or she'd never get through it. "He raped me. Many times. And before him..." She took a deep breath. Started again. "But I'd been on his arm, don't you see? His... his date, his *girlfriend*." The word felt like sawdust in her mouth. "Carlos was an upstanding member of the community. He owned businesses, paid taxes, gave to charity. The DA believed me, but there was no evidence. Just my word against his. His word and his army of attorneys."

"But surely, if they'd let you testify..."

"The DA thought a jury might think I was a jilted lover trying to get revenge."

Eric pulled Kelsey close again and rubbed her back.

She pressed into his soft sweatshirt and allowed him to

comfort her. Was she really here, with her husband, telling this story? How many times had she dreamed of this, just this? It felt right, and it felt wrong. Because she wasn't the woman he'd married. She could never be that woman again.

And when he found out about Daniel, he'd never forgive her.

He'd hate her. She pressed her hand against his chest, and he let her go.

"When the trial was over, we were free to go. Misty hadn't testified because her testimony hadn't been necessary. And she was just a child."

"How old?"

"Fourteen."

Eric swore under his breath. Paused to collect himself. "You testified?"

"I did. It was all hush-hush. Closed courtroom. They tried to protect us."

"And they never found your sister's killer." He said the words as if he knew.

"We never found out who pulled the trigger. The body and the gun had been dumped in the bay."

"That I knew." Eric squeezed her hand. "Then what happened?"

"The case wasn't big enough for federal witness protection. Florida's witness protection wasn't the same. It wasn't nearly as good."

Kelsey'd had to disappear. She couldn't risk getting any of her family involved. She faked her death. She knew Carlos wouldn't believe she'd died, especially when she tried to make it look like Carlos had murdered her. Misty had been happy to make the anonymous call. Kelsey's parents had believed, had grieved and moved on with their lives.

But Eric had never believed. Which meant he'd been waiting for her for a decade.

More tears fell, but she wasn't crying for herself. She was crying for her husband, crying because she knew as much as she'd already hurt him, she was going to have to hurt him again.

NINETEEN

SHE'D LEFT out a lot of details.

Eric knew better than to press her. But he was still unclear about one thing.

"Tell me about the connection to Nutfield."

"Right." She stood, snatched a fresh tissue, and walked to the window. "Sunny day."

"Warm, too," he said. "Relatively speaking."

"I wish we could go for a walk."

"Your ankle—"

"It's much better today. And I need to get outside. I've been cooped up for days."

He wanted her to talk and was in no mood for a walk, but she'd been stuck in that cabin, then in the jail cell. He felt a little guilty about that.

Okay, a lot guilty.

She said, "But we can't."

"Why not?"

She turned to face him. "What if they're watching your house?"

He tried to hide his smirk. "I live in the middle of nowhere.

How would they watch my house?"

"All those woods," she said. "Who knows who's out there?"

A fair point. "We could go for a drive."

"Yeah. We could." But she didn't move.

He got her coat and boots out of the front closet.

Magic jumped up and bolted to the back door. Then she turned and ran to the front. Back and forth, so excited her back legs moved faster than her front, making every few steps like a kangaroo hop. He couldn't help but smile.

Kelsey laughed out loud, and the sound, musical and familiar, brought back a thousand memories.

"My dog's an idiot. She thinks we're going for a walk."

She laughed harder. "She's hilarious. I wish we could."

"A drive, though?" He held up her boots like an offering.

She looked around, shook her head. "No. I like it here. And I don't want to be out more than I have to." She gazed out the window. "It's beautiful here."

"You should see it in the summer." A vision filled his mind. Kelsey pushing a toddler on a swing set in his backyard. Him grilling steaks. Magic wrestling with a little boy in the yard.

Funny how much that boy looked like Daniel.

He'd promised to go see the kid this weekend. And even though Kelsey was here, Eric wasn't sorry he'd made that promise. He liked Daniel. Felt connected to him. And felt sorry for him. He knew what it was like to have the most important person in your world disappear. Must have been much worse to lose a mother, and the way the woman had left him? If Eric ever got his hands on her, he'd wring her neck.

Kelsey turned, looked around at his living area, and crossed to the back door.

The dog decided that was a good sign and bolted to sit beside her, tail thumping on the carpet.

"I can see why you bought this place," she said. "It's amazing."

He crossed the room and stood next to her. "I've got three acres, mostly forest."

"Wow." The word was filled with awe, as if he'd accomplished something grand. Not that hard to save money and buy a house when you had a good job and only yourself to feed. And he'd been planning for something all that time. For her.

"I thought you'd like it."

She turned to face him. The smile that had been there faded. "I'm sorry, Eric."

"I know you didn't want to leave me."

Magic stood, nudged at the glass. Eric reached across Kelsey and slid the door open. The dog bolted out and straight into the woods.

"You need to go out there with her?"

Eric watched his dog disappear in the brush. "She'll be fine."

She turned away, took a little of his heart with her. She'd take the rest of it when she left again.

He forced a deep breath. "You were telling me about a connection to Nutfield."

"Right." She pulled out a chair at his small kitchen table and sat. "I've been gathering evidence against Carlos all this time."

He sat across from her. "How?"

"Before I faked my death..." Her voice trailed off, and she looked out the slider again. "You're going to be mad. Just remember, I was desperate. My sister was dead, and it was my fault. It was stupid."

"What did you do?"

When she didn't answer, he started counting. If he reached twenty, he'd press her further.

He was at seventeen when she said, "I broke into his house."

That got his attention. "You did what?"

"I knew he wasn't there. I watched until he left. He didn't usually leave a guard there."

"Not 'usually,'" he said. "But sometimes?"

"Not that day. No cars out front. There was an alarm, and I knew it was silent, and I knew it would alert him, not the police. I also knew which windows were wired and which weren't."

"You knew a lot."

"I'd...I'd lived there a couple of months." She gave him a minute to absorb that morsel before she continued. "I thought I could get in without him knowing. There was a small window in the half bath downstairs that he sometimes left cracked open. He didn't think anybody could get through it. But I could. I'd gotten through it once before, almost escaped."

"Why didn't you?"

"Danielle. He'd have taken out his anger on her. I was trying..." Her voice trailed, then continued stronger. "Anyway, I barely fit when I climbed in through that window."

"Barely? Why?"

"Oh. Well, I'd gained some weight."

He opened his mouth to question that statement, then snapped it shut. Kelsey'd always been thin as a willow branch. Not only that, but she was one of those people who didn't eat when she was worried. She used to lose weight in the weeks leading up to exams. He'd gotten to where he forced her to eat. But her weight wasn't important, and she wasn't a suspect. He needed to let her tell the story her way.

She continued. "I got in and downloaded the files from his computer onto a flash drive."

He remembered a flash drive in her backpack. His heartbeat was racing as if she were in Otero's house right now.

"I also downloaded his search history. I was going through his paper files when I heard a car door."

He clamped his lips together, mostly to keep from yelling at her.

She swallowed. "He almost caught me. I managed to get out the bathroom window and slide it down it to where it had been, thank God. Because I figured if he knew what I'd taken, he'd have changed his tactics."

"He could have killed you. He would have killed you."

"I know. I know. I was reckless. It was too close a call. That's when I decided to fake my death and run."

Eric couldn't stand the thought of it, of any of it. Of what that man had done to her, of all the fear she'd faced, of how alone she must have felt. He reached across the table, and she slid her hand in his. "I wish I'd been there to protect you. I would have, if you'd only called."

"I know. I didn't want to ruin your life, too. I'd already ruined my own."

He pulled his hand back. "You think...?" He looked away, looked outside at his dog rifling through the brush while he tried to rein in that flash of irritation.

"You have a good life, Eric."

Right. Perfect. As long as a man liked being alone, liked not knowing what had happened to his bride, to the woman he thought he'd spend his life with.

He took her hand again. He needed to get past his anger.

After a few moments, she continued. "I've been watching him. Tracking him. He conducts his business on the dark web. It's very difficult to keep track of everything. He communicates in code. A few years back, he started corresponding with a man who goes by TakeTwo. It's taken me years to piece together the clues about where they meet. Those clues led me to Nutfield."

"That's a heckuva coincidence."

She shook her head. "I don't think it is. Carlos had Danielle.

And Danielle knew about you and me. She knew we'd eloped. I think maybe Carlos got the information out of her."

He squeezed her hand. "It wasn't your fault."

She shrugged. "She didn't know where we got married, but if he was keeping an eye out for me, then when you moved here... I think maybe he has a connection here keeping an eye on you. It's why I tried to stay off the radar when I was in town. If I'm going to catch him, he can't know I'm onto him. I thought I'd try to get pictures of him with the person he's working with, maybe work backwards from there."

A ridiculous idea. No way could Kelsey bring these people down on her own. All she'd do was get herself killed. But he wasn't going to say any of that, not yet. "What kind of business do they do?"

She slipped her hand from his and crossed her arms. "From what I can piece together, it looks like he supplies someone in Nutfield with girls."

Eric sat back. "Supplies him...for what?"

She shrugged. "I'd guess videos."

"Why videos?"

"The name, TakeTwo."

"Oh." He imagined that, some man in his town, getting girls...buying girls, filming videos. He swallowed his nausea, remembered his conversation with Brady just a few days before. Maybe someone in Nutfield was involved in human trafficking. And maybe it had been going on under Eric's nose all this time.

"How did you figure out it was Nutfield?"

"It took me years. A word here, a number there."

"What words? What numbers?"

She ticked off phrases on her fingers. "Nutty. Clearwater. Ninety-three. One-oh-one. Crystal. There were more, too, but those are the most telling."

Nutty for Nutfield. Made sense. Clearwater—their lake.

The interstate, the state highway, and the name of the main street running through town.

"Wow," he said.

"Where else could it be?"

He couldn't think of another possibility. If nothing else, the word *nutty* seemed a dead giveaway. "I think I need to see those messages."

"Maybe," she said.

"Maybe?"

"I trusted the police once before. My sister is dead."

"You don't trust me?"

"Of course I trust you. But I don't know your chief. And I don't know your police force. For all I know, the guy here has an in with the cops. Carlos is good at that, bribing police officers. Making sure he always knows everything. This is the best lead I've gotten in years, and I'm not going to blow it. And neither are you."

Eric glared across the table at her. She glared right back.

"You can't seriously think you can bring him down all by yourself."

She broke eye contact, looked beyond him. "I'll figure something out."

The instinct to argue was hard to stifle, but he managed it. He wouldn't bother until he had all the information. "Is there a meeting set up?"

"When I left"—her sentence hitched a fraction—"Kansas City, I had nowhere to go, and I thought, why not get close?"

What had caused that hitch? Could she not remember where she'd been living? Or had she checked herself.

Kansas City was a lie.

Or Eric was being supremely paranoid. Equally likely. He tucked away that thought for later. "But you didn't settle for close. You were in Nutfield."

"I just wanted to see it. I never planned to stay."

"No car. No wallet. No cell phone."

She sighed. Paused. He could practically see her spinning a story. "I hitchhiked. The guy got fresh with me, and when I told him to lay off, he dumped me out of the car."

Eric could picture that. Maybe it was true, but he didn't think so. Because Nutfield was too far off the highway. It'd be a stroke of luck to find someone headed this way. And when she'd gotten here, when she'd seen what she came to see, what would she have done? Walked back to Manchester? The weather had been frigid that day, a blizzard forecast. And Kelsey was no fool. All that, and she'd been trying to stay off the radar. Hitchhiking in a little town like this?

No way.

He wanted to call her on all her lies. Instead, he filed them away, puzzle pieces he'd try to fit into the larger picture when he was alone, which he figured he would be soon enough. "That doesn't explain your lack of personal items."

The wait for an answer was long this time. Too long. More story spinning?

"I hid my things at the cabin. I thought if my backpack was stolen or if I was arrested, I could go back for them later."

"So they're still there?"

"I assume so, unless somebody found them."

Huh. She'd told him the truth. "Weird instinct, to separate your stuff."

"Honestly, I'd thought through what I would say if I got caught there—that I'd hurt my ankle and didn't have a way to contact anybody. Having a phone on me would have ruined my story. Same went with the iPad. The wallet has money in it, all the money I had left. I couldn't risk it getting stolen or confiscated by the police."

"We need to get that stuff back for you. I'll call Sam, see if she can smooth it over with the homeowner."

Kelsey flicked her gaze to his, a small smile on her lips. "If you just take me over there—"

"You're not breaking in, Kels."

"Such a straight arrow."

"You used to be."

"Lived a lot of life since then."

A life he still knew very little about.

"So Carlos... Your plan is to, what?"

"Catch him."

"How?"

She gazed out the window at the dog, who was barking at the treetops. "I have no idea. They haven't set the next meeting yet, and when they do, I'll have to decipher it. And do it in time. I just don't know..."

He heard the worry in her voice, the despair. "You don't have to do this alone anymore, Kels. I can help you."

She chuckled. "You a good internet stalker?"

"I've learned a lot these last few years." Then he imagined Sam's face. "And I know somebody who's better than I am. It's time to ask for help."

TWENTY

"I don't want to do this."

As if Kelsey hadn't spoken, Eric jogged out the front door.

She stepped outside, hugged herself in the chill, and watched as he leaned in his Jeep and started it up. He returned to the front stoop a moment later.

"Eric, I'm serious. This is a bad idea."

"You have to learn to trust people."

"I don't know these people."

He kissed her on her forehead. "It's going to be okay."

She wiped the spot his lips had touched, trying to brush away that tingly feeling and stay focused. All she managed to do was offend him. He stepped inside. She didn't miss the hurt in his eyes before he turned away.

She followed him in. "How do I know I can trust these people."

"I know them." He stoked the glowing coals, then closed the screen. "You should be able to trust me."

"I do. It's just—"

"You don't." He turned to her, squared his shoulders. "If you did, you'd have come home a long time ago."

"Oh, Eric—"

"Don't 'Oh-Eric' me." His face turned red, and he rounded the chair and stopped a few feet from her. "I'm not a twenty-year-old kid anymore, Kelsey. While you've been running away, singing in clubs and...and filing papers or whatever the heck it is administrative assistants do, I've been catching bad guys. I'm a detective. And a darn good one, too."

The anger in his voice had her stepping back until she bumped into the doorjamb.

He pointed at her, and she froze. "None of that, either. The Kelsey I knew would never back down from a fight."

"I'm not—"

"I would never hurt you. You know that."

"I know. It's just... Can you dial the rage down, please?"

He raked his hand through his hair, turned toward the back door, and checked the lock. Then he marched across the house, passed her, and stood on the stoop again, holding the door open. "Let's go."

She stepped outside. "I don't want to do this."

"Get in the car, Kelsey."

"You promised to take me to the bus station if I asked."

He closed the door, slowly, focused on the doorknob. He took a deep breath and faced her. The front stoop was small, and they were close together. Too close. She could smell his aftershave. He opened his mouth, closed it again, and swallowed. "Is that what you want?"

No. Never. But... "I can't do this."

"Do what? Trust me?"

"Trust anybody." How could she make him understand? Her every instinct told her to run.

She thought of Daniel. She had to go. "I've kept this secret a long time..."

He said nothing.

"I think I should..." Her eyes filled with tears, and she looked at the concrete beneath her feet. "I need to go."

"No."

"You promised."

"You promised to tell me the truth."

"I did."

"No, you didn't. You told me part of it. But not all of it."

"I told you—"

He stepped closer. "You going to lie to me again, Kelsey? After everything, don't I deserve the truth?"

"I didn't—"

"Kansas City."

What? How did he know? What had she said?

"And you didn't hitchhike to Nutfield."

"I—"

"You didn't keep your end of the bargain, and I'm not keeping mine. Now, are you going to walk to the Jeep, or do you want me to carry you?"

She would have stepped back further, but the wrought iron railing trapped her.

No. She wasn't trapped, because Eric would never hurt her, never in a million years. And she could trust him, she knew that. She did trust him, at least intellectually. But the fear churning in her stomach wasn't listening to her intellect.

He lifted his hand, and she flinched.

He sighed and dropped the hand. "Get in the car." He stepped back to give her room to pass. "Please."

Apparently, she didn't have a choice.

She started down the steps, then stopped. She looked up, toward the staircase inside, toward the room that had been hers. Should she grab her backpack, in case she had to run?

"You don't need anything else," he said. "You'll be back here later."

"Fine."

She swiveled, hobbled the short path, and climbed into the passenger seat.

Eric slid in beside Kelsey.

The first few minutes, the only sounds came from the engine and the road beneath them.

Kelsey was breaking his heart. Again. She knew that, but there was nothing she could do about it. "I'm sorry," she said.

He reached across the space, took her hand. "Me, too."

TWENTY-ONE

VANESSA HAD LEARNED to love silence.

Her home in Serbia had been small and filled with people. Tata and Mama, of course. Herself, her three little sisters, and her two little brothers. Also, her tata's parents, and her mama's sister, whose husband had been killed during the war. A city apartment with four bedrooms and eleven people. Even in the dead of night, it had never been quiet.

When Tata sent her away, things had not gotten better for young Vojislava. Sad, scared, squabbling girls crammed in close quarters. As she'd moved—away from Serbia and into better, more established organizations, her living conditions hadn't changed much. Lots of girls, very little space, no privacy.

Only when she'd been with Abbas had she been alone, and that had been far from restful. That had been more akin to solitary confinement in a luxurious floating torture chamber.

This, though. This was restful.

Vanessa awoke late on Friday morning, showered, and ate breakfast on the lanai overlooking the ocean. After she'd cleaned up her breakfast dishes and Carlos's—he was already gone—she headed to the beach for a walk.

The beach wasn't empty, of course, but in front of their home there were very few vacationers. The hotels down the beach were full this time of year, but most people didn't venture this far.

The silence was beautiful here. It was a safe silence. A silence like she'd never known.

She imagined bringing a child here, letting him play in the warm water, build sand castles and learn to swim. She'd teach her child to swim the way Tata had taught her.

The burner phone, which she'd kept with her, dinged with an incoming text. She shielded the screen from the sun and looked at the photos in her message app.

Snapshots taken from far away, through a forest, of a man and a woman. They were standing in front of a house on a tiny stoop. The house was surrounded by trees. She scrolled through the photos until she found close-ups.

The man had turned away from the woman, and she saw his face. Definitely the cop who'd married Kelsey all those years ago. Eric Nolan.

Then she found one of the woman. Vanessa had only seen photos of her from a decade before, but...she studied it. Yes. That could be her.

Vanessa rushed back to the house and into Carlos's office. She found the photographs he kept of Kelsey in the top drawer of his desk and compared them.

Kelsey had grown her hair longer and dyed it lighter. But she couldn't change her facial structure, the heart-shaped face with the high cheekbones, those blue eyes. She'd been attractive when Carlos had owned her. She was downright stunning now.

A fissure opened in Vanessa's confidence. Would Carlos want Kelsey again? Would he discard Vanessa for this woman?

No. He hated Kelsey, and as beautiful as Kelsey was, Vanessa was younger, much younger, and treated him like her master and benevolent king. Why would he throw her over for a woman who'd stolen his child and run away?

Vanessa was safe.

The words didn't dispel her fear. Regardless of what would happen now, Vanessa had to tell him about Kelsey. And she had to tell him her news, too. He would be pleased to know a baby was on the way. Maybe it would help him keep Kelsey and her kid in perspective.

Vanessa forwarded the photos from the burner phone to hers, then called the private investigator. When he answered, she said, "What have you learned?"

She listened to the man's information—everything there was to know about Eric Nolan, his friends, his associates, his habits. Maybe they could use this. Maybe this would help. Even if it didn't, Carlos would be impressed at all she'd done. He would thank her for it. He would love her for it.

What would it be like to raise another woman's child? Carlos didn't even know if Kelsey had given birth to a boy or a girl. They only knew the child would be with his mother.

Except he or she wasn't with Kelsey. Which was odd.

Vanessa made another call, this one to a private investigator in Savannah Carlos had hired before. The man had watched the house for a long time when Kelsey had first run away, but Carlos told Vanessa that he'd given up hoping she'd go home to her parents. Kelsey was too smart for that. When the PI's voicemail picked up, she left a message. Maybe Kelsey had left the kid with them. Wouldn't that be simple?

When she'd gathered as much information as she could, she started toward her bedroom while she dialed Carlos. She'd better start packing. They'd be leaving for New Hampshire soon.

TWENTY-TWO

Twenty minutes later, Eric parked in front of a beautiful home. Kelsey took in the scene. It sat in a clearing nestled in the woods. There was a barn off to one side. Together, the two structures looked as if they'd sat in this spot for a hundred years.

"This is Brady's house," Eric said. "His wife grew up here."

"It's beautiful."

"I think it was built in the late nineteenth century. It's had a lot of updates and additions since then. Oddly, there's a tunnel that leads from there"—he pointed at a small room that looked like an addition that jutted out from the barn-side of the house —"to there." He pointed to the barn.

"No kidding? How interesting."

"Rae didn't even know it was there until... Well, that's a story for a different day. But it's a good one."

She opened her car door, but he grabbed her hand before she could get out. "Stay there."

"I can walk."

"I'd like to open your door for you, if you don't mind. My folks would have my hide if they thought I wasn't treating my wife respectfully."

She couldn't help the smile as he jogged around the car. He pulled her door open and helped her out.

"Thank you."

"A pleasure, ma'am." He played up his accent.

"Well, I'll be," she said, playing up hers. "Such manners, even after years among these dirty Yankees."

He chuckled. "You might oughta leave the *dirty Yankee* talk out here. Inside, that'll go over like a hockey puck on a volleyball court. Unless you're talking about the New York Yankees. Then they'll join right in." He offered his arm. "I should have brought your crutches."

"My ankle's better." And crutches would keep him at a distance. She preferred him right here, supporting her, holding her.

They were just about to ring the bell when the door opened. A tall woman with strawberry-blond hair smiled at her and held out her hand. "Hi. I'm Rae Thomas."

Eric said, "Rae, this is Kelsey Nolan, my...wife."

The words jolted her, though everything he'd said was true. Except the Nolan part—she hadn't ever changed her name legally. She would have, though. If everything had been different.

She shook the woman's hand.

"Come in, come in."

Rae stepped back, and Eric guided Kelsey inside.

"Brady's in the living room," Rae said as the man she'd met the other day, the chief, filled the doorway at the end of the short hall.

He nodded to her. "Nice to see you again, Kelsey."

"You, too, Chief."

"Brady, please." He looked over her head to Eric. "But you can call me Chief."

"Yes, sir, Chief, sir."

Kelsey could hear the humor in her husband's voice. These two seemed to have a good relationship, like they were more than coworkers. They were friends.

It struck her again how different Eric was from when she'd left him, how much of his life she didn't know, probably would never know.

Eric guided her to a sofa on the far side of the room. She gazed out the windows behind it to the backyard. A couple of apple trees stood there, stark and leafless, but still somehow beautiful. "Your home is lovely."

"Thank you," Rae said. "It's been in my family for generations."

"My mother inherited her family home, too," Kelsey said. "She's never lived outside of Savannah. What a comfort that must be, to have a home like this."

Rae perched on the fireplace hearth and smiled. "I left for about twelve years. I won't leave again, not if I have anything to say about it."

Brady had disappeared up the stairs. He returned holding a child. A little boy with surprisingly dark skin who squealed when he saw the crowd. "Down, down, down," he said.

Brady complied and set the boy on the floor. He toddled toward his mother, then saw Eric and turned to him. "Uncew Ewic."

He held up his pudgy arms, and Eric swung the boy up and onto his hip. "How's my little man?" Eric tickled the boy until he giggled, then sat beside her. "Johnny, this is my wife, Kelsey."

The boy hid his face in Eric's shoulder, and Kelsey nearly cried. Eric was a natural with children. Of course he was, but she'd never seen it. Never witnessed it.

She thought of Daniel, tried not to cry, and said, "Nice to meet you, Johnny."

He peeked up, said, "Hi," and then snuggled again. About

ten seconds later, he squirmed, and Eric set him down. He toddled over to Rae, who settled him on her lap.

A knock sounded, the front door opened, and two more people walked in. The first was a short woman with long light brown hair pulled into a ponytail. Following her was a man a little taller than Brady, maybe six-four, with broad shoulders and a crew cut.

Rae stood, Johnny on her hip, and hugged the woman briefly before she turned. "Kelsey, this is Samantha."

The woman crossed the room, and Kelsey stood and held out her hand to shake. The woman ignored it and pulled her into a hug.

Kelsey couldn't help her little giggle.

"It's nice to meet you, Kelsey." Sam stepped back but grabbed her hand and squeezed it. "I'm too touchy-feely, I know. But I love Eric, so... I'm thrilled to meet you." She turned to Eric, who'd also stood, and smacked him on the shoulder. "All these years I've been trying to fix you up with women. Why didn't you tell me?"

"I didn't tell anybody."

She hugged him, too, and lowered her voice. Kelsey barely picked up her whispered words. "I'm glad she's here."

The man stood behind her, a small smile on his face. He caught Kelsey's eye and held out his hand. "Garrison Kopp. I'll leave the hugs to Sam."

Kelsey shook his hand, somehow soothed by his steady presence as she hadn't been with Brady. Well, no surprise there, considering Brady'd locked her in a cell.

But he'd done it kindly.

Garrison reached past her to shake Eric's hand. "Good to see you."

"How's Aiden?"

"Doing great." He stepped back and looked at Kelsey.

"Aiden is my teenage son." He turned back to Eric and said, "He's staying out of trouble."

"Glad to hear it."

Sam sat on the couch beside Kelsey, and Garrison took the nearest chair. Brady sat in the chair closer to his wife, and they all turned their gaze to Eric.

He cleared his throat.

Sam said, "Oh," and reached into her bag. While she dug around, she said, "I talked to the guy who owns the cabin where you holed up this week. They're not going to press charges."

"They're not?" Tears prickled her eyes, relief, gratitude. "Thank you."

Sam pulled out a plastic sack and handed it to Kelsey. "Your stuff."

Kelsey opened the sack, peeked inside, and saw her iPad, wallet, and cell phone. She turned to Sam. "You got these for me?"

"The owners are friends of mine. And we share the same management company. They let me in."

"Thank you." Kelsey was tempted to hug the woman again. "You can't imagine—"

"It was no problem," she said. "That's what friends are for."

"You don't even know me."

"You're Eric's wife." She bumped Kelsey's shoulder. "That makes us friends."

"Oh."

The woman smiled and looked past her to Eric. "Well, are you going to explain what we're doing here?"

He cleared his throat and squeezed Kelsey's hand. In clipped sentences and straightforward words, he explained the situation to his friends, glossing over her time of captivity. Not that he could have shared those details, since she hadn't told him. When he finished, Brady stood and met Kelsey's eyes.

"You're saying this Carlos Otero is working with somebody in Nutfield?"

Eric started to speak, but she answered first. "I think so, sir."

Brady paced behind the club chairs. Johnny'd long since tired of sitting on his mother's lap and was stacking blocks in the middle of their circle.

"And you don't think it's a coincidence?" he clarified.

Again, she spoke before Eric could. "I believe it's possible he knew about my marriage to Eric. I'd told Danielle, and I suspect Carlos would have gotten as much information out of her as possible before..."

When she didn't finish, Brady said, "Right." He looked at Sam. "Any experience on the dark web?"

She pulled a MacBook from her giant bag and opened it up. "Nope. But let's see what we can find." She turned to Kelsey. "Do you have a web address I can look at?"

Garrison stood. "While you guys do that, I'm going to make a call."

No, no, no. Who would he be calling? She turned to Eric, knew her fear must've shown on her face, because he smiled and said, "It's okay."

Garrison said, "Did they tell you I used to be with the FBI?"

She shook her head.

Garrison sat again and leaned toward her. "You can trust me, Kelsey. I'm going to see if this guy's on their radar, and if they can give us any more information about him. Okay?"

He watched her, waited for her to agree.

"It's okay," Eric said again. "Trust me."

She turned back to Garrison. "Okay."

He nodded once and disappeared into another room.

Kelsey opened the iPad, navigated to the page, and showed it to Sam. A moment later, the same page glowed on her screen.

"What's Carlos's screen name?"

"V-E-L-A."

"Vela?" Eric said. "What is that?"

"Sounds familiar," Sam said, "but I can't figure out why."

Kelsey said, "Vela is the name of a constellation in the southern sky that's supposed to look like a ship's sails. It also has something to do with ships." When Rae's eyebrows lifted, she said, "I looked it up." She turned to Sam. "But maybe you're thinking of those mythical creatures in the Harry Potter series."

"Oh, yeah," Sam said.

"Right," Kelsey said. "But that's spelled with two E's. This is just one. Honestly, I'm guessing it's a nod to his home, Venezuela."

Sam nodded. "Makes sense."

Eric turned to her with a smile. "You a big Harry Potter fan?"

She thought of Daniel. They'd read the books together, prompting his obsession with all things Hogwarts. And his round glasses and shaggy hair, which were straight out of the first book. "You ever read them?"

"Uh, no," he said.

"You should ask that kid you met the other day if he has. Lots of kids love Harry Potter."

His eyebrows rose. "Good idea. Thanks."

While she and Sam scrolled through the messages, Brady said, "How is that kid. Daniel, right?"

Suddenly, Kelsey couldn't focus on the screen, but she didn't look up. Couldn't show she was interested.

"I haven't seen him in a couple of days," Eric said, "but I talked to him yesterday morning. He's doing well. They got him enrolled in second grade, even though Marisa thinks he'd do well in third. Kid's sharp as a tack, despite his monster mother."

She swallowed the pain those words caused. Eric was right —she was a monster mother. A good mother would never have put her son in such danger. But he'd been born into that danger.

And what other choices had she had? She could have given him up for adoption, she supposed. Theoretically. But not in reality. She loved him too much.

She longed for her son with his little round glasses and his little boy smell, his sweet voice and tender kisses. Would she ever hold him again?

"Is he adjusting to life with Nate and Marisa?" Rae asked.

Nate and Marisa. Were they good people? Were they kind people? Eric considered them friends, and based on what she saw here, he chose his friends well.

"Seems to be," Eric said. "He hasn't told them anything else about his mom, and I've had zero luck finding the woman."

"Here," Sam said.

Sam pointed, and Kelsey forced herself to focus on the screen.

TakeTwo: Need 1 E, BL, BR, RH

Vela: Same $?

TakeTwo: Half w/ info

Sam read the lines aloud. "What does that first line mean? E, B-L, B-R, R-H?"

Kelsey had a guess. She'd seen those codes often enough in this chatroom. She wanted to see if this group would come up with anything better.

A minute later, Rae said, "Blonde, brunette, and redhead?"

Exactly what Kelsey had guessed.

Eric added, "Maybe one of each?"

"Yes. That makes sense." Rae's enthusiasm waned as she considered what it meant. "Oh, my God. He's talking about selling...people. Women."

"Not women," Kelsey said. "Girls."

The room was silent as they considered that.

Eric broke it when he said, "It's the last line that bothers me."

Kelsey read it again. "Half with info."

Eric looked at Kelsey, swallowed hard. "What information do you suppose he's selling?"

"Oh." Kelsey's insides squeezed tight.

"We can't know for sure," Brady said.

"What other information would he have right now? Information worth the price of..." Eric waved toward the laptop on Sam's lap.

Garrison returned, and Brady faced him. "What'd you learn?"

"I'll have to wait for a call back." He sat and looked at Kelsey. "I'd like to share what you've told us. They'll be able to do a lot more with this information than we will."

The very thought of it made her stomach churn. "Can we find out what they know without telling them about this? I'm afraid... Carlos was always bribing people. I'd like to keep the circle small, if we could."

Garrison focused on Kelsey. He inched forward in his seat and leaned toward her, imploring her. "The FBI are experts in this sort of thing. You don't need to do this alone. You can't do it alone."

The thought of not being alone nearly thawed her determination. But she'd already let too many people in on her secret. "I trusted them already. I told them everything I knew about Carlos and his people."

"And a lot of them were put away," Garrison said.

"Not by the federal government, though. By the State of Florida. The feds... It wasn't important to them. They didn't see Carlos for what he was. They saw him as...as a pimp. Not a slave trader."

Garrison was nodding slowly, listening carefully. "But things have changed in the last ten years. Attitudes have changed. If a prostitute isn't eighteen, regardless of her attitude about her...profession, she's a victim."

"I was over eighteen." Kelsey remembered very well how the police had treated her and Misty, the disgust on their faces, the shame that had covered her like a layer of grime. "That's not how it was."

"It's changed, Kelsey. You've seen it, I'm sure, all the information about human trafficking, awareness campaigns, that sort of thing. Attitudes have changed. I promise you, my friends at the Bureau will take it very seriously."

Maybe he was right. But...could she trust him?

She didn't know. And she wasn't ready to make that decision. "Carlos is free, and they didn't care a whit. I can't risk that happening again."

"So you're willing to risk your own life?" Garrison said. "Because if I'm reading the situation right, he won't have any qualms about killing you."

He wouldn't kill her, though. That was the biggest secret she hadn't shared. Carlos wouldn't kill her until he had what he wanted from her.

She'd die before she let that happen.

TWENTY-THREE

"I WONDER if this is what it's like to have teenagers." The next morning, Eric waited by the front door while Kelsey walked down at the pace of molasses. "I'm not changing my mind."

She stopped halfway and glared. "I'm perfectly capable of staying here by myself."

"Sam wants you to come."

"I won't take off. I promise, I'll be here when you get back." Kelsey continued to the bottom of the stairs and crossed her arms.

The thought of coming home to her, his wife... He was tempted to let her stay, just so he could experience that one time. But then his smarter self took over. "Sam thinks the two of you can gather more information."

"How can she possibly help?"

"You'll be surprised," Eric said. "Y'all will probably have the whole thing solved by the time I get back."

"I don't have to go if I don't want to."

"You don't have to go to Sam's, you're right. You can come with me to meet Daniel." He doubted the kid would appreciate the tagalong, but Kelsey came first.

For some reason, that suggestion made her eyes fill with tears, and that made him feel about two feet tall. He didn't want to leave her any more than she wanted him to leave, but he'd made a promise to the kid, and he wasn't going to break it.

Eric prayed for patience, for wisdom. He hadn't wanted to bring this up, but it seemed that whatever that miscreant Otero had done to her hadn't completely drained Kelsey of the stubborn streak he remembered. "Sweetheart, remember that line on the message board yesterday, the one about information? What if Carlos knows you're here? My house is secure, and I'm a cop. If someone were after you, they'd wait until you were alone. Therefore, you're not going to be alone. No arguments."

The color drained from her face.

Eric wanted to pull her in his arms, but the memory of the night before kept him from stepping forward. He took her hand and squeezed. "Garrison will be there. He'll protect you. Maybe we should think about finding a safe house somewhere. I bet Sam would let us use one of her cabins."

"You don't think I'm safe here?"

"You've been running from him for a decade, Kelsey. If you think he has someone in town looking for you, then what do you think?"

She considered the question, sighed. "You're probably right." She looked around his house. "I like it here."

That remark made his morning. He'd thought, when he bought the house, that she'd like it. It was nice to know he'd at least gotten that right. He squeezed her hand. "We don't need to make any decisions right now. Besides, Sam's waiting for you, and Daniel's waiting for me."

Kelsey ducked her head, searched for her boots. But he'd seen something unexpected in her eyes before she did. Something painfully sad. Like longing. Like maybe she was missing him already.

Was she planning to take off today?

He'd have to clue Garrison in, make sure the man didn't let her get away. Maybe that made him a terrible person, but Eric didn't care. She wasn't leaving.

He couldn't let her leave. When they'd caught Otero, put him behind bars, then if she wanted to leave him, to go back to whomever it was she'd left, then fine. He'd let her go. It would kill him, but he'd let her. Not now, though. Eric wouldn't be able to survive it if she left him now, on the run, nobody to count on. He'd never sleep again for worrying about her.

Finally, she was ready to walk out the door. He ushered Magic into the backseat of the Jeep, then helped Kelsey in the front. At Sam's condo in town, he escorted her to the door.

"I'll be back in a couple of hours." Eric kissed her on the forehead, and she disappeared inside.

Back in his Jeep, he texted Garrison. *Don't let her leave. No matter what she tells you.*

A minute later, Garrison texted back. *I'll do my best.*

Why didn't that response make Eric feel better? Because Kelsey was a grown woman, and Garrison wouldn't hold her against her will.

He considered calling Marisa and telling her he couldn't meet Daniel after all. But he'd made a promise. And if Kelsey wanted to leave that badly, then nobody would be able to stop her.

He turned away from the condo complex and headed toward Marisa and Nate's place near the lake. It was a nice day, sunny and relatively warm. The temperature was forecasted to be in the upper thirties. Eric figured it was warm enough to try out that skateboard for a little while. He hoped the kid would like it.

But he couldn't keep his thoughts on Daniel, not with the memory of the night before itching to be replayed.

He hadn't planned it, and if he could go back and undo it... No, he wouldn't, even if he could.

They'd picked up Chinese and a movie on their way home from Brady's house. After the food, they'd sat side-by-side on the couch to watch the movie, a comedy neither of them had seen. Somehow, they'd gone from sitting to lying, her in front, watching the movie. Him behind her, watching her laugh.

He'd looked down at her face, at the way her eyelashes fluttered every time she blinked, the way her cheeks turned pink with every off-color joke.

It felt natural, her in his arms, like they'd been lying just like that forever. Felt natural when he'd brushed her hair out of her face, run his fingers down the length of it, enjoyed the silky strands against his skin. He liked it long, liked the color she'd put in it. Then he'd rested his hand on her waist. Still as thin as ever. His hand had traveled over her hip, then landed on her upper thigh.

Her laughing stilled, and the atmosphere changed.

He inhaled her scent, shampoo and soap and Kelsey.

He brushed a kiss in her hair. On her temple. She shifted, and he found that space right behind her ear, kissed it, too.

She turned to face him, and all wisdom slipped right out of his mind. They kissed, hands exploring, movie forgotten.

Her simple, whispered question snapped him out of his daze. "Do you have protection?"

"Of course not." He hadn't seen his wife in a decade. Even condoms had expiration dates. "Do you?"

"No." Her expression looked pained. "But we could risk it."

But rational thought seeped in. "Bad idea."

Where he'd found the strength to say it, he had no idea.

The moment passed, though his need hadn't. He wanted her so much, he ached. And he didn't feel guilty about that. She was his wife. He could sleep with her without a twinge of guilt.

But until he knew the whole story, he had to wait. Until he knew if she was going to stay or go back to the person she swore didn't exist, he had to wait. Because if she left him again, if she left him for somebody else...

There was somebody. He knew that. He'd seen the longing in her eyes when she'd talked about her home in...wherever. Not Kansas City.

So it was good they'd stopped.

And he wouldn't let himself think about babies, though he wanted one of those. Or two of them, or more.

He was overwhelmed by want.

They'd sat up, watched the movie until the final credits rolled. Then she'd pecked him on the cheek and gone to bed.

He had taken a long, cold shower and slept on the couch. Partly to make sure she didn't try to escape again. Partly to make sure nobody came in to get her. Partly because he needed more space between them than her closed door provided.

It was with great relief that he parked outside of Nate and Marisa's home. He needed a distraction badly. The house wasn't lakeside, but it was within walking distance of one of the beaches. Unlike the cabins that ringed the lake, this house was newer, two-story, and had a lovely yard.

He climbed the front porch steps and rang the bell. Inside, he heard the smack-smack-smack of someone running across the hardwood floor. A moment later, the door swung open and Daniel stood there, a wide smile on his face.

"You came." The boy's voice was matter-of-fact, but his eyes gave away his excitement. Maybe his relief.

"Sorry I'm late."

Marisa rounded the corner from the kitchen. She was pretty with that long brown hair and those wide brown eyes.

Ana, her five-year old, trailed her.

"I told him you were on your way," Marisa said. "Do you want to come in?"

Eric glanced at Daniel, whose smile had vanished. Kids were easier to read than cereal boxes. "Thought we'd just go, if you don't mind. I'm hankering for some pizza."

"Me, too." Daniel turned to Marisa and said, "See you later," before he bounded out the door. Halfway to the Jeep, he yelled, "You brought Magic!"

Eric said goodbye to Marisa and followed, chuckling. "I told you I would."

Daniel climbed in, and the dog jumped into the front and nearly licked the kid to death.

When Eric had started the car, he said, "How hungry are you?"

Daniel angled away from the dog, petting her behind her ears. "Not a lot. Miss Marisa makes humongous breakfasts."

Eric turned the car toward the park. "Then I have a surprise for you."

ERIC COLLAPSED on a bench in the town common, and the dog collapsed on the ground beside him. Eric had been running alongside Daniel for an hour, hoping the kid wouldn't fall, snapping photos, and taking video. Magic had barked and chased. She probably would have knocked Daniel over if Eric hadn't kept her tethered on her leash.

Now, both man and dog were exhausted. While Daniel pushed himself up the small hill, the one he'd been too scared to ride down when they first got there, Eric opened his photos to see what he'd captured. A lot of great pictures. Would there ever be a parent for this child, one who would treasure the photos?

"Eric, watch!"

Eric looked up, and Daniel pushed himself off and rode down the hill, teetering just when it got steep. Eric stood, willed Daniel not to fall, prayed he'd be safe.

Finally, Daniel got his balance and made it to the bottom. His momentum carried him all the way to Eric.

"Did you see? I went all the way to the top that time."

Eric high-fived him. "Awesome job."

"Thanks! I love my new skateboard."

"I'm glad. And you promise to always wear your helmet?"

Daniel's answer was sarcastically patient, like he'd catapulted from eight to fourteen and found an attitude along the way. "I know, I know. Every time."

"I don't want you to get hurt."

"You sound like my mom."

The boy's smile faded, and a fresh wave of rage rolled through Eric at the thought of the boy's mother. "You hungry now?"

Daniel picked up the skateboard. "Starving. I think I could eat a whole pizza all by myself."

Eric chuckled. "Maybe we'll split one to start, but if you're still hungry, I'll buy you another one."

"You will? Really?" Daniel's smile was back, and he and the dog raced to the Jeep.

They drove the short distance to downtown Nutfield, and Eric parked a few doors down from the pizza place. The dog looked as eager as Daniel.

"Not this time, girl." Eric patted her head and scratched behind her ears. "But I'll save you a slice."

The dog looked forlorn when they left her in the car.

"I feel sorry for her," Daniel said.

"She'll curl up in the backseat and sleep. And I really will save her a slice."

"What's her favorite kind of pizza?" Daniel asked.

"Well, I never asked her, but I'd guess anything with meat. How about you? What's your favorite?"

"I like hamburger and sausage and pepperoni."

Eric couldn't help the chuckle. "I guess you and my dog have a lot in common."

Daniel beamed in response.

They were nearly to the pizza joint when Daniel stopped. He cupped his hands around his face to block the light and looked in a storefront window. Eric realized where they were.

"What's that?"

"The Nuthouse. It's a video arcade. They also have ice cream and snacks and an old-fashioned soda fountain."

"Cool."

Much as he longed to return to Kelsey, he didn't have the heart to refuse this boy. "We can stop in for a few minutes after pizza."

Daniel peered up with wide eyes. "Can we? Really?"

"After lunch, since you're starving."

The boy's smile was as wide as Eric had seen it.

They ordered the meaty supreme. While they waited for it, Eric took Kelsey's advice and asked Daniel if he was a Harry Potter fan.

The boy filled him in on the series for the rest of their lunch.

Kelsey was a genius.

Despite his prediction, Daniel only ate two pieces. Eric ate his fill and still left a slice for the dog. "Will you let her eat it here?" Daniel asked.

"After we go to the arcade, we'll let Magic get out of the car and scarf down her slice. It'll take about thirty seconds."

"Really? Cool!"

Everything was cool today. Eric paid the check, and they carried their small leftover box next door to the arcade.

As soon as the door opened, the sounds assaulted them.

Dinging and roaring and buzzing and laughing. It smelled like a combination of homemade sweets and teenage sweat.

They stepped in, and Eric spied Wally and Sally Price, the couple who ran the place for the church. Sally was behind the soda fountain. Wally wandered the room, chatting with the kids. He saw Eric and headed his way.

"What brings you in?"

Eric introduced Daniel, who was not-so-patiently standing by his side. "Wally, meet my new friend Daniel."

Wally held out his hand, and Daniel shook it. Eric felt a little wave of pride, as if he could claim any responsibility for the boy's good manners.

"Pleased to meet you," Wally said. "You hungry?"

"No, sir."

"We just ate." Eric lifted the leftover box as proof. "Looking to have some fun."

Wally pulled a handful of tokens from his pocket, looked around as if he were afraid he'd get caught, and handed them to Daniel. "My favorite is the racing game."

Daniel took the coins, his eyes wide and bright. "Thank you, sir."

Wally winked at Eric and walked away.

They started with the car racing game, which Daniel was surprisingly good at. There was a first-person shooter, which Eric wanted to avoid. But Daniel educated him.

"Mama says it's okay, as long as we aren't shooting people." He pointed to the zombies on the side of the machine. "I think zombies are okay."

Well, his monster-mama would know.

After the zombie game, they moved on to another racing game, then played two rounds of air hockey. Eric had to be careful not to destroy the kid—air hockey was his sweet spot.

When Daniel wanted to play a one-player game, Eric didn't complain. He stood to the side to watch.

This place had been built as a hangout for teens, a ministry connected to the church Eric attended. Their plan had been to give the kids a safe place to congregate, and for the most part it worked. But as Garrison's son had proved the previous summer, where there were teens, there were problems. Fights, PDAs—not the electronic kind, the public displays of affection kind—and drugs. Too many drugs.

Today, though, the crowd was light and seemed well-behaved. There were a couple of boys from the youth group at the church. Eric knew them well, since he volunteered on Wednesday nights. A gaggle of girls sat at one of the tables, sipping sodas and checking out a small group of guys hanging around one of the first-person shooter games.

None of them looked familiar. There was one in particular who caught Eric's eye, mostly because he'd caught the guy watching him. Five-ten, blue jeans, black jacket, nose ring, man-bun. The kid had probably pegged him for a cop, but Eric wasn't here to bust anybody. He turned back to watch Daniel play his game, stifling a yawn. Watching video games wasn't nearly as fun as playing them.

A ruckus near the door had him turning his head.

The guy who'd been watching him threw a punch. Another one went down. The first snatched something that had flown across the floor and ran toward the door.

"Hey." The kid on the floor struggled to stand. "That's mine!"

The thief pushed outside.

Wally started toward the ruckus. Eric headed him off, shoved the leftover pizza box at him, pointed at Daniel, and said, "Watch him and call 911!"

"I will," he said.

Eric slammed out the door and turned in the direction the kid had gone. He was already past the pizza parlor.

Eric followed, checking for his pistol. It was concealed beneath his jacket, as always. He didn't pull it, but he unsnapped the holster, just in case.

Eric gained on him. The kid ducked into an alley. Eric knew the town well enough to know it would dump him out on the street behind. From there, the kid could get lost behind a smattering of houses and businesses.

He turned into the alley and froze. Nobody. Something wasn't right. The kid couldn't have gotten though that fast.

Eric reached for his gun, started to spin.

Pain exploded on the back of his head, and he went down, barely catching himself before his face landed on the pavement.

Someone straddled him, pressed his head against the asphalt. All Eric saw was black pants.

The kid had been wearing blue jeans.

Eric didn't move. He couldn't move. The pain in his head was excruciating. He fought to remain conscious.

"You with me?" The voice was deep, gravely. Definitely not a kid. A man.

Someone ran past, probably the kid who'd lured him here.

"Answer me," the man said. "You with me?"

"Who are you?"

"Listen." The man spoke fast. "Carlos is coming. Kelsey needs to grab the kid and run before he gets here."

Kid? What kid? "There's no—"

"Keep your friends at the PD out of this. Carlos is coming. Tell her to run. Today."

The man lifted Eric's head and smashed it on the pavement.

TWENTY-FOUR

VANESSA STILL HADN'T TOLD Carlos her news.

He'd been too focused on Kelsey and her child the day before, and Vanessa hadn't wanted her news to be overshadowed. And even if she'd wanted to, Carlos might as well have forgotten she existed. He and Mateo had spent hours going over the little information she'd given them, trying to formulate a plan.

Carlos didn't fly commercial. The charter jet he'd hired was smaller than the one they'd taken from Europe. It had twelve seats, but a couple of them converted to tables. Carlos and Vanessa sat across from each other, him by the aisle, her by the window, so they wouldn't have to share legroom. They converted the seats beside them to tables.

She hadn't asked about Mateo, and Carlos hadn't mentioned bringing his closest friend and confidant on the trip. She willed the door to close and hoped Mateo wouldn't be joining them.

"Grab me a water, would you?" Carlos said.

She made her way along the narrow aisle to the back, and dug around in the tiny compartment the copilot had pointed out, looking for the cooler. Finally, she found it and wrenched it open. She was reaching into the icy water when she heard a voice at the front. Sounded like, "Welcome aboard."

The answering "Thank you" told her she'd been foolish to hope. Of course Mateo was joining them.

She pulled a third bottle out, pasted on a smile, and turned. "Water, Mateo?"

"Sure." He sat in the place she'd chosen for herself. Carlos either didn't notice or didn't care the man was taking her seat.

Vanessa returned with the waters, handed them out, and set hers on the table beside Mateo's seat. "Convert that to a chair for me, would you?" She addressed Mateo, who gave her a tight smile.

Did he have the nerve to refuse with Carlos right there?

He nodded once. Battle won, she said, "Do either of you want a snack as long as I'm up? They have bagels and pastries."

Carlos didn't look up from his phone when he answered. "Bagel with cream cheese."

"What kind of pastries?" Mateo asked.

She checked, listed his options. He chose an apple Danish.

She got the bagel, spread the cream cheese on it, and delivered it to Carlos, then retrieved her pastry and Mateo's before she returned to her seat. Normally, she would never eat such a high-calorie breakfast, but she was very hungry lately. Must be the little one needed more calories.

She sat beside Mateo, across from Carlos, and nibbled her breakfast until they took off.

Vanessa'd always imagined private jets to be wide and luxurious, but the two she'd been on were cramped. She couldn't imagine what it would be like if all the seats were occupied. Of course, with the animosity between her and Mateo, the three of them all mashed together seemed to fill the plane. Mateo never tired of reminding Carlos what had happened the last time he'd trusted a woman. Kelsey had put a lot of Carlos's men in prison,

Mateo included, though his stint had been short. Mateo didn't trust Vanessa, and Vanessa didn't trust him. Neither would voice their fears about the other to Carlos. He'd chosen them both, and neither was willing to test his loyalty.

When they were airborne, Carlos looked up from his phone. She'd never forget the first time she'd seen him. She'd been standing behind Abbas—always a few feet behind, like a well-trained pet. Carlos had walked into the private room in the large casino as if he owned the place. Dark hair, dark eyes, and that deep voice with his Spanish accent. Vanessa had never developed a true desire for men—that had been pounded out of her long before she'd been old enough to understand what desire even meant—but Carlos had been impressive. She'd never forgotten how he'd met the eyes of every man in the room, then turned specifically to her and nodded.

His attention had earned a painful pinch from one of Abbas's guards, as if she'd caused Carlos to notice her.

Well, maybe she had. She didn't know how to be invisible. Nobody'd ever asked that of her before.

And then, when Carlos ran the table and took all of Abbas's money, it was Carlos who suggested he throw Vanessa into the pot.

Abbas had been furious. Oh, his words had been respectful, laughing, even, but she knew his posture, the way he held his back, the way his neck turned red when he was angry. Backed into a corner, Abbas hadn't known how to offer something else instead without showing that she mattered to him, and a man like Abbas wouldn't let on that he believed a woman worth anything.

He'd flicked his hand as if she were no more valuable than one of his chips.

When Carlos won the hand, he stood, filled his pockets with the kitty, and had one of his guards grab her.

She'd felt Abbas's glare as they'd walked out of the room. And she'd been devoted to Carlos ever since.

"I got three of our most trusted men on a commercial flight," Mateo said.

More men. Vanessa would be pushed aside by the sheer numbers.

"*Sí*," Carlos said. "Good, good."

When the pilot announced they were at cruising altitude, Carlos grabbed his phone, put it on speaker, and dialed his man in New Hampshire. Vanessa took notes about the conversation while Carlos and Mateo questioned him.

He had no new information except that Nolan had taken a kid to get pizza that afternoon.

Carlos's eyes got wide. "How old? What did he look like?"

"He looked about eight. I heard it was a foster kid," Durant said. "Nolan hangs out with local kids a lot, even volunteers at his church. He's a freaking Boy Scout."

"You're sure it's a foster kid?" Carlos asked. "How can you be sure?"

"I'm not sure. I just said, I heard it. It's not like I got the kid's fingerprints. I can tell you, they weren't making any attempt to stay hidden. They went to the park to skateboard, then got pizza, then went to the arcade. Probably a hundred people saw them. If it was your kid, don't you think he'd have been more careful?"

The man made a good point. Probably, that kid had nothing to do with anything.

Carlos said, "Did you see where he picked the child up?"

"Nope. Just saw them get into town."

"You're supposed to be watching—"

"Nolan knows my car. I have to be careful."

"Rent another one," Carlos said.

"This is a small town, Carlos. And Eric's a cop. He'd notice a tail, no matter what kind of car it was."

Vanessa wasn't sure if she should be frustrated or relieved they didn't know where the kid was. She didn't want her child to have to compete with anybody, certainly not a boy ten years his senior.

Carlos sat back in his seat and spoke to the phone. "What else?"

"Nothing right now. No sign of Kelsey's kid."

"My kid."

"Right. That's what I meant. Anyway, no sign of him. Or her."

Carlos hung up and spoke to Mateo. "Not much."

Mateo glanced at her, then focused on Carlos. "You should just let this go, my friend."

"He's my kid. And she put you in prison. I'd think if anyone wanted revenge, it should be you."

Mateo shrugged. "It is water under the bridge now. No good can come of you finding her."

"You don't think it would be good to find my own kid?"

Mateo's gray head bobbed up and down as if he were thinking, choosing his next words carefully. "He is your child, I know. But he doesn't know you, and you don't know him. She has probably turned him against you. Taking the child will not be good for him."

Carlos flicked away his argument like a fly. "He's my son."

"Or daughter," Mateo said gently.

"All the more reason for me to find her. A daughter will need my protection."

"And the woman?" Mateo asked.

"Kelsey will be sorry for the way she crossed me."

Mateo bowed his head, almost a nod that stayed low too long. No wonder Carlos liked this guy—Mateo treated him like royalty. Mateo turned to Vanessa. "What did you tell the PI you hired?"

She addressed Carlos. "I told him that your girlfriend was pregnant, and that she took off years ago, and that you want to meet your child."

Carlos nodded. "Good. Good."

She glanced at Mateo, who'd already started dialing. He put the phone on speaker, and Vanessa took notes as the investigator spoke. He had a deep and businesslike tone, very different from Barry Durant's. He gave them names, addresses, and phone numbers of people Nolan had had contact with the previous day.

Nolan had been at the home of Brady and Reagan Thomas. Brady was the Nutfield Chief of Police.

The only other car in the driveway that day had belonged to Garrison Kopp, a former FBI agent. A woman had been with Kopp, but her name was unknown.

Great, a police chief and a fed. Even Vanessa knew enough not to mess with either of those. Bad enough Nolan was a cop.

The investigator continued. "This morning, he did pick up a child from a home in Nutfield. They went to the park, then he took the boy to eat pizza. There was some kind of scuffle, and Nolan ended up in an ambulance."

Mateo leaned forward. "What kind of scuffle? What happened?"

"Impossible to know for sure," the PI said, "but I heard a teenager stole something and ran, and Nolan followed. He was knocked out in the alley."

"The child?"

"He was picked up by the people who live in the house where Nolan had picked him up. He isn't their child, though. That house is owned by a Nathan and Marisa Boyle. They have one child, a five-year-old girl. I'm not sure who this kid was."

"Our other source says it's a foster kid," Carlos said. "Can you look into that?"

"Tough to get information like that, but I'll see what I can do."

"What about the other people?" Carlos snatched her notebook, read the names. "Brady Thomas or Garrison Kopp. Either of them have a kid they didn't have a few days ago?"

"Don't know yet," the man said, "but I'll keep my eyes open."

They ended the call, and Carlos tossed his phone on the table beside him. "If anything happened to my child, Kelsey is going to pay."

Vanessa knew better than to respond to that. She slipped her notebook off Carlos's table and read what she'd written. Not a lot to go on.

"When we find her," Carlos said, "I'll make her tell me everything. I'll know where my son is by the end of the day."

His son. Vanessa knew Carlos assumed it was a boy. Like she assumed the child growing in her womb was a boy. Because a boy would be better. A boy could grow up to be strong and powerful.

She knew what it meant to be a girl. She wouldn't wish that pain on anybody.

The problem was, Carlos's plan was flawed. She waited for Mateo to point it out. As the miles rolled below them like waves, her anxiety rose to an altitude even higher than the chartered plane's. Did she have the nerve to point out the flaw in his plan?

She glanced at Mateo, but he was typing something into his phone.

Carlos was staring out the window, hands clenching into fists, then unclenching.

If she wanted to prove herself invaluable to him, she had to speak up. "When you had her before"—she kept her voice soft, gentle, weak—"did it work to hurt her? Did that break her?"

Mateo slowly lowered his phone. They both watched Carlos's reaction.

The vein on his forehead pulsed, a sure sign he was angry. He addressed her. "This time, I will not be kind. I was a fool. I thought she cared for me." He regarded Vanessa through narrowed eyes, and she knew what he was thinking.

"It's different with us, Carlos."

The vein stopped pulsing. The man's moods shifted faster than the sand beneath the surf. His lips tipped up, the satisfied smile of a predator that had just cornered its prey. "How so?"

She shrugged, backed away the tiniest bit, and forced an easy smile. All subtle moves designed to show her self-confidence, her independence. All lies, of course, but ones she needed him to believe that she believed.

It was a very dangerous game.

"I chose you," she said. "Do you have any idea how many men have desired my devotion."

His eyebrow quirked. "Abbas?"

She knew her reaction showed before she could school her expression. She and Carlos had never talked about the man Carlos had won her from, and she'd prefer not to talk about him now. Certainly not with Mateo's curious gaze on her. "Abbas was a monster. He couldn't earn the loyalty of a golden retriever."

Carlos's laugh settled her fear. "I rescued you, then."

Rescued her? He had no idea what he'd rescued her from. She leaned forward, across the tiny space, and took one of his hands in hers. "You rescued me. You earned my loyalty in that moment, and you've earned it every moment since."

He stared into her eyes, seeking what, she didn't know. Duplicity? Fear? She knew better than to show either. Finally, he sat back, and she did too.

His gaze flicked to Mateo, and for the first time she was

thankful the man was with them. Otherwise, what would Carlos do? She'd let him do whatever he wished to her—she'd learned that lesson years ago. It was easier to comply than to fight, and either way, it always ended up the same.

Carlos looked back at her, leered at her. "You're much sexier than a golden retriever."

She laughed and picked up her notebook.

A few moments passed before she finally had the nerve to ask, "How did you keep her in line before?"

"I had her sister," Carlos said. "It's amazing the things that woman did, the ways she lied to me..." He shook his head, and Vanessa didn't press him. Obviously, reminding Carlos that he'd been a fool wasn't a wise move.

"She is a skilled manipulator," Mateo said. "She was willing to endure many things to save her sister."

"You think being with me is something one needs to endure?"

Mateo shrugged. "Under the circumstances..."

Carlos regarded the man. That vein had started throbbing again by the time he said, "Perhaps I was a fool to believe she could get over that."

Perhaps? Vanessa decided not to voice her sarcasm. Instead, she said, "How much more willing will she be to protect her child?"

Carlos started to argue, then snapped his lips shut. The moment stretched, Vanessa waited, and Carlos's vein pulsed.

Mateo said nothing. For the first time since she'd met him, she and Mateo seemed to be on the same side in an argument. Unfortunate, because that meant one of them was unnecessary to the conversation.

She prayed it wouldn't be her.

Finally, Carlos addressed her. "What do you suggest?"

She stifled a smug look. "We could wait, of course, until she reunites with her child. Then we could snatch them both."

"I have waited long enough."

"I agree."

He nodded.

Vanessa continued before Mateo would offer a suggestion. "We could make her choose. Her husband or her child."

"You're suggesting we threaten a cop?" Mateo asked.

She barely glanced his way before looking at Carlos. "I'm suggesting we take the cop. For all we know, he knows where your child is. Maybe he will be more easily persuaded. It's not his child, after all. It's a child she had with another man. He should feel no loyalty to him."

"We could hurt him," Mateo said.

"Or," Vanessa said, "we could convince him we'll kill her, if we don't get the child. Maybe her loyalty is to the child, but his will be to her."

Carlos nodded slowly and addressed Mateo. "If I were her husband, I would want that kid gone. Of course, if a woman of mine did what Kelsey did with another man"—he shifted, met Vanessa's eyes and smiled, though this one didn't crinkle his eyes—"I would kill her."

She didn't cringe under his gaze. He hadn't needed to make the threat. Carlos was a passionate man, and she'd seen him unleash his anger often enough. She'd seen him murder the man who'd held out for more money in exchange for information on Kelsey's whereabouts a couple of months prior. She'd seen his anger grow and morph into something terrifying, something with a mind of its own. She'd hardly been surprised at the bullets that followed the look in his eyes.

The informant had crumpled in a pool of blood.

Vanessa had no intention of ever being on the receiving end of Carlos's anger. She would work with him. She would help him, and he would be devoted to her all the more for it.

TWENTY-FIVE

KELSEY HATED TO ADMIT IT, but she was having fun.

With friends.

She hadn't had friends, real friends, in a long time. She hardly knew how to handle it.

Sam's condo was gorgeous—bright colors, clean lines, and modern touches. They worked at the kitchen table in front of the sliding glass door. The sunlight was cheerful, the mood, weirdly lighthearted.

If only Daniel were here.

The thought sobered her. At least she knew he was safe. With Eric, probably having the time of his life. For now, she knew he was okay. For now, she could relax.

She and Sam sat in front of Sam's laptop and searched the dark web while Garrison leaned against the doorjamb and made frequent remarks.

"The FBI could do that faster," he said.

A few minutes later, Garrison added, "They are professionals, you know."

Another couple of minutes passed when he added, "They have tools for this sort of thing."

Sam responded to that one. "Be a dear and get me access to their tools."

Garrison threw up his hands and stalked into the living room, where he turned on the TV.

Kelsey and Sam only giggled.

How could they be having fun doing this?

The fun fizzled fast when they found the photographs. Just a few minutes passed before Sam slammed her laptop closed. "I can't do this."

Kelsey didn't blame her. "Doesn't help that we don't know what we're looking for."

Obviously, Garrison had been listening, because he came back in the kitchen and sat beside Sam. "I'm glad you stopped." He met her eyes. "You don't need to look at that stuff."

"You're right."

They didn't even want to look at it.

Kelsey had lived it.

Her sister had died in it.

Sam grabbed her hand and squeezed. "I'm sorry. I can't imagine what you went through."

Kelsey wanted to pull her hand away, hide it, hide herself away from these good people. But she didn't want to hurt Sam's feelings. The moment turned awkward.

Garrison clapped his hands. "Well, enough of that. Let's eat."

Sam squeezed Kelsey's hand again and rolled her eyes. "The man is always hungry."

Kelsey opened her mouth. The words almost popped out. *Daniel is the same way*. She snapped her jaw shut just in time.

That was why she couldn't have friends. Nothing killed a friendship faster than secrets you couldn't share.

Sam, far too observant, narrowed her eyes. "You okay?"

"Just thinking about my sister." The lie came easily. Too easily. "She was always hungry."

Sam's gaze was kind. "I'm sorry. It must be hard."

"I don't know why...I guess just being here brings back a lot of memories."

"Not all bad, I hope."

Kelsey's smile was real this time. "Mostly good. The best days of my life were spent right here in Nutfield."

While Garrison and Sam fixed lunch, Kelsey told them about her wedding and the days they spent on the lake. She told them how she and Eric had fallen in love with Nutfield.

"I often wondered how Eric ended up here." Garrison carried three plates to the table. "Guy like him could get hired on anywhere he wanted."

"But he loves it here." Sam lifted two cups and followed Garrison. "Carry the chips, would you?"

Kelsey snatched the two bags off the counter and joined her friends at the table. "He likes it here. But still... That he would come here, wait for me..."

She let her words trail off as she slid into her seat.

"He loves you." Sam's words were matter-of-fact as she ripped open the potato chips. "Love means sacrifice."

Kelsey met her eyes. Was she worth it?

She didn't have to voice the question. It hung like a fog over the room.

Sam started to speak, but Garrison beat her to it.

"You are worth it, Kelsey. You are worth his sacrifice." His gaze was serious and steady.

He nodded, turned to Sam. "Pass those chips, babe."

They dug into their meal, but as Kelsey bit into the ham and cheese sandwich and munched the salty potato chips, she couldn't keep Garrison's words from flitting through her brain. Was she worth it? Was all she'd cost Eric worth it? If he could, would he rewind the clock, never get on his knees in the quad where they'd met, never beg her to marry him?

Would he take it all back if he could?

Would she?

Nope. She'd do a lot of things differently, no doubt. But becoming Eric's bride—she could never bring herself to regret that. Her love for him, and her love for Daniel, felt like the only bits of purity she had left in her ruined heart.

That love would cost her, but her friends were right. Love was worth any sacrifice. She'd have given her whole life to save her sister. She'd given up her marriage to protect Eric. She'd given up Daniel to save him.

And Eric had given up his dreams to wait for her.

Would any of it amount to anything, in the end?

A phone rang. Garrison stood, pulled his cell from his pocket. "Kopp here."

Kelsey smiled at Sam. "His last name is Cop?"

"It's K-o-p-p, but yeah. Could he be named more aptly?"

The girls giggled while Garrison stepped out of the room.

He returned a moment later, slid his phone into his pocket. His expression was far too serious. He looked at Kelsey. "Eric's been attacked."

"What?" She stood, nearly toppled the chair behind her, and caught it before it crashed into the sliding glass door. "Is he okay?" Then another thought occurred to her. "Daniel. Was Daniel hurt?"

"The kid was at the arcade," Garrison said. "I guess a teenager assaulted someone and bolted. Eric followed him into an alley and got whacked on the head."

"Is he all right?"

"They're taking him to the hospital."

Sam stood, started throwing cold cuts into the refrigerator. Garrison helped while Kelsey stood there, uselessly.

This was her fault. Whatever had happened, it was about her. It had nothing to do with Eric. But just like she'd always known would happen if she came back to Nutfield, she'd pulled him into her nightmare. Now it was his nightmare, too. If anything happened to Eric, she'd never forgive herself.

And then what would become of Daniel?

She should go. She should just go. Run. Never look back.

"Kelsey."

Sam was staring at her. Had she said her name more than once?

"I'm sorry. What?"

"We're ready."

She would only make it worse. She should leave now. Would her disappearing protect Eric and Daniel?

Garrison walked to her side and grasped her arm. "You're going with us. Eric'll kill me if I let you take off."

"I wasn't—"

"Please don't lie to me. I'll know if you do." He gave her a look, and she wondered... Had she lied? She had. And he knew it.

Their gazes held. He lifted his eyebrows.

She swallowed. She would have to leave, but she couldn't leave without seeing Eric one more time.

Just one more time.

TWENTY-SIX

ERIC WOULD PUNCH something if his head weren't pounding.

After the attack, he'd been frantic to make sure Daniel was all right. He'd staggered to the sidewalk, been grabbed by hands, seen faces he didn't recognize. As the fuzziness cleared, all he could think about was Daniel.

Wally met him on the sidewalk. "He's inside with Sally. He's fine. He thinks you're a hero."

Right. Some hero.

Thank God the boy was safe. Nobody else had been injured. Eric had told Wally to call Brady since he didn't know Nate and Marisa's phone number off the top of his head, and he needed to get Daniel home. Well, that had been a mistake.

Brady rode in like the flippin' cavalry.

Eric was adamantly refusing to go to the hospital. Had no time for ERs and CTs and whatever other letters they wanted to throw at him.

But Brady had showed up and spoken in his *I'm the Chief and you'll do as I say* voice. He'd contacted Nate and Marisa, sent Daniel and Magic home with them, and ordered Eric to follow the paramedics' orders.

And then Eric lay on a gurney, figuring it'd be easier to follow orders than to argue.

The ambulance ride had been mercifully short. Thanks to Brady, who'd lost no time throwing out words like *first responder* and *line of duty injury*, Eric saw the doctor right away.

The older bald man asked him all the same questions the paramedic had asked, performed the same tests, or near enough. "I think we ought to do a CT scan."

"I'm fine. It was a bump on the head."

"A bad bump."

Eric had to fight to rein in his temper. "What's a CT scan going to tell you? That I have a concussion? I think that's obvious. How will we treat it differently if we know?"

"There are other things. You could have bleeding on the brain."

"I don't."

The man's lips quirked like they were fighting amusement. "You a medical doctor, too, Detective?"

"He didn't hit me that hard." Okay, it had been hard. And it had been twice. Still...no sensitivity to light. No nausea. No dizziness. No memory loss.

The doctor sat on his stool and rolled to the side of the bed. He watched Eric's face a moment, then said, "How do you feel, son?"

Furious. Afraid. Desperate to be alone, to look at the package he could feel pressing against the small of his back. He'd touched it as soon as he'd stood in that alleyway, knew it was an envelope. But he hadn't pulled it out. Because his attacker had hidden it for a reason.

He couldn't tell the doc any of that. "My head is pounding."

"I imagine it is. We'll get you some Tylenol. Anything else?"

"Just the headache." Eric actually managed a smile. "And of

course the embarrassment. But y'all don't have medicine for that, do you?"

The doctor's eyes were kind as he stood and clasped Eric on the shoulder. "Can't imagine why you'd feel embarrassed. Men who follow bad guys into dark alleys are few and far between. Be proud you're that kind of man."

Eric wasn't sure how to respond.

"We'll keep you for an hour."

"If you'll just give me the Tylenol, I'll be on my way. No need for me to hang around here and take up a bed."

The doctor chuckled. "Good effort, son. But we have plenty of beds." His smile faded. "One hour. There's nothing so important it can't wait one hour."

"I'll stay with him." Brady stepped in the doorway, arms crossed. "He won't go anywhere until you release him."

With that assurance, the doctor left them alone.

"You should have had the CT scan," Brady said.

Eric closed his eyes, tried not to wince with the headache. "I'm fine."

"What happened?"

He needed to be alone for five minutes. And then he needed to talk to Kelsey.

The attacker's words were playing like a skipping record in his brain.

Grab the kid and run.

The kid.

Kelsey had a kid.

She'd had a child with another man. She'd gotten pregnant, given birth to another man's child.

And then, what? She'd stolen the baby?

If that were the case, where was that baby now?

Maybe the man in the alley had no idea what he was talking about.

If only Eric could convince himself of that.

It was all he could do not to shove past Brady and go find her, demand answers.

A nurse walked in with a little paper cup and a glass of water. "How's our patient?"

"Impatient," Brady said.

She smiled and handed Eric the medicine. "I can understand that," she said. "Nobody plans to spend the afternoon in the ER."

He tossed back the pills, then took a big gulp of water to wash them down.

The nurse took the cup. "You need anything else, just holler." And she left.

Brady was waiting. Eric went through the story, not that he hadn't done that at the scene multiple times.

"The guy say anything to you?"

"Nope. Just walloped me and ran."

Brady regarded him, eyes narrowed.

Eric wouldn't tell him the truth, not right now. Maybe later, maybe after he'd talked to Kelsey.

"I need to call my wife."

"She's in the waiting room. I'll send her in when you've told me everything."

"I told you everything. And now I'd really like to see Kelsey."

"Did this have something to do with her?"

Eric blew out a long breath. Brady might be the chief, but this was Eric's life. It was Kelsey's life. "I told you—"

"Right." Brady's expression gave away his suspicion, but he didn't say anything else.

"Just get her. Please."

Brady stared at him, and Eric thought he might refuse. Fine, then he'd leave this stupid place and find Kelsey himself.

Maybe the chief read his mind, because he nodded. "I'll send her in." He closed the door behind him.

Alone. Finally. His head pounded. His heart pumped. He wanted nothing more than to lie back and sleep. Instead, he pulled the package from his waistband. It had Kelsey's name written on it.

Well, the man had given it to Eric. And considering what it had cost him to get it, he figured he was entitled. He opened it, and everything seemed to stop.

Photographs.

First, Kelsey's mother. Then the whole family, her mom and stepfather and stepbrothers in various places at various times. The pictures were grainy like they'd been taken from a distance. Snapshots, images stolen without permission. One had a Christmas tree in the distance. Based on the flowers in another, Eric would guess they'd been taken in the summertime. The message was clear.

They were being watched.

Eric flipped to the next photograph.

It was his own image staring back at him, walking his dog. Beside the road, the foliage was ablaze with fall colors. October, probably. Four months before. Or a year and four months. Or more.

He flipped to the next. Eric again, this time in his backyard.

Whoever had taken this had been behind his house.

No snow on the ground. Not recent.

He'd been watched, too, and for quite some time.

The last photo was Eric and Kelsey, face to face, on his front stoop. This had been taken the day before.

He lifted that photo to find a piece of paper folded in fourths behind it. He opened the paper, read the typed words.

Grab the kid and run before he finds you.

BY THE TIME Kelsey knocked on his door, he'd stashed the photos and note under the blanket. Maybe he'd show them to her, maybe he wouldn't. He had to gauge her reaction to the rest first.

She stepped in, rushed to his side, and leaned in to hug him. "Thank God you're okay."

Gently, firmly, he grabbed her by the shoulders and pushed her away.

Hurt registered in her eyes.

Welcome to the club, sister.

She found the doctor's stool and sat slowly. "It was about me, wasn't it?"

He nodded, couldn't seem to find the words. Because once he said it, everything would change. They'd had two days together. Not normal days, not even close. But at least they'd been together.

Those two days had been a mirage. He'd known it at the time, but he hadn't wanted to admit it. Now, everything would change. The truth would come to light. When it was out there, they could deal with it.

Or, she could just take off again.

Whatever happened, he had to know everything now. "Close the door."

She stood, pushed the door closed, and sat again. "Please tell me."

"It was a warning." He rubbed the lump on the back of his head, wished they'd just mailed a letter.

She tilted her head to the side. "A warning? From who?"

"No idea. I didn't get a look at him, and I didn't recognize the voice."

"Okay. What did he say?"

"Apparently, Otero is coming."

She glanced behind her, as if maybe he'd walked in. Shook her head. "We knew that, though. We knew he probably knew I was here. That's what that message meant yesterday—the guy who lives here and his offer of information."

"Right. But who would warn you?"

She stared past him. A moment passed before she said, "I have no idea."

He should question her further. There had to be an answer. But the bigger question pushed out all the others. "He said you should grab your kid and leave."

The color in her face drained. Then her eyes filled, and she mashed her lips together until they turned white.

"So, it wasn't a lie? It wasn't a mistake?" He'd hoped...what? That the guy was wrong? That she didn't actually have his kid? Yes, that's exactly what Eric had hoped. What a fool.

"What did you do with it?" he asked.

"Him." Tears dripped silently down her cheeks. She wiped them with her fingertips. "My son."

"Your son with that man."

Her eyes looked wider, brighter, against her pale skin. She looked down again, but not before he saw the haunted look return.

"It's not like I planned it," she said.

"Right. Well, apparently your boyfriend—"

"No." She stood and the stool rolled back. "How dare you?"

"I'm not the one—"

"You have no idea what you're talking about, Eric Nolan." She pointed at him, hand trembling. "No idea what that man did to me."

"Hmm. And why is that? Certainly not because I wasn't here for you. I've been right here, all along, waiting—"

"I couldn't come back." Tears were dripping off her chin now. She didn't look away, though. Didn't wipe them. Didn't do anything but glare at Eric. "This is why... This is why..." She turned toward the wall, then started toward the door.

He swung his legs over the side of the gurney, lurched forward, grabbed her arm. Tried to speak, but the sudden onslaught of pain nearly took him to his knees. He hunched over, waited through a wave of nausea. But he didn't let go of her wrist.

"Come on." She put one arm around his back and urged him to turn around. "Come on. Back in bed."

The worst of the pain passed. He stood straight, sat on the side of the bed, never let her wrist go. "You're not running away this time." He paused through another wave of nausea. He would not be sick. A deep breath, then, "I'll have Brady throw you in jail again before I let you leave."

"On what charge?"

"Suspected kidnapping."

"I didn't kidnap anybody. He's my son."

"Last I checked, it takes two to make a baby. Which means he's Otero's son, too."

"He's not."

The woman was still stubborn as a mule. He lay down, leaned his head on the pillow, closed his eyes. Kept her wrist firmly in his grip.

"Being here is making everything worse. I have to get out of Nutfield. Then you'll be safe. Then everyone will be safe."

Safe. Right. He remembered safe. Based on the photos, that had been a mirage, too.

He grabbed the envelope he'd stowed beneath his blanket, slapped it on the bed. "If you disappear again, nobody will be safe."

She stepped away like the package might bite.

"Go ahead."

She looked at her wrist, his hand firmly wrapped around it. He thought about making her manage the envelope one-handed but figured her curiosity would keep her here at least long enough to look at the photos. He let her go. "You try to leave again, I'll tackle you."

He'd expected a flippant answer, but she said nothing as she pulled out the photos, flipped through them one by one.

She reached the one of Eric. Her hand flew to cover her mouth, but she forced herself to look at every photo. Then she got to the note. Opened it. Read it. Shook her head. "I don't understand. Why would somebody warn me? Who would do that?"

He searched her face, tried to guess what she was thinking. He hoped to find resolve. The fight he knew she possessed. All he saw was defeat.

"Where's the child, Kelsey?"

"I was trying to protect him. To protect everybody."

"Where's the child?"

"I thought it would be better, don't you see? If I just left him. Left him with somebody I knew would love him. Would care for him. I had no choice."

"Where's the child?"

But before she could speak again, her words registered.

It all started because of her sister, Danielle.

Danielle.

Daniel.

"It was you." He swung his legs over the side of the bed, took a deep breath. Prayed his guess was wrong.

He wasn't wrong, though.

"It was you?"

She wilted. Slid right onto the floor. Curled into a ball as she had that first night. As if she thought he might hurt her. He didn't need to use his fists to hurt her. The truth would do the trick.

"You're the monster mother."

TWENTY-SEVEN

KELSEY HAD TO GET UP.

Eric stood in front of her. She could see his tennis shoes and was thankful he hadn't worn his boots. Those would hurt much worse. She waited for a kick. Knew one would come. She'd found it, his breaking point. At least she was already in a hospital.

But no. He stomped past her. The door banged open.

She had to stop him. She had to explain.

She had to make sure Daniel was safe.

"Sir?" A nurse in the hallway. "Sir, you haven't been released."

"There's a woman in there." Eric's voice. "I think she collapsed."

"A woman? Wait..."

Get up. Get up. She had to get up.

Daniel...

Eric would take care of Daniel. They would protect him. They would have to, because she couldn't do it anymore. She'd been fighting too long. Fighting Carlos for ten years. Fighting to keep her son alive, fighting to keep herself alive, fighting to put food on the table and pay the bills and make a normal life for them. And all she'd done was fail.

She'd put everyone in danger.

Monster mother.

Footsteps outside the room, coming closer. She wanted to lie there and die. But she wouldn't die. She'd just put more people in danger.

The nurse came in. "Hey, you okay?"

Her time was up. She had to move or they'd think she'd gone mad. Maybe she had. She shifted to her knees and looked up. "I'm all right." She forced herself to stand, brushed off her clothes because it seemed like the thing a normal person would do.

The woman held her wrist, the same wrist Eric had held. Her touch was no more gentle as she wrapped her other arm around Kelsey's back and urged her forward. "Have a seat on the bed. I'm going to get a doctor."

"No." She tried a smile, but the nurse didn't buy it. Kelsey didn't care. She pulled away. "I just had my heart broken." Shattered and smashed. "Unless you have an ointment for that, I'll be on my way."

The nurse looked unconvinced, but Kelsey didn't have any more words for her. She'd taken two steps toward the door when Sam came in.

"I saw Eric leaving. What happened? You okay?"

She could only shake her head.

"Come on." She opened her arms, and Kelsey stepped into them. She let Sam comfort her, wondered how her new friend would feel about her when she discovered the truth.

Monster mother.

Add that to her list of sins.

You had a kid with him. Apparently your boyfriend...

Sam thanked the nurse and led Kelsey toward the door. "I

have no idea what happened, honey. All I know is Brady said you're coming home with me."

KELSEY WOKE to muted light outside the window the next morning. Cloudy and gray. The clock told her it was after nine.

Sam had finally given up trying to comfort her and sent her to bed. The sun had barely gone down.

Kelsey slept off and on until around eleven when Sam knocked gently and entered carrying a glass of water and a pill bottle. She sat on the edge of the bed and brushed Kelsey's hair from her eyes the way she might for a small child.

"Are you sleeping at all?"

Kelsey shook her head. The tears that were always close to the surface leaked out and dripped toward her ears.

She should leave. She should be getting her son and running as far away as she could get. But she couldn't make herself get out of bed. And even if she knew where Daniel was, she couldn't face the people who had him. Or face him. Or take him. Her whole point of coming to Nutfield had been to ensure his safety. She'd thought, she'd hoped, it would all be over and they'd be safe by the time she held Daniel again.

She was such a fool.

"You don't have any trouble with pills, do you?" Sam asked.

"What do you mean?"

"Garrison's son's an addict. Since I met him, I'm more cautious about these things than I was before."

"Oh. No, I don't take much but aspirin."

"Not an alcoholic?"

"I never cared for the stuff."

Sam smiled. "Good. I called a doctor friend and asked if it would be okay to share one of these with you. It's an anti-anxiety, not the kind you take every day. The kind you take when... well, when your brain won't stop and you just need to sleep."

"Oh."

"I could get you an over-the-counter something, but my friend thought this would be better. Make your mind quiet down and let you rest."

Kelsey hated taking pills, but she was desperate to silence the accusations. She swallowed it.

She'd slept soundly the rest of the night.

If only she could go back to oblivion and not face the consequences of all she'd done. Instead, she climbed from the bed and pulled the door open. Her backpack was resting in the hallway right outside.

Had Eric been here? Had she missed him?

She remembered how, the day before at the hospital, he'd launched himself out of the bed and nearly collapsed from the effort to keep her from leaving.

Probably now, he wished he'd let her go.

She took her backpack with her to the bathroom to clean up.

Showered and dressed, she went downstairs. Garrison was in the living room, working on his laptop. The TV was on, and a weatherman was pointing at a multi-colored map. The sound was muted. Garrison looked up when she came in. "Good morning."

"Hi."

Sam came around from the kitchen, crossed the room, and pulled Kelsey into a hug. Silly to hug somebody good morning, but Kelsey wasn't complaining.

"Come get some coffee." Sam took Kelsey's hand, settled her at the kitchen table, and reached for the pot. "Wait. Eric said you prefer tea. All I have is black. Is that okay?"

"Coffee's fine. I just need a lot of sugar."

While she sipped from her steaming mug, Sam made her

two pieces of toast, set them in front of her with the butter and a jar of apple jelly, and prattled about the weather. Apparently, a storm was coming, and it could be a big one.

"Could be," Sam said. "But you know how weathermen are. Every storm is the storm of the decade."

Kelsey swallowed a bite. "The last one was pretty bad." She could still feel the chill.

"On Monday?" Sam said. "I think we got three inches, maybe four. They're talking about more than that this time. Assuming it even comes."

Garrison called from the other room. "It's coming. You don't have to be a meteorologist to see that."

"The question is, how much." Sam walked around the wall and peered at the TV. She whistled, lifted her eyebrows. "Estimates have gone up."

"To?" Kelsey asked.

"Nine to twelve."

"Inches?" Kelsey said. "Holy smoke."

Sam laughed. "Don't worry. We can handle it."

Too bad. A snowstorm might keep Carlos from getting there. She'd have to get Daniel and get out of town, fast. Today, before the storm trapped her.

Where would they go? How would they get there? She had no idea and couldn't think, still fuzzy-headed after the pill she'd taken the night before.

She hadn't eaten since the few bites of sandwich at lunch yesterday. Maybe food would help. She forced another bite of the toast.

Sam returned to the table. "You want some juice or something?"

"A glass of water. I can get it if you'll just..."

Sam was already up. She grabbed a glass. "Ice?"

"No, thanks."

A moment later, Sam rested the glass in front of her.

"Thank you. I'm sorry to be such a bother. I really appreciate you guys letting me stay here."

"Just me, actually," Sam said. "Garrison doesn't live here."

"Oh?" She'd just assumed.

Sam stood, pointed out the slider. "See that building there?"

Kelsey looked out the back, past a playground and basketball court and covered pool to another condominium about a hundred yards away.

"The corner unit on this side...Garrison lives there."

"Is that how you two met?"

Sam returned to the table and sat. "Actually, we met through friends, Nate and Marisa. They... Oh."

Kelsey's face must have registered her surprise at the names. Nate and Marisa. They were the people who had Daniel.

Daniel.

Was he safe? Surely Carlos didn't know where he was. Carlos couldn't have put together that the boy who'd been abandoned nearly a week earlier was her son. Except... Eric had been with Daniel. What if someone saw them together? What if...?

"Your son is safe," Sam said. "Eric told Nate what's going on, and Nate took his whole family away for the weekend."

"Away?" How could she grab him and leave, if he was gone? "Where are they?"

Sam shrugged. "Eric wouldn't say. He figured your son would be safer if nobody knew where he was."

Tears filled her eyes. Of course Eric had thought of protecting Daniel. And these foster parents, Nate and Marisa... What a sacrifice they were making for her son.

So many people were involved now. People trying to help. People she'd put in danger.

Why, why, why had she come back here?

But she knew why. Because she couldn't live like this

anymore. She'd thought, even if she died, she could give Daniel a future. Even that was at risk now. And with Daniel out of town, she couldn't grab him and leave. She'd set this in motion, and she couldn't back out now. Tears burned Kelsey's eyes.

Sam handed her a napkin. "Nate and Marisa are friends of ours. Very nice people. Good people."

Kelsey swallowed, nodded, couldn't think of a thing to say. She wiped her eyes with the napkin and pushed her plate away. Maybe she'd eat tomorrow. "Garrison sure spends a lot of time here, if he doesn't live here."

Sam shifted subjects with her. "He's here a lot. But right now, he's here because of you. Eric didn't want you left alone. And apparently nobody's impressed with my superior fighting skills."

Kelsey attempted a smile at the joke. "I'm sure you're deadly."

Garrison piped up from the other room. "You haven't tried her spaghetti. Terrifying."

"Watch it!" But Sam smiled.

Garrison stepped into the doorway. "Sam makes the best caramel brownies you've ever had. But her pasta?" He shook his head, and Sam rolled her eyes.

"Apparently, Garrison is too good for store-bought sauce."

Kelsey tried to laugh, but she couldn't force the sound out. "Y'all didn't have to skip work to babysit me."

"It's Sunday," Garrison said.

"Oh," Kelsey said. "Right."

"We usually go to church," Sam said, "but we didn't mind missing today."

"Thank you." She sipped her coffee, thought about church. "Do you go to the same church as Eric?"

"We do. He's there now."

Of course he was. Probably praying she'd disappear.

"He'll be over when it's done."

He would?

Sam smiled. "He came by on his way, brought your backpack, and reiterated the importance of you remaining here."

Garrison said, "Not sure what he thinks I should do if you decide to leave. I never perfected my hog-tying skills."

"I'm surprised he doesn't want me gone."

Sam reached across the table and laid her hand over Kelsey's. She'd called herself touchy-feely, and the label fit. "He cares for you. Very much."

Kelsey pulled her hand away. She couldn't talk about this anymore. Not with these two.

She needed to talk to Eric.

Or maybe, she just needed to leave.

TWENTY-EIGHT

SUNDAY MORNING, Vanessa sat in the backseat of the rented sedan and glared at the back of Mateo's head. The two men had been up late, up long after Carlos had suggested she retire to their shared bedroom in the hotel suite in Manchester. Suggested, as if she'd had a choice.

What had they talked about after she'd gone into the bedroom? She'd tried to listen at the doorway, but their voices were too soft to understand. How could she prove her worth to Carlos if he wouldn't even let her into the conversation? This always happened when Mateo was around. At first, Carlos would ignore the older man's gentle suggestions that such conversations were no place for a woman, and didn't she have better ways to spend her time? Over time, Carlos would either agree with Mateo or simply quit arguing the point, and Vanessa would be banished.

It was Kelsey's fault. Neither of the men trusted Vanessa, not because of anything she'd done, but because of what Kelsey had done.

Last night, shortly before Vanessa had been sent to bed,

Mateo's phone had rung. The private detective she had hired was now giving updates to him. One more blow to her plan.

The PI had given them an address, a condo where he believed Kelsey was staying for the night.

"She's not with Nolan?" Carlos had asked.

"Doesn't look like it," the PI said over the speakerphone. "He's back at his place, alone."

Carlos had smiled at that. "Trouble in paradise, I suppose. No sign of my boy?"

"Boy? I thought—"

"Right. Yes, you're right," Carlos said quickly, flicking the remark away with his wrist as if the PI could see him. "Perhaps it is a girl."

"No sign of a kid. I'll let you know."

"Stay there and watch tonight."

A short pause answered that. Then, "I'm expected at home."

Carlos named a price, and the man agreed to stay.

Apparently, women weren't the only ones who could be bought.

Now, Carlos, Mateo, and Vanessa were driving from Manchester to Nutfield, a ridiculous name for a town. Mateo had gently suggested—all his suggestions were polite, all made with that irritating head-bob that was nearly a bow—that Vanessa should stay at the hotel, but she'd flat-out refused. And Carlos had been inclined to agree with her. Perhaps it was the eager way in which she'd woken him up that morning. She'd learned early on that generosity in the bedroom was often repaid.

Often, but not always.

The image of Abbas came to mind. She pushed it away and focused on the towering trees surrounding the car. It reminded her of Serbia. Before her life had fallen apart, before the lost jobs and sanctions, her family had occasionally left the city to spend the day on the lake, where they would picnic and relax. Her mother and the other adults didn't swim, but her father always went in with the children. Tata taught them to swim and dive off the dock. They used to play games and have races. Back then, Vanessa had always believed she was her father's favorite.

The thought didn't bring the tears it used to. She'd cried all the tears she had many years before.

Finally, Carlos turned the sedan into the entrance of a condominium complex in Nutfield, a collection of identical buildings, each of which had four doors in front, four separate entrances for four separate homes. Carlos snaked through the twisting streets. She read road signs and studied the area.

One of the road signs caught her eye. Mountain View Drive. It wasn't the obvious lack of a mountain view that had her staring at it. It was the name itself.

It was familiar.

She pulled her notebook from the seat beside her and started flipping until... Yes, right there. The man, Garrison Kopp, lived on Mountain View.

But the address they were going to now... She flipped to the next page back. This home belonged to Samantha Messenger. They hadn't heard her name until the night before when the PI called. Now, Vanessa wondered if she was connected to Garrison Kopp.

She let the information simmer for now. Eventually, she'd tell Carlos.

They stopped down the street from the address the PI had given them and stared at the door.

Vanessa was silent, wondering how she could use her new information to her advantage.

Mateo was silent, probably remembering how Kelsey had put him in prison.

Carlos was silent, too, and it was his silence that frightened her most.

TWENTY-NINE

"I CAN'T EVEN LOOK at her." Eric stomped back and forth across the floor of the dusty barn, ignoring the puffs of breath that came with every word in the chilly space. He'd attempted to sit through the service at church, but he hadn't made it through fifteen minutes before he'd slipped out and come here. They had too much to do. Figure out who in town was helping Otero, figure out what their plans were, and figure out how to thwart them, all while keeping both Kelsey and Daniel safe.

"She had a kid," Eric said. "With another man."

Brady perched on the old metal desk that looked like it had been in that spot for a century. Brady and Rae had been cleaning out the barn ever since they'd married more than a year before. Eric had seen it at its worst, stacked nearly floor to ceiling with junk accumulated over generations. Most of the junk was gone now, but there was still a lot of furniture they hadn't figured out what to do with.

"It's not like she had a choice," Brady said.

"I know that! Don't you think I know that? I don't blame her."

"Don't you?"

Eric stopped, glared at him. Right now, Brady wasn't the chief. He was Eric's mentor and closest friend. And Eric didn't like the challenge in Brady's short question.

"I know she was held against her will. But... This is different. She wasn't just... It wasn't..." He raked his hands through his hair. "She lived with him. In his house, like...like a lover."

"She told you that?"

"She could have escaped. She chose not to." He stomped all the way to the barn window, looked outside at the gray skies. Snow wasn't supposed to start until that night, but the air already felt heavy with it. A storm was brewing.

Brady's voice was annoyingly calm behind him. "She was trying to rescue her sister."

"Why not make a phone call? Why not—?"

"You assume she didn't do all she could to get away? You think, what? She loved that man?"

When Eric didn't respond, Brady said, "I think that concussion did more damage than we thought."

Eric rested his forehead against the frigid glass. His head was pounding, but that pain was nothing compared to the rest. "She didn't love him. I know that."

Brady said nothing while Eric let the chill of the window, the cold air in the barn, seep all the way through him. If nothing else, it lessened the ache in his skull from the knock on the head he'd gotten the day before. "She lived with another man. She had a kid with another man." He looked out the window at the driveway, at the bare trees that circled the house. "Daniel is only eight. And it doesn't make sense. Because..." He'd been obsessing over the timeline since he'd walked out on Kelsey the day before. Daniel was eight, which meant Kelsey was with Otero a lot longer than she'd let on. Which meant...what?

"She was trying to save her sister," Brady said.

Eric spun to face him. "What about me? She risked everything—"

"Her sister was a child, Eric. You were an adult."

"I know that. I know all of that. I could forget... I'd planned to let it all go, to forgive her for everything."

Brady's eyebrows shot up. "Forgive her? For being kidnapped? Enslaved?"

"Not like..." He leaned against the windowsill. "Forgive her for not calling me. For not coming back, even when she was free. You don't understand. I was married, Brady. I was married, and I thought... I loved her with every cell in my body. I'd never been happier. I was on my honeymoon, dreaming about our future, and I rolled over one morning and she was gone. Gone. And I never saw her again, not until three days ago. And, what happened? She left me, left me to rescue her sister. She shacked up with another guy, she had a kid, then she came back and kept all of that a secret. Like...like she felt guilty. And why feel guilty, if she didn't do anything wrong? And now I'm just supposed to, what? Just take that kid like he's mine? Assuming we don't all die in the next twenty-four hours. Assuming Kelsey hasn't lured all of us to our deaths."

"You're not being fair. She's—"

"Fair? You want to talk about fair?" His voice roared in the cavernous space, and he pounded on the wall beside him with his fist. "My wife had a baby with another man." He took a breath, tried to quell his temper. "While I waited here and fought crime and protected other people and had no"—he swallowed the curse word dying to escape—"no idea where she was. She stayed gone for ten years, when all she had to do was pick up the phone. I would have been by her side for all of it, if she'd only asked."

"Of course—"

"And I'm supposed to forget it. Just...what? Love her kid and raise it like he isn't another man's child, isn't the spawn of evil?"

Brady pushed off the desk and crossed the room. "That's what I'm doing."

Eric snapped his mouth shut. Closed his eyes and took a breath. He was an idiot. Brady had adopted Rae's son, and that boy's biological father had been an arms dealer. A murderer. "I'm sorry. You're right."

"How do you feel about the kid?"

"That's irrelevant."

"Is it? Is the boy really irrelevant?"

Eric shook his head to clear it, then fought the wave of pain he probably deserved for being such a jerk. "He's a great kid. A great kid she abandoned in the woods."

"No." Brady squeezed Eric's shoulder. "She left her son with a man she trusted, a man she knew would take care of him."

"It's not like I could keep him. It's not like...I mean, I had no choice but to put him in the system. And now it's out of my hands. We're just lucky Nate and Marisa got him."

"True." Brady dropped his hand. "But she never intended to be gone forever, right? She thought she could bring Otero down."

"Right. Her and her great plan."

Brady stepped back, blew out a puff of vapor into the cold air. "Here's what we know. From what you've told me, Daniel's smart, well educated, and very advanced for his age. He's also healthy, and he's been well cared for. He's polite, and he adores his mother. Is all that true?"

Eric shrugged.

"She loves her son. She's taken good care of him."

"She abandoned him."

"To protect him. Don't you think that was the hardest thing she's ever done?"

He tried to imagine what that would have been like, but he couldn't think beyond his anger. "Who does that? I mean, if she loved him, how could she leave him?" How could she leave Eric, if she loved him?

"You know Rae's story, right?"

Eric thought of how Reagan had faced her murderous husband and then a madwoman to save her baby. "Yeah."

"And Marisa's? She was willing to die for Ana."

"I know."

"And what about Garrison and Aiden? And let's not forget Sam, who would have walked into certain death if not for a lot of good luck."

Not luck, Eric thought. God's intervention.

Where was God now?

Brady continued. "And Sam did that to save someone *else's* kid."

"This is different."

"That your wife was willing to sacrifice her own life and abandon her son with the man she loved in order to save them both? Not that different, my friend."

Brady sounded like he thought Kelsey was some sort of a hero. But how could Eric let go of this rage?

Brady crossed his arms, said nothing. As if he were sure he'd made his point.

Which he had.

Which just irritated Eric more.

Eric's cell phone beeped, and he looked at the screen. He read the message a second time, just to be sure he understood.

"Anything important," Brady said.

"It's Garrison." Eric looked up to meet his friend's eyes. "Looks like he has a lead. He wants us to come over ASAP."

Eric led the way to Sam's condo. Brady followed in his pickup. When they arrived, Sam opened the door and ushered them inside. Garrison was already seated at the kitchen table, laptop open in front of him.

"Kelsey's getting her things together," Sam said.

While Brady slipped past, Eric gave Sam a quick hug. "Thank you for all you've done for us."

"Don't be silly," she said. "I like her. How's your head?"

He stepped back and rubbed the bump on his skull. "Nothing a little time won't cure." He walked to the kitchen and leaned against the counter, too keyed up to sit. He addressed Garrison, seated at the table. "So...?"

"A friend at the Bureau called me a few minutes ago. Turns out, there is someone in town on their radar. A guy named Barry Durant."

"Durant!" Eric looked at Brady. "He's the one who had the fifteen-year old—"

"His niece, if I remember correctly." Brady settled across from Garrison.

"So he claimed," Eric said.

"So her mother said," Brady reminded him.

"She gave me a phone number," Eric said. "Who knows who answered that call? Could have been anybody."

Brady took a deep breath, and Eric knew he was struggling to keep his patience. Every cop in town knew that when Brady paused to breathe, it was time to back off. "But if she was being held against her will," Brady said, "then why wouldn't she tell you when she had the chance? You separated her from Durant, right? She could have told you the truth, and you'd have rescued her."

"Maybe she was afraid."

"It's not unheard of," Garrison said. "After a while, the girls are broken. They don't have the courage to fight back, even when someone tries to help them. They don't know how to be free anymore. Captivity is horrible, but at least it's familiar."

"The evil you know..." Eric said, disgusted by the whole thing.

"What should I have done?" Brady's question felt rhetorical. "The man hadn't done anything illegal. You'd separated the girl, asked her in private for her mother's phone number. The woman who answered the phone told the same story as the girl told. We can't just arrest people because we don't like them. And your gut feeling does not constitute evidence."

Eric heard a noise. He turned as Kelsey set her backpack down at the foot of the stairs. How long had she been listening?

She stepped into the kitchen, where she leaned against the doorjamb. Her hair was wet, her face scrubbed clean, her eyes puffy and red-rimmed. "Hey."

He nodded, unable to form words at the sight of her. How could he love her and be furious at the same time? He turned to the table, tried to remember what he'd been thinking.

Durant and his *niece*. Right. "You didn't see her, Brady," Eric said. "The girl looked..." He gazed at Kelsey, seemed to implore her with his eyes, then back at Brady. "She looked like my wife did when she was telling me the story of what happened to her. Haunted."

"Dead," Kelsey said. "After a while, the girls just look dead. How any man would want..."

Eric's frustration with his wife faded when he saw the look on her face. He crossed the space and wrapped his arm around her back. She leaned into him, and he kissed the top of her head, inhaling the scent of shampoo.

Brady focused on Garrison. "What are they investigating Durant for?"

"They're not investigating him," Garrison explained, "but his name came up in a sex trafficking investigation focused on a player in the Boston area."

Brady blew out a long breath. "Maybe he's Otero's connection." His voice sounded defeated. "Maybe he's been operating right under my nose for years."

"You do the best you can," Garrison said. "There's not a cop alive who doesn't regret the bad guys who slip through his fingers. But we can't stop them all."

Brady ignored the pep talk. "I'll make a call, get someone to keep an eye on him." He stood and stomped past Eric and Kelsey. A moment later, the front door slammed.

"It's not his fault," Kelsey said. "If the girl was being held against her will, she was probably too afraid to say anything."

"We know that," Sam said. "But Brady won't forgive himself easily." Sam slid Garrison's laptop in front of her. "We've also been deep in the dark web, combing through images and videos posted by that user, TakeTwo." By the pinched look on her face, Eric figured nothing about that had been pleasant.

"Did you learn anything?" Eric asked.

She shook her head. "Nothing helpful, unless we can find this place." She turned the laptop to face him, and he bent over to study the photo. He saw a plain room. Behind a large bed where a woman—girl, he figured, though he didn't let his gaze linger—lay in a seductive pose covered by a thin sheet, there was a window high on the wall. Probably a basement. There wasn't much else to differentiate it from any other room.

Eric straightened. "How does this help—?"

"Helps a lot," Garrison said. "I know it looks very ordinary, but there are clues." Garrison slid closer to Sam and pointed at the screen. "The position of the heating unit in the ceiling, the exact color of the walls, the position of the windows. Not just that, but the perspective. Other pictures have told us the door is about here"—he indicated just to the left of the photo—"and over here is another window." He pointed to the right. "Of course, the room is large enough to have camera equipment and lights. If we could find this building, find out who owns it, we could bring this guy down on multiple charges."

"Based on what?" Eric said. "That one girl on that bed doing nothing?"

Garrison smiled. "Oh, we have a lot more than that. The FBI has this thing, a program called Memex. It's created just for this kind of search. I don't really understand how it works." He looked at Sam, who shrugged. "She gets it more than I do. They can search images for these elements and see what else this guy's posted and sold on the dark web. My friend at the Bureau is working on it. Maybe he can connect those photos to others. Best case, he can link those photos to something connected with the suspect, Barry Durant."

"How soon?" Eric asked.

Garrison's pleased expression faded. "It takes time."

"We don't have time," Eric said. "Otero and his men are coming. They're probably in Nutfield right now."

Garrison closed the laptop. "These things don't happen overnight, Eric. You're a detective. You know this."

Eric closed his eyes, took a deep breath. "I'm sorry. I'm just—"

"I know," Garrison said.

They'd made headway. If TakeTwo was Durant, and if they could connect those photos to his house or some property he owned... If they could figure out when and where Durant and Otero were planning to meet...

Brady came back inside bringing a gust of cold air with him. "I've got somebody headed to Durant's house right now."

Eric asked, "Who? What's the plan?"

"Jimmy." Brady focused on Kelsey. "He's one of my uniformed cops." He turned back to Eric. "He's going to watch the house, see if he can ascertain if Durant is home. If he is, then Jimmy'll just sit on him 'til he moves. If not, then we'll be looking for his car. Once the pre-storm traffic dwindles, we might be able to locate him in town."

Eric felt a vapor of hope blow through his heart. Could they really stop Otero? Could they really bring him down?

"Meanwhile," Brady said, "we'll be keeping an eye on your house, in case anybody shows up there looking for you. And I talked to Nate this morning. They'll stay gone until I call him."

"Do you know where they are?" Kelsey's voice, full of longing, took Eric off guard.

"Nobody does," Brady said. "We figured it'd be safer that way. And they are safe. I promise."

Kelsey nodded, and Eric glanced down at her. Her expression was filled with fear.

Brady continued. "I've briefed the guys at the station. They'll be on the lookout for strangers. They have a photo of Otero and another man who's associated with him, Mateo Ruiz."

"He's out of prison?" Kelsey asked.

"Uh..." Garrison opened the laptop, clicked a few times. "Yeah. Ruiz was released after five years on good behavior."

A mugshot of the man filled Garrison's screen, and Eric leaned in to study it. Older, short gray hair, brown eyes.

Kelsey chuckled, but the sound was dark. "No doubt his behavior was perfect. Most polite criminal I've ever met. Doesn't make him a good guy, though."

Brady nodded. "If Otero and Ruiz are in town, we should know. We're faxing their photos to all the local hotels. And I have a man visiting local businesses as well."

Sam jumped in. "I can call the management companies, see if anybody rents a condo or cabin."

Brady nodded. "Yes. Good idea."

"And if you find him?" Eric asked.

"We'll watch him. No need to let him know we know he's here. No need to give him the opportunity to put up his guard. Let him think he's free to roam. With a lot of luck, we'll follow him right to his meeting with the local contact and bring them both down at once."

Eric took in all the information. "Okay. Good. You'll keep an eye on Durant, let me know if he moves." At Brady's nod, he said, "Until then, I need to get Kelsey someplace safe."

Kelsey stepped away and faced him. "I'd rather stay here, be involved."

"Not a chance," Eric said. "You need to stay out of sight. The whole point of this is to keep you safe."

"No, the point is to bring Otero down." Kelsey shifted her gaze to Brady. "I can help. Please, let me help."

Brady was already shaking his head. "It's our job to bring him down. Your job is to stay safely out of the way."

She crossed her arms and huffed her frustration.

Eric shifted to face Brady. "If anybody spots Otero or this Ruiz guy," Eric said, "if something happens, I want to be involved."

Brady nodded once.

Sam stood and grabbed a key off the kitchen counter. She slid it to Eric. "I need to rename my business." She bent over a piece of paper and wrote down an address. "Sam's summer rentals and safe houses."

"The cabin wasn't such a safe house for Garrison and Aiden," Eric reminded her.

"I sold that one. I'm sending you to the one Marisa and Nate used."

"If I remember correctly," Eric said, "that didn't end up being safe, either."

She handed him the Post-It with the address. "Hmm. You're

right, though it worked out well in the end. I pray you and Kelsey will be safe as two bugs in a plush rug."

Amen to Kelsey's safety. What Eric wanted was to be doing something to bring down her enemies. If that meant he wasn't safe, that was fine with him.

THIRTY

VANESSA HAD SEEN the blue Jeep first.

They'd been watching the front of the condo for a half hour, and Carlos had started to get antsy, tapping his fingers on the steering wheel, gaze darting all around. He didn't sit still well, and he hated to be confined. She could feel his anxiety rising as she and Mateo stared at the front door.

"You sure everything's in place?" Carlos asked for the third time in ten minutes.

Mateo, the picture of patience, smiled at him. "I set it up myself."

"And we have time to get there?"

"It would be foolish, my friend. If the police aren't already watching Durant, they will surely swarm the area as soon as it's finished. We don't want to be anywhere near there."

It irritated Vanessa to no end that she didn't know what they were talking about. She'd asked the first time they'd had this conversation, but before Carlos could answer Mateo had suggested the matter was too delicate for her ears.

Bah. What did Mateo know of what her ears could handle? She'd been a play toy for men for a decade. Her ears were no more innocent than the rest of her. But reminding Carlos of that was not such a good idea.

That anybody thought her delicate almost made her smile.

Carlos resumed his tapping. "We know where she is," Carlos finally said. "I need to rent another car. One of you guys can watch her. I can't sit here any longer."

It was just as he'd shifted into drive that she'd seen the Jeep turn toward them. It was still a few buildings down, but she knew where it was going. The PI had told them what kind of car Eric drove.

"Wait," Vanessa said.

Carlos glanced over his shoulder, eyes narrowed. "For what?"

She'd smiled and nodded in the direction of Eric Nolan's car. "He's here."

Sure enough, the Jeep parked in front of Samantha Messenger's condo. A silver pickup parked beside it. A man got out of each car. The one in the pickup was very tall and had dark hair. The other man was about six feet, light hair. He looked just like the pictures she'd seen of Eric Nolan.

Carlos looked at her again. "How did you know?"

"The PI told us he what he drives."

A slow smile spread over Carlos's face. He looked at Mateo. "I told you she could help."

"I never doubted it." Mateo shifted, looked toward her. "Well done, Vanessa."

The man made her skin crawl. *Ulizica*. She couldn't think of the English word for what Tata had always called his manager—a man who was always agreeing with and trying to impress the boss.

Oh, yes, the term came back to her now. *Bottom-kisser*? Something like that. The term described Mateo perfectly.

She nodded at the *ulizica* with a smile. "*Hvala*. Thank you," she amended quickly. Carlos didn't like it when she spoke Serbian.

"You're welcome." Mateo turned to face forward again. "We should wait, see what happens next."

Carlos sighed, tapped the steering wheel with his fingers. Turned on the radio, scanned through the stations for a few minutes, then flipped it off. The men talked about the friends Eric Nolan had involved and wondered what those friends were discussing now.

The friends, though... They made Vanessa think. A cop and a former FBI agent. But what did the woman do?

"Mateo, do you mind if I use your laptop?"

"Help yourself." Then he added, "There's no internet service, but you can probably find a game on there."

A game. She paused, smiled at the back of Mateo's head. One of these days she'd prove to Carlos that he didn't need the bottom-kisser at all. She couldn't wait.

She slid Carlos's laptop out of the bag resting on the seat beside her. She used her phone as a hotspot—apparently the *ulizica* hadn't thought of that—and navigated to the internet.

First, she found a local car rental company and reserved two cars. She'd tell Carlos about that when she'd finished with the laptop, lest Mateo realize she was connected and take it away from her. Not that he'd need it—he had no ideas. He'd take it out of spite.

Vanessa searched Samantha Messenger's name. There were too many. She added *Nutfield, New Hampshire,* and searched again.

She scrolled through the choices. The woman's Facebook profile wasn't helpful. She started to click on something called LinkedIn, but then she scrolled further down, saw a newspaper article dated the October before.

Samantha Messenger, Entrepreneur Extraordinaire.

She clicked the link. Apparently, the woman owned rental properties on the lake nearby.

Interesting.

Carlos and Mateo kept repeating all the information they already had, looking at it from every angle, wondering if they'd missed something.

She searched Google, discovered a website, and searched for deeds with Messenger's name on them.

The results made Vanessa think she'd done something wrong.

She clicked on each one, and each one listed *Samantha Messenger Properties* as the owner. Vanessa counted... Seventeen. The woman owned seventeen properties.

Just to be sure, Vanessa scrolled through the list. Sure enough, the condo they were watching right now was one of the properties listed.

Wow.

Could Vanessa ever do something like purchase her own home? Maybe do more than that? She'd known women worked in America, worked all over the world. Hadn't Mama had a job? But in America, women often had the same kinds of jobs as men.

Maybe that had been true in Serbia, too. Vanessa had been a child. What did she know?

The world in which Vanessa had spent half her life had kept her from believing women could own anything, do anything, be anything. Women weren't buyers and sellers. Women were property.

But this Messenger woman... she had done this. Had she done it alone? It appeared so—no man's name was listed with hers.

Women really could stand alone.

Vanessa could too. If she wanted to badly enough.

If she could get away.

She rubbed her still-flat belly. *Would you like that, little one? Would you like a mama who isn't your tata's property?*

If it killed her, Vanessa would raise her child in Samantha Messenger's world, not in the one she belonged to.

Slowly, painstakingly, Vanessa searched all the property addresses and starred them in her map program. Then, she studied the map.

Every property except this condo was located on Clearwater Lake.

Vanessa didn't know what to do with the information. She copied the list, sent the information to her phone, and then cleared her search history.

Maybe it would come in handy. She was not going to share it with Mateo or Carlos, not yet. No, this she'd keep to herself until she knew how she could use it.

THIRTY-ONE

THE JEEP WAS STILL WARM when Kelsey climbed in. She petted Magic, who started to jump into the front seat to greet her. Only Eric's quiet "stay" kept her from hurtling into Kelsey's lap.

Eric maneuvered out of the condo complex.

"Do you think Daniel's safe?" she asked.

"He's perfectly safe, I promise."

"Okay." Her voice cracked on the word, and she told herself not to cry even as she imagined her little boy missing her the way she was missing him. If anything happened to Daniel, she'd never survive it. "But I mean... These people who have him—"

"You couldn't choose a nicer family." Eric's voice was as confident as it was gentle. "And they're already falling in love with him."

"That's good. He's so lovable." She could trust Eric with this. She knew that. She also knew she was putting him and all his friends in danger. Carlos was ruthless when he wanted something. "I should take Daniel and go. If Carlos doesn't find me when he gets here, he'll think I slipped through his fingers again."

The very thought of leaving Eric had tears filling her eyes. How could she still have tears left?

"That's what you do, huh?" Eric's voice was harsh. "You run away. Is that why you left me ten years ago? Second thoughts?"

"Don't be a jackass." The quick flash of anger surprised her. She thought of the cowardly woman she'd been at the hospital the day before. No, she wouldn't be that person, not with her husband, a man who should respect her. She was sick of his judgment, his accusations.

He glanced at her quickly. His voice was gentler when he said, "I'm just trying to understand."

"If you don't by now, Eric, you never will."

He turned the Jeep toward town, the only sound in the car the huffing of the dog in the backseat. Snow fell outside, soothing and steady.

Like her husband.

For years, all she'd longed for was to be with Eric again. Her love for him hadn't faded, but perhaps while she'd been gone she'd romanticized him, romanticized their relationship. She didn't remember these long brooding silences, and she couldn't recall a time when he'd been anything but polite to her. Had she blocked out the unpleasant things, or was Eric different now?

Of course he was different. The years had changed him. His job had changed him.

Missing her, not knowing where she was... Yes, that had changed him, too.

"You could have called me." Eric's tone was measured. No accusation, no sadness. "I would have come, wherever you were. I would have been with you. I would have protected you."

"I know."

He kept his focus forward. She'd never seen this much traffic on the little two-lane road that went through Nutfield. "Where did all these people come from?"

"Storm's coming. People are shopping, getting prepared."

"We need anything?"

"I took care of it. We should be fine for a few days."

They were inching slowly through town with nothing else to distract them from the pachyderm between them that felt more corporeal than the dog in the back seat. How could she make Eric understand? "I know you would have come," she finally said. "You would have quit school, abandoned your dream, to be with me. I couldn't let that happen to you."

"You were my dream." His jaw was clenched like he was fighting the urge to say more. "It would have been fine. I could have gone to school—"

"No, you couldn't. You wouldn't have been able to go to school somewhere else. Don't you see? You would have had to give up your identity. Your family. Your future. Fake IDs don't come with transcripts. This wasn't the federal witness protection program. When I changed my identity, I paid a guy five hundred bucks for a counterfeit driver's license, birth certificate, and social security card. Every job, every brush with the police, every time I've been asked to show ID, I cringed, knowing eventually somebody would discover my secret. I couldn't go back to college, even if I hadn't had Daniel. Under my new name—"

"Carrie Anderson."

The name caught her up short. But of course, Daniel had told him. "Right." She'd intended to buy new papers in Manchester after she'd left her son, after she'd made that critical call. The one she could never make now. "Under that name, I had no high school records, no job history, nothing. I couldn't ask that of you."

"I would have—"

"I know that." There was more to it. Maybe she didn't want to explain the rest of it. But he deserved to know. To know who she was, what she'd become. "You don't understand what it was like. I wasn't the same person. I went from being this...this successful pre-law student to being property. I went from feeling loved and cherished to feeling like a whore. No, to *being* a whore."

"Don't say that." His words were quick and harsh. "Don't ever say that."

"See?" He couldn't even stand to hear the word, but if he understood all she'd been through, all she'd done... "You don't... I couldn't..." It was impossible to explain. Impossible because she didn't want Eric to know. What would he think if he knew everything? "How could I come home to you as if I were the same person? You always made me feel valued, treasured." Her voice cracked. She swallowed the emotions. "Thanks to Carlos, I was worth less than the dirt you'd scrape off your boots."

"You weren't, though." He hit the brake in the stop-and-go traffic and turned to her.

She met his eyes for a moment, then ducked away. She couldn't look at him and talk about this. She'd never be able to overcome the shame. And if that were the case, what was she doing with this man, this good man?

"I would never have seen you that way." His confidence, his vehemence, had her shaking her head.

"Such big words. But do you know how the police treated us when Misty and I escaped? Like worthless garbage. I'm convinced if they'd acted faster, they might have rescued my sister. But we were whores. We didn't matter."

He inched ahead in traffic. "So you expected me to treat you the same way."

"Maybe you wouldn't have, but—"

"Maybe?"

Her voice rose, cracked. "I didn't know. How could I know?"

"You could have expected the best of me. You could have tried."

Expected the best of him. That's what she'd done, all those years ago when she'd agreed to marry him. Because she'd known Eric was one of the best men she could ever know. Over the years, she'd wondered...how many times had she wondered what he would have said to her, how he would have treated her if she'd simply gone home? On good days, she imagined him folding her into his arms and declaring his eternal, unconditional love.

But on bad days, the scenario she imagined was very different. Scorn in his face. Hatred.

She'd never had the nerve to risk that. "Knowing you were here. Knowing you'd loved me... What if I called you, what if you came to me, and what if when you learned the truth, you looked at me like those cops did? How would I have survived that?"

His frown, the quick shake of his head, told her he didn't understand. He never would. He reached across the car, took her hand. "I had a good idea of what you'd been through. I did enough searching. I figured you'd been taken by the people who took your sister, and I knew what kind of people they were. I searched for you—until you faked your death. Over the years, I never stopped believing. I never stopped loving you."

Tears filled her eyes, and she sniffed.

He glanced at her. "There are some napkins in the glove box, if you need one."

She managed to open it and pull out a napkin and wipe her tears without letting go of his hand.

Maybe if they could just keep holding onto each other, they could survive this.

She composed herself, studied his face as he inched along in traffic. His eyes were red as if he were fighting tears as much as she was giving in to them.

"Years passed, though," he said. "Years and years, and still..."

"I never thought it would be a decade. I thought that with the information I'd stolen from Carlos, I could bring him down. I thought it would be six months, maybe a year, maybe two. And then Carlos would go to prison, and I'd come back. I thought if I brought him down then maybe you'd believe... you'd understand. You'd forgive all I did. I thought, by then, you'd have gotten your degree, and we could be a family. But then two years turned into three, then four... I figured too much time had passed. You'd have met someone else. Gotten married. Forgotten all about me."

His face showed no reaction. "So you moved on."

She scoffed. "I raised my son. I had no choice but to figure out how to live, how to support us. And I kept trying to find a way to bring Carlos down."

He glanced at her then. "But there's a man, right?"

She met his eyes. "What are you talking about?"

He stopped the car, though the one in front kept moving in the traffic crawling along Crystal Ave. He stared at her, and the moment stretched before he said, "I saw that...that expression on your face when you described your home. You're in love with somebody."

"I'm in love with Daniel. I was thinking about my son."

"Oh." He blinked twice and focused ahead and let up on the brake enough to catch up with the car in front of them. At this rate they'd never get through downtown Nutfield. "You're saying there's nobody else?"

"Never."

He turned to face her again, held her gaze, and then nearly smiled.

After everything, her optimistic heart fluttered with joy.

But of course, just because she hadn't moved on didn't mean he hadn't. "How about you?"

She studied him, waited for the quick answer. He didn't

give her one. Instead, he let go of her hand and pulled into an empty parking lot.

She didn't want to know. She wouldn't be able to survive if he told her there was somebody else.

He shifted the car into park and met her eyes. "I never told anybody about you, because... Well, it didn't seem wise. People were always fixing me up. I refused so many blind dates with women, a friend tried to fix me up with a guy."

The very thought of it made her laugh.

He smiled, but it faded. "So... I dated some. Women," he clarified, which made her smile again. "Movies, dinner, a couple of church things."

She swallowed, braced herself.

"But there was never anything to it. Two, three dates, and I was done."

"I see."

"Nothing... It was just dates. No..." He swallowed. "Nothing happened with them. I mean, I never even kissed them."

The words penetrated. *Never even kissed...?* "Seriously?"

"Our wedding vows meant something to me. There's never been anyone but you."

How could she have ever doubted this man? She leaned forward, unable to keep her distance any longer. The dog huffed in the backseat. Snowflakes landed on the windshield. The car was nearly silent, warm from the heater and the desire she couldn't temper.

His mind seemed to be going to the same place.

He placed his hand on the side of her face and claimed a kiss. It was sweet and tender and nearly made her cry.

Just like that, he pulled away. He might as well have slapped her.

He turned away, jaw tight.

"What?" Her word was harsh. "What have I done now?"

He faced her again. "Daniel is eight. Which means either you were still with Carlos after your sister died, or he's somebody else's kid. Which means, once again, you're lying about something."

"Ah." She couldn't help the smile. "I can see why that would anger you."

He crossed his arms and glared.

"Or," she said, "Daniel isn't eight."

He dropped his arms. "Wait. What?"

"I told him to lie about his age."

Eric seemed to process that. After a moment, he asked, "Why would you do that?"

"Because Carlos is looking for a nine-year old. I figured that one little lie would protect him better than anything else could."

"Huh." He nodded slowly. "But...he's tiny."

"He's always been little for his age."

"Oh. I was like that, too," Eric said. "Until I hit puberty, people always thought I was younger than I was."

"Otherwise, I would have gone the other direction, told him to tell you he was ten. Because he's super smart." She failed to keep the pride out of her voice. "Eight seemed easier to pull off."

He stared at her. His Adam's apple bobbed. He said, "You just left him there."

"No. I didn't. I watched the whole thing."

He tilted his head to the side. "What did you see?"

He didn't believe her? She forced herself not to get defensive. Eric was having to reframe the whole scenario. "Magic ran straight for him. I nearly screamed out a warning, but then your sweet dog just licked him."

"Where were you?"

"Far enough away that Daniel thought I'd gone. I walked until he quit looking, then doubled back."

"I didn't..." He pursed his lips, shook his head. "I'm sorry."

"It's a lot to take in."

"Yeah." He looked beyond her, and she waited. He wasn't finished. That she could see in the wrinkles beside his eyes, the way his lips seemed to tighten at the corners. Finally, he asked, "Does Daniel know who his father is?"

She looked down, shook her head. "No."

"But he knows his father's not a good guy. He must know something, if he was willing to lie about his age."

She met Eric's eyes again. "He doesn't know anything. I told him I had to take care of something and I'd be back for him."

"But he lied. Why would he do that if he didn't understand?"

"He's nine, Eric. I told him it was important and that, eventually, he'd be able to tell everyone his real age. He trusts me."

Eric nodded slowly, processing. "So the story..."

"It's all true."

"And there's nothing else?"

Oh, that she could tell him everything. She'd have to. Soon. But not yet. Not when they'd finally come to a place of peace. She looked at her hands, folded in her lap, and tried to think of how to answer.

"What?" he said.

She met his eyes. "There's a lot I haven't told you. Details I just can't..."

He reached across the console and took her hand. With his other hand, he lifted her chin until their eyes met. "You'll tell me, in time. There's no rush." He pulled her as close as he could with the center console between them. She tucked her head against his neck and inhaled his woodsy scent. She felt warm, safe. When he spoke, she could feel the vibration of his voice on her cheek. "Maybe if I quit being so angry," he said, "that'll make it easier."

She surprised herself with a short burst of laughter. "Wouldn't hurt."

"I'm sorry."

She backed up, met his eyes. "I knew you'd have given up everything for me. I didn't want you to do that. You understand that, right?"

"Not really."

"I thought you'd move on."

"Then you don't know me very well."

But she did. After everything they'd been through, he deserved better than her. But he wanted her.

And for all her plans to leave him, she knew she couldn't do it again. She wouldn't. Somehow, this was going to have to all work out. She had no idea how, but she also knew she'd never have the strength to walk away from Eric again. "Can we just...?" She paused, collected her thoughts. "I know it's ridiculous, and I know everything is up in the air, and I know there's still Daniel, and I have to figure out how to get him back and get us safe and..." Her voice trailed off. "I don't know what's going to happen, Eric. I just know I need you. I don't want to leave you again."

He brushed her hair behind her ears, looked deep in her eyes. "Whatever happens now, we're in it together.

THIRTY-TWO

Eric's phone rang, and he and Kelsey both jumped as if they'd been caught committing a crime. As if there were something wrong with a husband and wife kissing. His pulse raced, and that had nothing to do with the ringing phone and everything to do with the beautiful creature in his arms.

It was probably good they were in the Jeep with a console between them.

Probably good there was a dog in the backseat, watching their every move.

The phone rang again.

Eric shifted just enough to see Kelsey's face. He smiled, kissed her forehead.

She smiled in return, blushed and looked away.

Eric forced himself to focus. Beyond his very alluring wife, beyond the windows of his Jeep to the snow falling outside. Right. There was a whole world out there. A world filled with evil and danger. A world that seemed like it couldn't exist in the same realm as this peaceful place.

The phone rang again.

She sighed, and the soft sound made him want to start all

over again. He sat back in his seat and hit the button on his steering wheel to answer. "Nolan here."

"It's Brady. You're not at the cabin yet, are you?"

"Not even downtown yet," Eric said. "We, uh..." He glanced at Kelsey, and her cheeks turned a beautiful shade of pink. "The traffic is terrible."

"Good, excellent." Brady's voice held an intensity that focused Eric's thoughts. "Durant's on the move. Jimmy's following."

Eric glanced at Kelsey. "I need to get her—"

"Got a plan. Head to McNeal's. Park right in front, if you can. Go inside, both of you. Rae's almost there." There was a pause before Brady said, "No idea how she got ahead of you."

Eric wasn't about to explain. "And then what do we do?"

"I gotta go. I'll call you in a minute."

Brady hung up, leaving Eric and Kelsey staring at the now silent dashboard.

"He'd better not be thinking of sending you and Rae off by yourselves," Eric said.

"I'd rather stay with you."

Eric ignored the comment as he maneuvered back into traffic. They finally made it through the one stoplight in town, and he parked on the street in front of McNeal's.

Kelsey reached for her door handle, and he grabbed her arm, lifted his eyebrows.

"Oh, for heaven's sake," she said.

"It's that bad having your husband open the door for you?"

"I'm sorry. Of course not." He heard the anxiety behind her words, the fear.

He held her gaze. "I'm going to make sure you're safe."

"What about you?"

He smiled. "I'll be fine. Don't you worry about me." He walked around and opened her door.

She stood beside him, her gaze on his face. "But I am worried about you. Now that I have you back..." Her eyes filled again.

The woman cried more than a newborn.

He pulled her into a hug. "I'll be fine. Nothing's going to happen to me."

She pulled away. "You promise?"

Her fear was palpable. Suddenly, he was very aware of the line of traffic moving slowly beside them, the people in the restaurant who could easily be watching. He felt very exposed.

Too exposed as he led her to the sidewalk. But Brady wouldn't have had them come to the busiest restaurant in Nutfield on the most crowded street in town if he hadn't wanted them to be seen.

Kelsey was still waiting for an answer.

He kissed her forehead. "I promise I'll do everything in my power to stay safe."

"That's not exactly the same thing."

He wasn't about to make promises he couldn't keep. He took her hand and led her to the door.

They stopped just beyond the threshold, and he took in the crowd. McNeal's was doing quite a business, considering the storm building outside. About half the tables were full. He scanned the customers. No Otero or Ruiz, not that he'd expected them. Nobody suspicious-looking at all. Behind the counter, the staff was buzzing like they'd never been busier. The line of take-out sacks on the counter probably explained that.

The waitress, Bonnie, shuffled over when they walked in. "How many?"

"Two," he said.

She winked and lowered her voice. "Brady told me to seat you guys by the window. Don't know what's going on, but I'm glad to help." She led the way to the seat in the window, and they each sat. "Coffee?"

Eric shrugged, frustrated. "Uh..."

"Coffee."

After Bonnie walked away, Kelsey sighed. "Are we supposed to sit here and enjoy a meal? What's going on?"

"No idea."

His phone rang. He angled it to show Kelsey Brady's name on the screen, then answered.

"You made it?" Brady said.

"Just got seated."

"You guys order something, then have Kelsey go to the restroom. Rae's waiting for her. They'll go out the back. Be sure to slip her the key to the cabin that Sam gave you."

"Okay."

"No big goodbye scenes," Brady said. "We don't want to tip off anybody watching that she's leaving."

"Do you think we're being watched?"

"Very likely. And we need to throw Durant off her trail, especially since you won't be with her."

Good point. His blue Jeep Wrangler wasn't exactly inconspicuous. "Who's going to protect them?"

"Donny'll follow them to the cabin and stay with them there."

"Just Donny?"

"We need everybody else. This deal is going down today."

"How do you—?"

"Later."

That whiff of hope Eric had experienced earlier grew into something powerful. They could actually do this. They could catch Otero and Durant in the act of handing off the *merchandise*. The thought made him ill. But if they pulled this off, they could rescue three women, maybe underage girls. They could put at least two men behind bars.

They could protect Kelsey and Daniel.

Eric could get his life back.

He was afraid to hope. But his fearless, hopeful heart pounded in overdrive. He stared at Kelsey and spoke to Brady on the phone. "How long do I wait?"

"Five minutes after Kelsey and Rae leave, I'll be there. We'll go together."

"Got it." He ended the call and kept his voice lowered. "Things are looking up."

Her eyes widened. "Yeah?"

He nodded, wished he could explain. Wished he knew enough to explain. He figured Rae would take care of that for him.

Bonnie returned with the coffee and two glasses of water. "What do you kids want today?"

"Baked potato soup for Kelsey," he said. "I'll have the fish and chips."

Bonnie winked and turned toward the kitchen.

Eric tried not to roll his eyes. He leaned closer to Kelsey. "I think she has a latent desire to be a spy."

Kelsey watched the waitress's retreating form. "Nobody would suspect her."

He nodded, took a deep breath, and reached into his pocket. He pulled out the single key Sam had given him, then took Kelsey's hand. He slipped the key into her palm, closed her fist around it, then set his other hand on top.

He smiled as if all were well. If everything went the way they hoped it would, then all would be well. But he'd been a cop long enough to know that things were never that easy. He leaned forward, laughed like he was making a big joke, and lowered his voice, keeping his smile in place.

"You're going to go to the bathroom. Rae'll meet you there. You're leaving with her. Out the back."

"Why—?"

"Just listen, okay?" He smiled again, and she followed suit, though he saw the worry in her eyes.

"I..." Eric swallowed, squeezed her hand, worked to keep his expression neutral. "You asked me to make a promise—that I would be okay. I won't make promises I can't be sure to keep."

Her eyes widened, and her lips parted, but he continued before she could interrupt.

"I don't know what's going to happen today. I can promise you I'll do everything in my power to keep you safe, you and your son. And I'll do everything in my power to come back to you in one piece." He brushed a teardrop off her cheek. "And you can make a promise to me, too."

She swallowed. "Anything."

"You can't leave me again. If you have to run, then we run together. Whatever happens, you and I have to stay together. Okay?"

She blinked back fresh tears, nodded. "I can't leave you again. I won't."

He took a deep breath. It felt like the first real breath he'd taken in nearly a decade. Then he remembered the show they were supposed to be putting on. No big goodbye scenes. Just a casual lunch. He plastered on a fake smile, and she returned it. He focused on her eyes. "I love you, Kelsey. I've loved you every single minute since the first moment I saw you when I was eighteen years old. No matter what the cost, no matter the lost years, no matter what the next hours and days bring, I will never regret putting that ring on your finger. I will never regret loving you." He squeezed her hand. "You are worth it."

Her fake smile faded. Her mouth opened, but she didn't speak.

"Now." He let go of her hand. "I can't kiss you goodbye because you're just going to the bathroom."

"Oh. But..." She still seemed unable to come up with a response.

"I know, Kels. You don't have to say anything. I know."

She stared another moment, then slid to the edge of the booth and stood. "Be right back."

He watched as she weaved among the tables. Right after she reached the hallway that led to the bathrooms, Bonnie hefted a huge tray and stopped in the perfect place to block everyone's view.

Eric sat back, swallowed, and told himself that he would see Kelsey again, that she wouldn't disappear.

So why did he feel like something had just ripped a hole in his chest?

Eric nodded politely when Bonnie delivered their meals.

Frustration and irritation rolled over him as he snatched a piece of fish, dipped it in tartar sauce, and took a bite. It was delicious, as always. If he ever moved back to north Texas, he'd quit eating seafood all together. Being a stone's throw from the coast had spoiled him. He munched on french fries, glared at his phone as if that would make it ring, and then turned his attention outside.

He hated sitting by the window. Normally, he'd have refused this table, but this had been Brady's idea. Apparently, exposed was the point.

Another few bites of fish, more french fries. And then Brady's tall frame passed by outside. A minute later, he walked in.

Eric started to slide out of the booth, but Brady shook his head and joined him. He slid into Kelsey's seat. "Soup? really?"

Eric lowered his voice. "I didn't know we were actually eating."

"We are." Brady took a spoonful of soup. "Never ordered the soup before. It's not bad." He took another few bites, then sipped Kelsey's water. He studied Eric over the glass. "Relax. Eat." He lowered his voice. "We'll go soon."

"Fine." Eric took another bite of fish, but he couldn't enjoy it, not with all that was going on, knowing something had happened, and he was in the dark. And the way Brady was studying him wasn't helping. "What?"

"What held you two up?" Brady's eyes narrowed. "I can't figure out why you weren't halfway out of town by the time I called you. I was sure we'd have to wait for you to get back."

Eric huffed out a breath. "Aren't we in a hurry?"

"We have time."

"Will you tell me—?"

"In the car." Brady lowered his voice to say that, then returned it to a normal level. "Car trouble?"

"No." Eric didn't want to explain what they'd been doing. "We pulled over for a minute. We were talking."

"Talking, huh?"

Eric glared at him.

"Okay." Brady held out his napkin. "Not sure if that's a hickey or lipstick on your neck there."

Eric wiped his neck, glared at his friend.

Brady laughed out loud. "No judgment here, man. She is your wife."

"You're in an annoyingly good mood." Eric glared at him, but Brady ignored him.

Bonnie returned, greeted Brady, and left the check. Brady pulled out his wallet—Eric didn't even reach for his. Brady'd just earned the right to pay for their meals. Brady set the wallet down and kept eating.

Finally, his phone dinged with an incoming text. Then he stood and tossed a few bills on the table. "Let's go."

They left the restaurant. Eric glanced at his Jeep, saw the dog in the backseat. "Crap. Magic."

Brady paused, followed his gaze. "We'll get someone to take care of her. Run the keys inside and give them to Bonnie."

Eric did, explained the situation in a hurried whisper. Two minutes later, he opened the door of Brady's truck.

Brady was setting his phone in the console when Eric slid into the car. "I called my dad," Brady said. "He's going to get the dog and take her over to the cabin. Kelsey likes her, right?"

"They made fast friends."

"Good, good." Brady maneuvered into the traffic and headed south. "After you left, TakeTwo left a new message on the message board. If we deciphered it correctly, the deal is going down soon."

"Then what were we doing, wasting time?"

"Our friend Barry Durant has an office right across the street from McNeal's."

Eric looked behind him, though the building was already receding from view. "I'd forgotten that. He works in that accounting firm on the second floor."

"Yeah. He left his house, went to the office. He's been inside all this time. With all those windows, we thought maybe he'd see us at McNeal's or out front. No idea what he was doing, but we figured we'd make it look like we had no idea what was going on."

"But if he's watching, he knows Kelsey isn't with us now."

"That text I got inside told me he just left. Jimmy's following him."

"Tell me the details."

"First, you should know that Garrison's friend at the Bureau is working on connecting that screen name, TakeTwo, with our friend Durant. The message today leads us to believe Durant and Otero are going to make the exchange outside of town. We don't know exactly where, but we know it'll be off Route 24 near Post Road."

Eric thought about that location. It was on the far side of the lake. Not close to Kelsey by car, but as the crow flies, close enough. He shook off the thought. It didn't matter. Kelsey was safe. Nobody knew where she was. "There's that abandoned horse farm just west of there."

Brady was quiet a minute. "That's right. I was focused on the corner. I didn't think of that place."

"It'd be perfect for a clandestine meeting."

"Good, good."

Brady dialed his phone and relayed the information to the team. "Jimmy confirms they're headed that way. I've got a couple of guys already out there."

"What if they tip them off?"

"They're in plain clothes and driving personal vehicles. We know what we're doing."

Eric nodded, silent. Brady was good at what he did. Eric had seen him bring down drug rings and rescue hostages and catch thieves. He'd never doubted his boss before, but this was different. This was Eric's life. This was Kelsey's life and Daniel's life.

Brady took back roads to approach the horse farm from the opposite side. When they were close, he turned onto a narrow strip that was more path than driveway, barely wide enough for his new pickup. Trees and bushes lined both sides and brushed the paint job.

"I should have brought the old truck," Brady said, wincing with every scratching sound.

He continued slowly, bouncing over the rough terrain as they neared the old barn. He parked where the trees would hide them, about ten feet from the edge of the unused pasture. The snow had picked up. It would help to conceal them but make it harder for them to see what was going on.

They both focused on the weathered building a hundred yards away.

"We should get closer," Eric said.

"For all we know, Otero and Ruiz are already here. That barn door is easily big enough for a car to drive through. There's not enough cover."

Brady was right. Eric was just antsy, dying to do something, anything, besides sit there. "If we're wrong..."

"Jimmy's following Durant," Brady said. "If we're in the wrong spot, he'll know it. I have ten guys on this, Eric. We're good."

"Why isn't Durant here yet? He left before us."

"Good question." Brady called Jimmy. Apparently, Durant had stopped at the grocery store. Even criminals needed to stock up for storms.

"He's leaving the store now," Jimmy said.

After Brady ended the call, Eric voiced his fear. "What if Durant picks up the tail?"

"The other guys are all around. If Jimmy thinks Durant's onto him, he'll turn off, and someone else will pick it up."

Eric imagined a game of tag, cars moving in and out. They might be a small-town force, but with Brady's expertise—the guy'd been an MP in the military and then a detective in Boston—they were all well trained. They could do this.

Brady's phone vibrated. He connected the call through Bluetooth. "What's going on?"

"You were right." It was Jimmy's voice. "Durant's headed to the farm."

A wide smile split Brady's face. "Excellent. Everyone's in place?"

"I'm circling to watch from the other side. We got guys stationed on the road in both directions. They won't get away."

"Good job. Keep a low profile." Brady ended the call, leaned forward. "There he is."

Sure enough, a black SUV—looked like a Lincoln Navigator—turned into the driveway and drove toward the old barn. A moment later, it stopped, and a man climbed out.

"I got eyes in the glove box," Brady said.

Eric opened it, grabbed the binoculars, and peered through.

And there he was. Barry Durant. Round face, clean shaven, brown hair with a bad comb-over, pale freckly skin. The guy's butt looked like it would require two seats on an airplane. His gut would keep the tray table from lying flat.

"A man with a voracious appetite," Brady said.

An appetite for food, obviously. And money. And girls.

Eric took his handgun from its holster, clicked off the safety.

Brady did the same, then looked through the binoculars himself.

Durant walked toward the barn. Halfway between it and his SUV, he stopped, looked around, checked his watch. Then he took out his cell phone.

Durant talked, his blubber jiggling, snow falling all around. It was a light snow, and he brushed it off his shoulders.

The man pocketed the cell and lumbered toward the barn.

"Maybe you're right." Eric had to force his voice to sound normal. Excitement pulsed with adrenaline through his veins. "Maybe Otero and Ruiz are in there already."

Durant reached the barn door and pulled it open.

Eric's excitement laced his next words. "We gotta get closer, gotta get eyes—"

An explosion ripped through the silence.

THIRTY-THREE

Before he could think, before he could process it, Eric was out the door, running flat-out toward the burning barn. Because Durant was his only hope. Durant was the only connection to Otero, their only chance of bringing him down, putting him in prison, saving their lives.

He couldn't be dead.

Eric burst out of the trees, aimed for the barn.

"Wait!" Brady's voice was muffled, as if he'd shouted through water. Everything was muffled now. The explosion had deafened him.

Eric pressed on, running faster.

A force hit him from behind. He landed in the snow-covered grass. A heavy body rolled off him.

Brady had tackled him.

Eric fought to get away, to run again. Because to stop meant to think. And to think meant to face it. Face that their only chance for a normal life had just gone up in smoke. Face that, once again, his life had blown up.

He rolled over, pulled his fist back. Froze.

Brady froze, too. Then, slowly, he sat back on his knees,

breathing hard. "You throw that punch," he said, his voice still faint to Eric's weak ears, "I'll have your butt thrown in jail."

Eric dropped his arm. He rose to his knees. His head fell forward.

"You can't just barrel in there. There'll be evidence. There could be more explosives."

Eric huffed a breath. Of course Brady was right.

They both sat there, breathing hard, staring at the flames rising from the ancient boards, the only color against the backdrop of gray clouds and fluttering snow.

"You're fast for a little guy," Brady said.

If Brady hadn't had four inches on him—and Eric was nearly six feet tall—he'd have made it.

"We can't all be mutants." The wind shifted, carried the scent of smoke, the taste of ash, across the pasture. "You think there's any chance...?"

"No," Brady said. "That explosion was the definition of overkill. I can't imagine how anyone could have survived."

Eric's muffled hearing picked up a loud crack, then a smash as a rafter fell.

Brady stood and started walking forward. "Come on. Let's see what we can find."

They jogged across the pasture as cars pulled down the drive. There'd been ten cops on this. Ten men wasted their Sunday to watch Barry Durant die.

To watch Eric's life float away with the ashes.

The place where the door had once stood was empty now. That entire side of the structure had been blown apart. The rest was collapsing in front of their eyes. Eric peered through the smoke for signs of life, of movement. As if anything could have survived.

He couldn't even see the body.

He didn't want to think about what had become of Barry Durant.

He took a step forward, but Brady's grip on his arm stopped him. "We're not getting any closer. For all we know, there are more bombs."

Eric stared at the flames, already burning out in the cold damp air.

What was he doing? There was nothing for him here, not now. His life wasn't Nutfield. His life wasn't his job. His life was Kelsey. Kelsey and Daniel. They were what mattered now.

Brady said, "What are you thinking?"

His hearing was coming back, and Brady's voice suddenly sounded too loud. "Can I borrow your truck?"

His friend narrowed his eyes, considered him. A moment passed while police officers milled about on the road. Far away, a siren roared.

"You have a plan?" Brady asked.

He nodded but said, "Not really."

"You'll need a different car as soon as possible."

"I'll buy something."

Brady turned back to the barn. "They must have known we were onto them. Maybe they're long gone."

"You believe that?"

Brady met his eyes. "Keys are in the ignition. Just let me know where you leave it."

Eric turned toward the truck, but Brady grabbed his shoulder, pulled him close, and slapped him on the back. "We'll catch this guy. It won't take long. So keep in touch."

Eric nodded once, turned, and jogged away.

THIRTY-FOUR

KELSEY PACED across the small cabin, her heart pounding, her feet itching to run.

Magic matched her step-for-step as if she were worried, too. Worried about her master and best friend. Kelsey and the dog were in this together now. They'd both lost him.

She was getting way ahead of herself. But hope was as elusive as the skittering snowflakes outside. Only it melted much faster.

"I'm sure they're fine," Rae said, but the fear in her voice belied her words.

"You can't be sure of anything," Kelsey snapped. She took a deep breath. She should apologize, of course. Except apologizing might mean this well of anger would empty. And she knew what lay beneath that anger. She couldn't let the despair win.

Everything had been fine.

She and Rae had come to this cabin a charming updated two-bedroom with a patio that reached all the way to the dock suspended over the lake. Rae explained that she'd taken Johnny to his grandparents' house to spend the night. When Kelsey had protested, Rae'd brushed off her concern.

"Are you kidding? Grandma and Grandpa are loving it."

"How about you, though? Don't you miss him?" Her voice had caught as the image of Daniel had filled her mind.

Rae'd only squeezed her shoulders. "You'll see your son again soon."

Then Rae had told her a story about this cabin, a story about Nate and Marisa and their daughter, Ana, who'd been kidnapped. Kelsey'd been amazed at what the couple had gone through. These were the people who were caring for Daniel right now. And to hear Rae tell it, they were brave and kind and wonderful.

Back then, minutes ago that felt like hours, Kelsey had been filled with hope. This was all going to work out. Rae didn't know all the details, but she knew Brady had been optimistic about whatever he'd had planned. Brady'd believed that by the end of the day they'd have Carlos and Barry Durant in custody.

But that was before.

Because in the middle of some story Rae was sharing—some childhood escapade involving herself, Sam, and Brady—something had exploded.

It had drowned out Rae's words, rattled the dishes, and changed everything.

A moment later, Donny'd knocked on the door. Rae'd let him in, and he explained what had happened.

A barn. A bomb. Eric and Brady had been close. Everyone thought Durant was dead. No reason to believe Brady and Eric were hurt, but nobody'd been able to reach them. No reason to worry, though. That's what Donny said. No reason to fall apart.

Rae seemed to believe the man.

Kelsey wished she could. If only Eric had promised to come

back to her. Irrational, she knew, to be angry about that. Irrational to think the promise would have protected him.

Another two minutes passed. Maybe three.

Kelsey continued to pace. Magic walked with her, bumping her side, whining. What did the dog know? Could she sense her master was in trouble? Worse?

A cell phone rang, and Kelsey whirled around as Rae reached for hers. She answered and held the device to her ear. Her breath whooshed out, and she met Kelsey's eyes, smiled and gave her a thumbs-up as she spoke to whoever was on the line.

Thank God, thank God, thank God.

More tears fell. Eric was all right. Whatever happened, it would be all right, as long as he and Daniel were alive and safe.

Rae ended the call, dialed another, and handed the phone to Kelsey.

She took it, swallowed. It rang twice before...

"Nolan here."

"Eric..." She couldn't get anything else out.

"I'm okay," he said. "I was just about to call. We were in Brady's truck."

When she still couldn't get any words out, he said, "Are you okay?"

She nodded as if he could see her. Sniffed. "Yeah. Just... Yeah. We felt it here, the explosion. I was sure..."

"Not a scratch. Listen." He took a long breath and blew it out. "I'm sorry, Kelsey. I know the last thing you want is to go on the run again, but this was our last play. I want to stay and fight this guy, but I can't do that and make sure you and Daniel are safe. I won't be separated from you again."

She imagined her husband's house, the comfort she'd felt there, the sense of home she hadn't known in a decade. All gone now, not just to her, but to Eric, too. Everything she'd hoped to avoid, it was all happening. She'd spent a decade trying to protect Eric from this. She'd failed so completely it was almost laughable. Except she only wanted to cry. "I'm sorry. I ruined—"

"Don't start with that, Kels. We discussed this already. You and me. Together."

She swallowed her protest. He was right. They could survive if they were together. She doubted either of them could survive alone.

"I'm going to come get you, but I need to make sure nobody's watching me first. I'm going to town. I'll hang out at the station. If anybody's watching me, they'll think I'm working. I'm going to leave my Jeep in town. Hopefully, if anybody's watching, they'll focus on the Jeep. When I feel like it's safe, I'll head your direction."

"What about Daniel?"

"When you and I are safely away, when we have a fresh car and we're sure nobody is following us, we'll call Nate. But not until then, okay? No reason to take unnecessary risks."

"We need to know where he is. We need to know..." Panic laced her words.

"If we don't know where he is, then we can't tell anybody. God forbid they get their hands on us, we don't want to be able to tell anybody where he is."

"Right." She could hardly speak through her tight throat, the layer of fear and panic. "You're right. Thank you for protecting him, Eric. I can't even—"

"He'll be safe," Eric said. "I'll call when I'm on my way."

"How long do you think?"

"I don't know. An hour, maybe? Two? Not too long."

"Feels like forever."

"No, Kelsey." His words were suddenly soft, gentle. "Forever is what we'll have when we're together. This will be nothing."

"I love you, Eric."

"I love you. Always." The call ended, and she held the phone to her chest and let his voice settle deep. An hour, maybe two, and then they'd be together forever.

THIRTY-FIVE

VANESSA WAS in the front seat.

Carlos had practically beamed at her when she'd told him about Samantha Messenger's properties. He'd dispatched Mateo in one of the rental cars she'd reserved to search for Kelsey.

"But, my friend, don't you think I can be of more service at your side?" Mateo had asked. "Perhaps Vanessa can go instead."

"I need Vanessa with me."

Carlos's reply had sent hope through her heart. Perhaps Carlos could see her as more than property. Perhaps they could be partners in his business. Because as much as Vanessa longed for escape, for an independent life like Samantha Messenger enjoyed, she had no idea how to be alone.

Mateo had been his usual polite self, bowing slightly before he'd left. But Vanessa had seen that glare in his eyes when he'd glanced at her.

She'd returned it with a smile of triumph.

The feeling of triumph didn't last long, because as soon as Mateo left, Carlos explained why he needed her. It had nothing to do with her intelligence or the fact that she'd helped him. It had everything to do with her body and her face. She was only there as bait.

She cursed the God who'd made her female.

She and Carlos waited in the car while snow fell all around them and accumulated on the roads. She wanted to ask Carlos if he knew how to drive when it was slippery. She doubted he did. She didn't know much about where things were in the world, but she'd looked up Carlos's home country of Venezuela once. It had a tropical climate.

Of course, Carlos's mother and sister lived in America, somewhere in the west. Maybe he'd learned to drive in the snow there. Vanessa could offer no help. She'd only recently learned to drive, and only because Carlos had been kind enough to give her lessons. She'd passed her driver's test and, as a reward, Carlos had given her a little sports car. At least she could feel free, even if she wasn't free. Even if guards followed her everywhere she went.

Carlos was getting antsy. He scanned the radio stations, tapped the wheel in time to the beat of the song he'd chosen. He munched on a bag of chips she'd brought from the hotel's mini-bar. He didn't offer her any.

"You're sure this is the best place to wait?" he asked her, as if she'd chosen it.

"You chose it for a good reason, Carlos," she said. "If he is going to the lake or to his own house, then he will have to pass here. It's secluded, and we can move into place as soon as we get the word."

"If we get the word."

"Your man is in Durant's office, yes? He will see when Nolan passes."

"*Sí, sí*. But if it doesn't work..."

She didn't respond. She didn't want to show her doubt, nor did she want to be too confident. If she doubted and it worked, then Carlos would be angry with her for her lack of faith. If she was confident and it didn't work, then he would blame her, though the idea hadn't been hers.

Carlos's phone rang, and he answered quickly. "Well?" He waited while the other man talked. She could hear just enough in the silent car to know the caller was Mateo. A wide smile split Carlos's face, and Vanessa knew they'd had success. "Excellent work. Stay, keep watch. We may need her."

Need her.

The last thing Vanessa wanted was for Carlos to see Kelsey alive again. She couldn't complain—it had been her information that had led them to locate her. It was hard to balance, this desire to be helpful to Carlos and the desire to have Kelsey gone from his life forever.

She'd chosen to help him. She hoped it wouldn't fire back in her face.

THIRTY-SIX

The police station buzzed with activity. As if the explosion hadn't been enough to keep everybody busy, the roads were getting slick, and there'd been a couple of auto accidents. The small force was stretched thin, but even though Eric was there in body, he was too distracted to help.

He needed a plan.

He'd already walked to the bank on the corner and withdrawn the daily limit for his account—five hundred dollars. After midnight, he'd get five hundred more. That should last them a while.

After he picked up Kelsey, they'd head south, probably find a hotel in northern Massachusetts. Tomorrow, he'd purchase a cheap car, then call Brady and tell him where he could pick up his truck.

Only when they had a fresh car would they contact Nate. They'd keep to back roads, get Daniel, and then...

What?

He had no idea where to go from there. They'd all need new identities. So... Boston? New York? How would they procure fake driver's licenses and such? Maybe Kelsey would know.

She'd done it before. Or Garrison. All his years with the FBI, surely he could give Eric some ideas.

He closed his eyes, prayed for help, for guidance, for direction.

And thought about Kelsey.

As awful as it was to have to run, Eric couldn't stem the eager hope that rose in him. Because they were going to be together, just like they were always meant to be. They'd rent an apartment, maybe even a house. They'd get jobs. They'd raise Daniel.

Daniel.

The boy would call him daddy.

Eric squeezed his eyes closed and imagined it. Imagined that great kid as his own. Maybe not by blood, but in every other way, Eric would make Daniel his son.

And maybe, someday, he and Kelsey would have another child. Maybe a whole passel of them. They would be together. They would be a family.

Finally.

He just had to get from here to there. Eyes still closed, Eric breathed a silent prayer, the image of his family taking the place of all the words he couldn't seem to form. God was with them, and he would lead them to safety.

When Eric opened his eyes, he focused again on the chaos surrounding him.

One conversation rose above the others. He listened to a fellow detective who was on the phone discussing the explosion. According to him, only one body had been found in the ruined barn. The door had been connected to a tripwire. When Durant opened it...

Boom.

Which meant Carlos and his men were still out there, and they were willing to kill to get what they wanted.

A patrolman came in brushing snow off his hat and shoulders and announced that the roads were nearly empty of traffic. Most folks were tucked in for the night. Eric stood, crossed the crowded squad room. Every officer in town was on duty tonight, and a few state investigators were there as well, working the explosion. Eric ignored them all and cornered the patrolman who'd just walked in.

"Did you see anything suspicious? Anybody hanging around town?"

The cop, one of their younger guys, narrowed his eyes. "We're all on alert looking for your friends. We've seen no sign of anybody suspicious. The only cars out there right now are covered with an inch of snow."

"Okay. Good." Eric inhaled a deep breath. It was time to go.

He called Rae's cell phone—he'd get Kelsey one at the first opportunity.

Kelsey answered on the second ring. "Are you on your way?"

He smiled into the phone. "I'm leaving now. If all goes well, I'll be there in fifteen, maybe twenty minutes. Be ready, okay?"

"I'll be watching at the window. Be safe."

After Eric hung up, he headed out the back door. Would he ever return to this place? Would they ever be free to reclaim their lives?

Eric didn't even turn around. He'd give up everything to be with Kelsey.

He crossed the snow-covered parking lot. Night had fallen while he'd been inside, and the light from the police station's windows reflected off the fresh snow. The storm had moved in soundly now. A good two inches covered the cars in the lot. Eric brushed off the window and climbed in. He turned onto the road, saw the snow that fell like glitter in the glow of the streetlights along Crystal Ave. Not a great night to escape unnoticed, but fortunately, he knew all the back roads between here and

Manchester. He'd keep to them, away from traffic and prying eyes, until they were safely in the city. He passed his Jeep with barely a glance and made it through the small downtown and to the country road leading to the lake in less than five minutes.

Up ahead, something reflected off the snow-white world. He approached slowly, letting his headlights illuminate the space. A red sedan, New Hampshire plates, pulled over on the side of the road. A figure stepped out and waved. Based on the long hair and slight figure, it was a woman. Impossible to tell her age from here.

No way was he stopping. He'd call the station, have them send someone out.

Twenty feet in front of him, the woman stepped into the road.

Eric swore and slammed on the brakes. The truck slid, and the woman dove out the way just in time. The truck spun to the right. Eric spun the wheel to the left, but it was too late.

The truck slid off the right edge and crashed into the snowbank.

He wrenched the door open and stepped outside. "Are you insane?" He wasn't even sorry he'd shouted.

The woman's eyes were wide. "I'm sorry. Please do not be angry. I didn't mean... My car is broken. Perhaps the engine. Maybe can you help? Maybe can you...?"

Her words trailed off. She spoke with an accent he couldn't place. Sounded...Slavic? He stopped about five feet from her. She was young, maybe twenty, and very attractive. Perhaps she was a student at UNH. Tall and slender with long blond hair, dark blue eyes, and pale skin. She wore a fitted jacket that looked barely warm enough for early fall, certainly not warm enough for this weather.

Her beauty didn't distract him from the fact that she'd run him off the road, nearly killing herself in the process. He clenched his teeth to keep more angry words from coming out. His hands were shaking with fury.

Kelsey. He had to get to Kelsey.

He took a deep breath, glanced toward Brady's truck.

"I'm sorry," she said again. Her words sounded frantic. "I didn't think. I'm not good in the snow. Maybe can you can fix my engine. I can pay."

He forced a neutral tone. "I'll call you a tow truck. You wait here."

She stepped toward him. "Please, you will help?"

Something wasn't right. His slid his hand inside his jacket and over his firearm. "Have a seat in your car, and I'll call you a tow."

She took another step toward him.

He lifted his free hand and held it out in the universal sign for stop. "Ma'am, I'm a police officer. Sit in the car, and I'll call someone."

Her eyes widened, blinked. For a moment, he was sure she'd comply. Her voice was a fervent whisper when she said, "Please, do not move." Her gaze widened, darted, left and right.

Every muscle tensed. He stifled the urge to spin.

"I will open the hood," she said loudly. "And you can look?" She took another step, a small step. She was within a foot now. Her voice was barely a whisper. "If you pull out that gun, they'll kill us both." Her smile hadn't changed, but now her eyes were filled with fear.

Options. Dive, hit the ground, come up shooting at... whoever it was this woman was afraid of. Except that would leave her exposed.

He could tackle her, protect her with his body, and turn to fight. But he had no idea how many he was up against. If he were alone, he'd chance it. But he couldn't put this woman's life in danger, too.

Assuming she wasn't lying about everything. Assuming she wasn't in on this, whatever *this* was. He was nearly positive this was a trap, that the woman was up to no good. But there was no way he could know for sure. No way he'd risk this stranger's life based on his gut.

Which left only one option. He started to slip his hand out of his jacket, but she shook her head, stepped closer still. "Give it to me. Quick. He's coming."

No, no, no!

"You have to trust me," she said.

He slid the gun out. She was only inches away. She snatched it, slipped it beneath her jacket, and turned to lean into her car. Over her shoulder to him she said, very clearly, "I will open engine, no?"

The hood popped, but his gaze was on her as she slipped the gun into a purse. At least she hadn't shot him.

He balled his hands into fists, itching to fight. He strained to hear, but the fresh snow muffled every sound. It was deafeningly quiet.

Thank God he hadn't picked up Kelsey yet. That was his only solace as he waited for whatever would happen next.

A voice came from behind him, probably on the other side of the road. "I have a gun pointed at the back of your head." The man spoke with a slight Spanish accent. "Do not move."

Eric forced himself to stay still and calm.

"Search him," the man said.

The woman approached, patted him down like a pro. Eric had been duped. Except...she'd hidden his gun. Maybe she would help him. Or maybe she'd help herself, somehow, and leave him to die.

The second option seemed more likely.

She took his wallet and cell phone and stepped back. "No weapons."

Eric stayed very still, refused to give anyone any reason to hurt him. He had to stay focused, to think.

Though he couldn't see the man behind him and he couldn't hear him walking in the soft snow, he could feel him approaching.

The seconds seemed to tick by in slow motion. Finally, a man stepped into view. Mid-forties, Hispanic, longish dark hair, dark eyes, dark skin.

Otero.

THE TRUNK.

Eric shifted, tried to keep his limbs from falling asleep as they rested against the hard metal floor in the tiny space. Maybe the red sedan's trunk wasn't tiny, but it had definitely not been made to hold a grown man's body.

The road crunched beneath the tires. They drove forward a little ways, then took a right and stopped. A moment later, the distant sound of a car door slamming. The truck probably. They couldn't leave it on the main road, of course. One of the sedan doors opened, then slammed, confirming his suspicions. They'd dumped Brady's truck somewhere out of sight.

Their voices were muffled. They didn't talk much, and he talked more than she did. She sounded...frightened. Maybe she would help him. Maybe all wasn't truly lost.

They did a U-turn, then turned left, he thought probably heading back the way they'd come. Then another left, away from the highway, though he didn't have any idea on what road.

Since that turn, they'd continued straight. Eric tried to imagine the options. Where could they be headed? Not toward any neighborhoods in Nutfield, not considering how long they'd been driving.

Time inched along faster than the car on these slick roads.

At least Kelsey hadn't been with him. Eric wanted to grasp onto that hope, but he kept asking himself the same question. If they wanted Kelsey, why not just follow Eric? Then they'd have them both.

Maybe they didn't want Kelsey. Maybe they only wanted Daniel.

That didn't make sense, though. Kelsey would be their best shot at finding Daniel.

Eric refused to face the only logical conclusion. Because if Otero hadn't followed Eric to Kelsey, then that meant he already knew where she was.

Eric couldn't think about that. He had to focus.

A moment later, a clue rumbled beneath the tires. The unmistakable sound of the rickety bridge on the road to Eric's house.

They wouldn't be going to his house, though. Too risky. But somewhere nearby. The bridge was a good five minutes from home, more like seven in this weather. He watched the seconds tick by on the glow-in-the-dark hands of his watch. About four minutes later, the car turned left.

He bounced and jostled over little bumps and big dips. Where were they?

He closed his eyes, thought of the road he'd traveled every day, and tried to remember. Yes, there was an old logging road, barely wide enough for a car.

He tried to focus on that and not on the bumps that had him bouncing painfully off the metal floor of the trunk.

Three minutes had passed when the car finally stopped.

Eric took a deep breath, braced himself for what was coming.

A moment later, the trunk opened, and Eric squinted against the flashlight beam pointed at his face.

"Get out." The male voice didn't belong to Otero.

Eric blinked, tried to see who was there, how many he was up against.

A man grasped his upper arm and yanked.

Eric pulled back, lifted his hands. "Okay. I'm getting out."

The man—men, Eric realized—stepped out of his way, and he climbed out.

Beyond the two men stood a log cabin surrounded by tall pines and oaks.

The men grabbed his arms, one on each side, and ushered him toward the structure. Up steps, through a door. Inside, stairs went both up and down—a split-level. He was shoved toward the flight that went to the basement.

He counted the enemies. Otero and the woman, who he thought were still outside. Plus the two men with him.

Four enemies. Assuming the woman wasn't going to help him, and he couldn't count on her now.

At the bottom of the stairs, Eric was pushed down a short hallway and into a brightly lit room that spanned the width of the house.

The déjà vu hit him as soon as he entered.

The bed, the windows, the heating vent on the ceiling. He glanced to his right, saw camera equipment pushed against the back, unfinished wall. This was the room Sam and Garrison had found photos of on the deep web. This was TakeTwo's studio.

Barry Durant's studio.

Durant wouldn't be needing it again.

In front of the bed he saw a wooden ladder-back chair. The men turned him, shoved him into the chair. One of them yanked his arms around the chair back and pulled on his hands, trying to get them close enough together to bind, Eric assumed. But the chair was too wide. His arms wouldn't reach each other, not that the man didn't try. Eric winced at the pain in his shoulders as the man yanked his arms back.

"They're not going to reach, dude." The man pressing down on Eric's shoulders, keeping him in place, was watching the whole thing. He looked mid-twenties with hair shoulder-length and bleach-blond. He wore a bright red parka and a pair of sunglasses on his head like he was waiting for the perfect wave to hang ten. "Just cuff him to the chair."

A moment later, zip ties bound each of Eric's hands to the back of the chair, one on each side. He had to slouch to keep the ties from cutting into his wrists.

He could hardly imagine a more vulnerable position.

Unfortunately, he could imagine what was coming next.

The man who'd been behind him came around the chair and faced him. He was chubby, red-faced, and bald. He wore a sadistic smile.

As soon as he was secure, Chubby lifted his cell phone. "Smile."

Eric glared, but Chubby snapped a picture anyway.

Eric didn't have time to think about where that photo was going, because a moment later, Otero walked in.

Chubby and Surfer Dude stepped away as if they were in the presence of a sovereign.

Otero stopped a few feet in front of Eric and looked down at him. "Pleasure to meet you, Eric Nolan."

"Wish I could say the same," Eric said.

The man chuckled. "Yes, I assume this isn't how you imagined our meeting would go."

"Not exactly."

"Fortunately for you, I am not a sadistic man. I do not wish to harm you. If you will just tell me where my child is, I will let you go, and you can live your life in peace."

"Right. And if you let me go, I promise not to hunt you down and make you pay for what you did to my wife. We can just part as friends. Is that it?"

Otero's smile stretched across his face. "Yes, well, it was worth a try."

"She gave your kid up for adoption right after he was born."

Otero's face turned red. "You are lying."

Eric would've shrugged if he could have moved his shoulders. "Why would I bother? Why would I care what happens to your spawn?"

Surfer Dude stepped closer. "Like, I'll get the truth out of him. Just give me a few."

"Patience." Otero turned, walked out, and closed the door behind him.

THIRTY-SEVEN

In the bedroom upstairs, Vanessa sat on the king-sized bed. Aside from that, the room was bare—no clothes, no bureau, no clock.

She hated to think what Durant had used this room for. She didn't have to try hard to imagine. She only had to search her own memories. She was sure the girls who made it into Durant's videos had also seen the inside of this room.

Nausea rose, and she rubbed her stomach. "You, little one, will never be treated like that." She whispered the words like a vow. She would see to it or die trying.

She'd been banished to this awful room after they'd returned with Eric Nolan. Banished to wait where she was *safe*.

She didn't even have Mateo to blame it on. This was all Carlos's doing. Mateo was outside the cabin where Kelsey was hiding, which they only knew about because of her.

She'd expected to hear something coming from the basement, but either this place was more soundproofed than it looked or Carlos had chosen not to hurt Eric. Vanessa wished she knew his plan. Then perhaps she could help, could offer some insights.

Of course, banished to the bedroom, she could do nothing.

She couldn't stand it any longer. She crept to the door, turned the knob. Unlocked, because Carlos knew she would do what he'd told her to do. And she would. Normally, she would. But her entire life hinged on what happened tonight. If she couldn't prove herself helpful, how would Carlos ever come to depend on her, ever make her an equal partner? And now that Kelsey was coming, Vanessa needed to prove her worth more than ever.

Because what if Carlos decided he didn't need her anymore. What if he replaced her with Kelsey, sent her down to live with the girls?

She thought of that place, the tiny locked closets for the girls still being broken, the odors and screams. The dorm where the compliant girls slept. The filth and drugs and despair. She couldn't go back there. She wouldn't.

She had to stay with Carlos. She had to prove her worth. She would find a way. She just needed more information.

She turned the knob and stepped into the dark hallway to listen.

THIRTY-EIGHT

THERE WAS no clock to count the minutes.

Eric focused on the far wall. Behind him, the space had looked like a bedroom—a ceiling, painted sheetrock walls on three sides of the bed. But the part of the room that would be out of sight of the cameras, the part that he could see now, was all basement. Concrete walls to each side and in front of him, concrete floor below, rafters and pipes and ducts above. There were full-sized windows near the ceiling. Beyond them, he could see only darkness, but he figured each was just inches above the ground outside.

Silence filled the space.

Surfer Dude was standing by the door, arms crossed. The kid was bored.

Eric's shoulders ached, and the plastic ties binding him to the chair were cutting into his wrists. Eric shifted, a futile attempt to get comfortable. The chair creaked beneath him. The thing would probably collapse any minute.

Yeah, focus on the furniture. Don't think about Kelsey. Don't think about what Otero is planning. If Surfer Dude had been given the go-ahead to torture Eric to get information, Eric would feel better about the situation. But he hadn't been. Which meant they didn't need to use pain as a motivator. Which meant they had a better motivator.

Kelsey.

Not that it looked like Surfer Dude's punches would hurt much, and Eric was used to being beat on. As the youngest brother, he'd gotten beat up plenty in his life. And this guy had nothing on Eric's oldest brother. On TV, all the thugs were skillful and brutal fighters. In real life, most people, even thugs, didn't get that much opportunity to practice their fighting skills. Eric figured Surfer Dude spent more time working on his tan than on his boxing skills.

Eric didn't know where Daniel was—for that he was thankful. But he needed Otero to believe Daniel had been given up for adoption and lost forever. Only that would protect the boy. Maybe Eric wouldn't survive this. And what would become of Kelsey?

He wouldn't let himself imagine the possibilities.

But if Eric could protect Daniel, then maybe, maybe all Eric and Kelsey had lost—their marriage, their lives together, their future—maybe their loss would have meaning.

Footsteps sounded on the ceiling above him, then on the stairs.

The door opened, and Otero stepped in. He wore a satisfied smile. Eric itched to punch it off the guy's face.

Clenching his fists only made the plastic dig into his flesh more.

"Dude, you gonna let me hit him?" the surfer asked.

"I'm not your dude," Otero said. "Step away."

Surfer Dude backed to the opposite wall.

Otero stared down at Eric. "Why are you trying to hide a child your wife had with another man?"

"I'm not hiding anybody. I don't know where the kid is."

"Oh, but you do. You know exactly where he is."

"You'll have to kidnap and torture someone from the adoption agency. Course, I don't know where she was living when she gave the kid up. It'll be a heckuva search. Maybe you should hire a lawyer."

Otero smiled, chuckled softly. "I don't think that'll be necessary." He stepped out of Eric's line of vision, then returned, dragging a chair that matched the rickety one Eric was in. He set it a few feet in front of Eric and settled into it, stretching his legs out in front of him. "You're quite attached to Kelsey."

Eric made eye contact but said nothing.

"I can appreciate that," Otero said. "A man like you. You married her. Where I come from, vows are important. Marriage means something, yes? And you, you have stayed loyal to our Kelsey for nearly ten years."

Our Kelsey. Like they shared her. The words filled him with a fresh rage. He fought the desire to struggle against the restraints, the creaky chair.

Otero noticed the reaction. He crossed his ankle over his knee. "But you must ask yourself, has she stayed loyal to you?" The man made a *tsk, tsk, tsk* sound. "This, I can answer for you. And I'm afraid you won't like it."

Eric didn't want to hear what Otero had to say. If he survived this, eventually Kelsey would tell him all that had happened between her and Otero. He didn't want to hear it from this man.

But he didn't allow his gaze to falter nor his emotions to show. This was a game of chicken, and Eric couldn't afford to flinch.

"Most of my girls, I don't even know their names," Otero said. "I don't bother with them. These days, I usually don't even see them. They are merchandise, valuable only as long as they can bring income. But your Kelsey, she was different from the very start. Back then, I examined all my girls. And when I examined her..." Otero smiled. "I knew she was different from that first day. I kept her for myself. The other men, those who'd tried to break her, they didn't recognize her value. So I took on the project. I wanted that pleasure to be mine." He shook his head sadly. "It wasn't as much fun as I'd anticipated. Do you know why?"

Eric wouldn't respond. Wouldn't react.

"Because she didn't fight me. Not once. She was as compliant as a trained dog from the first time. Not just compliant. No, no. Our Kelsey, she was eager."

The man was lying. Of course.

"You don't believe me." The man had the audacity to chuckle. "Of course not. Only a short time before, you had pledged your undying love to her. For her to move on that quickly—"

"She was trying to save her sister."

"Yes, I can imagine this is what she told you. She had to come up with a story. But she never asked me to have mercy on her sister. Never even mentioned her. I think she liked the power."

"You're a fool if you think I'm going to believe a word you say."

"One of us is definitely a fool," Otero said. "But it is not me."

"Kelsey is pure and precious and brave."

Otero laughed. "Kelsey is none of those things. Pure? Let me tell you how pure she is." And then Otero launched into a story, sharing details Eric never wanted to know about what he'd done to Kelsey, what he claimed Kelsey had done with him. Eric would have blocked his ears if his hands had been free.

The surfer leaned in for every disgusting word.

Kelsey is pure and precious and brave.

Pure and precious and brave.

But Otero's words brought images that caused nausea to rise in Eric's throat. He couldn't help but see the pictures the words described.

No.

He couldn't allow himself to think of her the way Otero saw her. Because Otero didn't know her, couldn't know her, and certainly had no right to define her.

The thought came gently, fell like the snow beyond the windows.

Kelsey was pure and precious and brave, and nothing Otero had done, nothing he said, nothing he believed could change who she was. Because nobody had the right to define Kelsey except her Creator. And her Creator saw her very differently.

"Kelsey is pure and precious and brave."

Otero stopped his story, frowned. "You are a fool."

"You are a worthless excuse for a man."

Surfer Dude stepped forward. "Lemme have a go with him."

Eric wasn't afraid of the surfer. He kept his gaze on Otero.

Otero continued to stare at Eric. Seconds ticked away before he stood, shook his head. "No need." He threw the words at his thug without breaking Eric's eye contact. "If he won't tell us, Kelsey will. I'll have her brought here right away."

No. No. Kelsey had to be safe. If she wasn't safe... "You're lying."

Otero smiled. "I always wanted a lake house."

Lake house. He knew where she was.

"But of course, I live on the sea, and that is better, no?" Otero turned to the surfer. "Make yourself comfortable. I may need your services when she arrives."

THIRTY-NINE

Kelsey and Magic had resumed the pacing. Every time Kelsey reached the window, she shifted the curtain and looked outside, just in case.

The driveway was always empty.

She glanced at her watch for the thousandth time. Nearly an hour had passed since Eric's call. "Where is he? He said fifteen minutes."

"Maybe the snow slowed him down." Rae's words were placating, but her voice carried traces of fear.

Because if the roads were the problem, Eric would have answered his phone. But every call had gone straight to voicemail.

Donny finished a whispered phone call and slipped the phone in his pocket as he stepped around the bar from the kitchen into the small living area. His uniform still looked as crisp as if he'd just put it on, but his face reflected the worry in Rae's voice, in the dog's expression, in Kelsey's heart. His glance skipped past Rae and landed on Kelsey.

"What?"

"No sign of him or the truck."

"Did they check his house? Maybe he went home to get something."

"Not enough manpower. They're stretched thin with the explosion and the storm."

"So that's it?" Her voice rose, and she didn't even try to lower it. "He's just gone?"

Magic whined as if she knew.

Donny shook his head. "Course not. They're looking for him. For Otero, too."

She turned, started pacing again.

The dog matched her, step for step.

Rae and Donny were silent, though she imagined that when she turned her back on them, they were sharing looks, silent conversations.

After a few circuits across the small room, Magic whined again.

Kelsey knelt and petted the dog. "I know. I'm worried, too."

Magic looked at her with frightened eyes. Kelsey couldn't comfort the dog. She had no comfort to give.

As the minutes ticked away like the final heartbeats of the condemned, Kelsey paced and prayed to the God Eric was convinced was not only watching, but cared.

Kelsey couldn't make herself believe it, but for Eric, she tried.

She'd believe anything if only Eric would walk through that door.

She peeked out the window again. She didn't see Brady's silver truck, but something did catch her eye.

She gasped, stepped back. "Someone's out there!"

The dog growled, focused on the front door.

Donny yanked Kelsey away from the window, pulled out his gun, peeked outside. He spoke into the radio attached to his uniform, then looked at Kelsey and Rae. "Get into the bedroom and lock the door. Backup's on the way."

They both headed that direction.

A knock on the door had them freezing. Kelsey turned, looked at Donny. He pointed to the bedroom, but she shook her head.

Rae stood beside her, held her hand. They watched Donny.

Magic growled again. Her hackles rose. She barked once. A warning.

Donny kept his gun at the ready and stood behind the wall beside the door. "Who's there?"

"I'm not gonna hurt you," a man said. "I just gotta show you somethin'."

"What is it?"

"I'm gonna leave it on the porch, then I'm gonna walk to the road. Then you can open the door and grab it."

"What is it?" Donny repeated.

"A phone. We need the woman, Kelsey, to look at it. Like I said, I mean you no harm."

"How do I know it's not a trap?"

"We don't wanna hurt anyone."

Donny turned, met Kelsey's eyes.

She needed to see whatever it was.

Now.

She stepped forward. "Tell him to leave it. I'll go out for it."

"No." Donny stared at her, then at the door. He was silent so long, her chest started to burn. She realized she was holding her breath and forced herself to inhale and exhale.

Rae squeezed her hand, held her in place.

Donny glared at her. "Go in the bedroom."

But she didn't move. She couldn't move.

Donny spoke to the man on the other side of the door. "Leave it, then."

There was no answer.

Donny shifted to the window, inched the curtain aside, and looked out. "He must've already left it. He's standing in the middle of the road, hands up."

Kelsey started toward the door, but Donny held up his hand. "Don't move. We'll wait for backup."

"I need to know what he left."

Donny pointed again to the bedroom. "Backup will be here any minute."

Kelsey looked at the closed and locked door, then at the policeman whose job it was to protect her. That was the problem, wasn't it? Donny wanted to protect her, but she wanted to protect Eric, and they both needed to protect Daniel. She took a deep breath. "It's not going to hurt to hear what they have to say," she said. "Just let me..."

Donny blew out a breath and inched the door open. He kept his gun at the ready, crouched down, reached out, grabbed something, and then slammed the door.

He held up a clear plastic bag. Kelsey got just enough of a glimpse beyond the plastic to get her moving. She crossed the space and snatched it out of Donny's hand.

An image glowed on the screen. Eric, sitting in a wooden chair, glaring at the camera. His hands were pressed unnaturally to his sides.

Tied to the chair.

Otero had Eric.

A piece of paper had been slipped behind the phone. Her fingers were trembling as she flipped the plastic bag to read what was written there. In his neat penmanship, Otero had written a short message.

First, we will kill your husband. Then we will kill the cop and the woman protecting you. When it's over, you will still be mine. But if you come out now, I will release your husband and leave the others alone. Nobody has to die.

Two minutes.

Yours,

Carlos

He would do it. He would kill Eric. He would have his men attack the cabin and kill Donny and Rae. Kelsey knew Carlos well enough to know he didn't make threats unless he were willing and able to follow through.

Kelsey couldn't risk Rae and Donny's lives. Eric... She didn't believe for a moment that Carlos would let him live, but he had no reason to kill these two.

Before Donny or Rae could stop her, before she could think about what it would mean, she lunged for the door.

Donny reached for her, but Magic stepped between them. The dog snapped at Donny, slowed him just enough.

Kelsey reached the door, opened it, and stepped into the blowing snow.

FORTY

Eric watched, waited. Prayed. Because he couldn't let Kelsey be hurt. He couldn't bear it. He feared what he would do, what he would say, if they brought Kelsey here, if they threatened to hurt her.

The very thought of it terrified him.

Surfer Dude sat in Otero's chair. He still wore that red parka. Eric was still wearing his jacket, too, and glad of it. There was no heat in this basement.

For a few minutes, the surfer had watched Eric, but now he was scrolling on his phone, chuckling occasionally. Eric's whole future was in question, and that idiot was checking Instagram.

And the surfer *was* an idiot. Eric had thought Otero would send the chubby guy back down, but he hadn't. Eric and this guy were alone. Unfortunately, Eric was strapped to a chair.

A rickety chair that creaked when he moved. A chair that felt like it might collapse under him.

Was it as fragile as it felt?

He glanced to his left and saw a metal post between him and the concrete wall. But to his right, the way was clear. If he could just...

It was an insane idea, but it was all he had.

He took a deep breath, sent up a prayer, and clenched his fists.

This was going to hurt.

With his bound hands, he gripped the chair legs. In one swift motion, he stood, lifting the chair with him, and launched himself backward as fast as he could. He smashed against the concrete wall.

Pain shot through his back and shoulders.

The chair shattered.

He shook his hands to remove the ties. His left wrist came up with the chair's support beam attached, but the right one slipped free.

With the wood gripped tight in his hand, he lunged forward.

Surfer Dude was on his feet, phone in one hand, nothing in the other, mouth gaping.

Reflexes like a sloth.

Eric lifted the chair leg, swung it toward the surfer's head. The man ducked, but not in time. The wood made contact with a thunk. Dazed, he stepped back. Eric grabbed his shirt, launched him into the corner.

The surfer stumbled, collapsed.

Eric kicked him while he dislodged the wood from his left arm and looked for the man's phone. It had skittered out of his hands when Eric had hit him. He didn't see it anywhere.

Surfer Dude was moving.

Pounding from upstairs. "You okay?"

No time to find the phone. Eric ran to the window, pushed it open, and climbed outside.

He bolted into the woods. Brush scraped against his face, his clothes.

Shouts behind him, a screen door opening and closing. But

Eric had the advantage now. He'd lived near these woods for years, and if nothing else the darkness would hide him.

Unfortunately, his footprints in the snow would lead them right to him.

He ran until the shouts faded in the background.

Deep in the woods, there were areas free of snow, thanks to the thick canopy created by the trees. He jumped from barren spot to barren spot, trying to hide his route.

North Texas was flat and empty. But here in beautiful New Hampshire there were hills and trees everywhere. He'd never loved them more. He found a good-sized hill, went up one side, down the other, and caught his breath behind a tree.

Now what?

FORTY-ONE

ALL HER RUNNING, all her attempts at staying safe, at keeping Eric and Daniel safe... All of it had been for nothing.

Kelsey pressed as far from the man in front of her as possible, but it was no use.

When she'd burst out of the cabin a few minutes earlier, she'd had no idea what to expect. But she had thought a car would be waiting for her.

There hadn't been a car, though.

She'd immediately been grabbed by a man she'd never seen before. He'd started running. She'd stumbled along beside him, surprised when he turned not toward the main road but in the opposite direction.

Magic was still barking. A door opened. Then a gunshot.

She stumbled, turned.

The man gripped her tighter. "Don't worry. That was a warnin' so the cop doesn't follow." Based on his accent, he wasn't local. "Nobody wants to kill a cop."

Eric was a cop. Did that extend to him? She hoped so.

She doubted it.

She didn't speak. Neither did he as they bolted through the

snow past cabins along the lake's shoreline. She was freezing. She had no coat, no hat, no gloves. On top of that, her ankle ached, and the pain increased with every step.

She'd almost been safe.

Almost was the story of her life.

The man yanked on her arm and angled toward the lake. What in the world? She was confused until she saw where he was headed.

A snowmobile was hidden in the trees between two cabins.

The man yanked her to its side. "Don't go jumping, lady, or I'll havta chase ya." The man pulled a gun from the inside pocket of his warm jacket. She shivered in the cold, more focused on the jacket than the gun. "I don't wanna hurt ya."

"I surrendered willingly. Why would I escape now?"

He shrugged. "Fear can make a person do crazy things." He turned his back to her and climbed onto the snowmobile.

In the distance, sirens wailed. If she could just...

Her captor grabbed her arm. "Get on."

She wrenched out of his grip and climbed onto the snowmobile

He started the engine, and the machine roared beneath them. They shot forward, down a hill, and onto the frozen lake.

When they reached the far side, the man angled between two deserted lake houses, across a narrow road, and sped into the woods. The snow was spotty out here, but the snowmobile sped across the frozen ground with little problem. Her captor seemed to be aiming for the dirt, not the snow.

So he wouldn't leave tracks, she realized.

Another few minutes passed before he stopped in a small clearing and powered down the snowmobile. They were far from any houses or roads. Surely this man wouldn't hurt her. But what was he doing?

He stepped off the snowmobile and waited.

Minutes passed in the silence.

The man checked his cell phone. She watched him, wished she could get her hands on it. And do what? Call the police and say she was in the woods with a bad guy? They already knew that. The problem was, the woods went on for miles and miles and miles.

The distant whine of an engine had her turning in the direction they'd come from. A moment later, another snowmobile entered the clearing. He stopped maybe twenty feet from them, facing away, which gave her a good look at the rifle slung across his back. He must have been the one to keep Donny from following them.

The man stepped off the snowmobile and turned to face her. "Kelsey. It's been a long time."

Her teeth were chattering, and she had to focus on not stuttering her words. "How are you, Mateo?"

He closed the distance quickly. "Still recovering from prison."

"That's what you get for protecting Carlos."

He shrugged. "I suppose that's one way to look at it." He took off the harness holding his rifle in place, then slid out of his jacket and handed it to her. "You must be freezing."

Mateo. Ever the gentleman. She slid into the oversize jacket and forced out a "thank you."

He put the rifle back on and looked at the other man. "Any problems?"

"Nope. She did just what you said she would."

"Good." Mateo pulled his phone from his jeans' pocket. He snapped her photograph, then pressed a few buttons.

He was sending her photo to Carlos.

Any minute, she'd see him again. She swallowed the bile that rose at the thought.

Mateo returned his phone to his pocket and gestured toward his snowmobile. "You'll ride with me."

She walked the distance with him silently. When they reached it, rather than climb on, he turned to face her, leaned in, and lowered his voice. "Why didn't you run on Saturday? Surely you got my message."

Mateo had sent the man to warn her? He'd been behind the attack on Eric? But... "Why?"

"My dear, you've done us nothing but harm. Why Carlos doesn't see it, I cannot understand. He can be very focused, very determined, even when it is not in his best interest." He shook his head. "It's too late now, I suppose. I am tempted to kill you right here just to keep us all safe from your schemes, but if I want to retain my position and keep my life, I'd better get you back safely."

It made no sense. Not only had Mateo warned her, but now he'd given her ammunition she could use against him. "Why would you tell me?"

He sighed, smiled slightly. "I suppose I wanted you to know I tried to help you. When you're back by his side, you'll have the opportunity to help me."

"I'll never be by his side."

"Perhaps if you'd run, that would be true. But now, I don't see another option."

She tried to laugh, but the sound was more sob than chuckle. "I'll die first."

He shrugged. "You did whatever he asked of you to save your sister. Would you not do just as much for your husband and child?"

The nausea rose again. Death she could handle. But to be Carlos's slave again...

No.

She swallowed, tried to think. Mateo had said something...

"You're hoping I'll do you a favor, assuming I ever have that power. But you just told me you want to kill me."

"I don't want to kill you, my dear. I also don't want to go back to prison, and the last time I saw you, that's where I ended up. I hope you won't do that again."

"I doubt I'll get another opportunity."

"True," he said. "So it hardly matters." He brushed off her words with a flick of his gloved hand and climbed back onto the snowmobile.

She climbed on behind him.

"Hang on tight."

The machine shot forward. She wanted, needed, to see Eric. She wanted to protect her friends back at the lake house. But the thought of facing Carlos had her itching to run. It took all her will power to stay still. She was here because she hadn't been willing to risk Rae's life or Donny's for her own safety. Otero had Eric, and nothing she could do would protect him now. But she wouldn't let him die alone. And she wouldn't be Carlos's slave, no matter what he threatened. She couldn't. And Eric wouldn't want her to.

She prayed she'd get to see her husband one more time. To tell him how much she loved him. To tell him that unlike him, she did have regrets. Big regrets. She'd give anything to have the last ten years back. Anything to have raised her son by Eric's side.

At least Daniel was safe. Maybe that couple, Nate and Marisa, would adopt him. Maybe they could give him a good home, a home she'd never been able to provide—and now, never would be.

Tears streamed down her face. She knew how futile they were. It was too late for tears.

Mateo seemed to be in no rush. His confidence stirred her fear. Was Otero really so good that he could get away with all of this? He'd blown up a building, killed a man. How could he possibly think he'd escape?

But Otero was slicker than a greased pig. She'd tried to put him away once, and he'd escaped prosecution and let others go to prison in his place. Nobody'd ever been able to pin anything on him. Maybe that would work in her favor. Maybe his confidence would hurt him this time.

Maybe he'd be held to account for her murder and Eric's. She could only hope.

FORTY-TWO

THE NIGHT HAD GROWN SILENT.

Eric had never known true silence until he'd experienced his first snowy night in New Hampshire. The snowfall muffled every sound. The animals were quiet, safe in their dens and hollows. The few birds that hadn't flown south were huddled, waiting out the storm. No bugs buzzed by his ears. The only sound was the occasional rustle of leaves in the breeze.

Tonight, the silence was unnerving.

What was happening back at the house? They must have been searching for him, but Eric heard nothing. Had he lost them? Must have. If he wanted, he could stay right here and never be found. But without the surfer's phone, he had no way to contact Brady and get help. And Otero knew where Kelsey was hiding.

Eric thought he knew roughly where he was. They'd driven over the bridge that led toward his home, then turned about a mile before his driveway. These woods were dark and empty. He'd never come this far from his house, had never discovered the log cabin. Otero and his men had no idea that Eric knew where he was. They'd imagine him running blindly into the forest.

Eric faced what he thought was north. If his calculations were correct, his house would be that way, probably less than a mile. At home, he'd have access to a phone, not to mention a sizable arsenal.

But if he was wrong, if his house was further, or if his internal compass was off by just a few degrees...

He blew out a breath and turned back toward the house he'd just escaped. Trying to be as quiet as possible, he picked his way through the forest. He had to find out what was going on.

In the silence, every move he made was amplified. He scanned the forest for signs of his captors. As he neared the house, he saw footprints, but nothing else. Surely they hadn't quit looking for him. If he could find one of them first...

Eric heard the hum of motors.

He closed his eyes, focused on the sound. These weren't car motors. The pitch was too high, and the sound was coming from the wrong direction.

He looked to his right, peered into the dark forest, saw nothing.

But it wasn't a coincidence. Whoever that was had to be headed this way. Maybe Brady had figured out where he was. Maybe...

No. Brady would come in a car. Unless his friends were coming from multiple directions. Unlikely, but it didn't hurt to hope.

Eric crested a hill. The cabin sat in a small depression in the distance. He dropped to the ground behind a bush and peered between the bare branches. Through a window, he saw the woman from earlier pacing, chewing a fingernail. One man was carrying things to the cars out front, packing up. Seemed Carlos was worried Eric would make contact with someone. He was running.

The motors were getting close now. Eric watched as two snowmobiles came into view through the woods to the east. A woman rode on the back of the snowmobile in front.

Her hair flew out behind her.

Kelsey.

FORTY-THREE

Vanessa had watched through the window as Mateo led Kelsey to the door.

The woman looked old and tired, scared and angry. Vanessa, on the other hand, was young and vibrant and beautiful and willing.

How could Carlos ever choose Kelsey over her?

She stood back and sighed. She'd done it. She'd helped Carlos find her biggest rival, but Mateo would be the one to get the glory. She'd been the one to discover the lake houses owned by the Messenger woman. But Mateo delivered Kelsey, and Mateo would be rewarded.

Vanessa had returned to her room when Eric escaped, afraid of what would happen if Carlos realized she'd disobeyed him. Nobody had checked on her, and she wasn't surprised. She wasn't a threat. She didn't matter.

One of Carlos's men was still in the woods trying to find Eric, but the fact that Carlos had called the other one back told her he didn't believe Kelsey's husband would be found.

She looked out the window again. The man who'd been with Mateo loaded the snowmobiles onto a trailer attached to a pickup truck, then came inside. She could hear their voices as they called commands to each other—*wipe this down, remove that*. Preparing to leave. Mateo would take charge of that activity, too, now that he was back.

She chewed her cuticles and tried to think of a way to remind Carlos of her value. Would he ever see her as an equal, as a partner? Perhaps she'd be wiser to escape, to try to make her own way, try to raise her child alone. But with Carlos, she had access to everything she needed. Food, shelter, clothing. She'd seen what it was like to go without those things. Better to be a slave than to starve on the streets. On the other hand, with her looks, with her body, perhaps she could find someone else to take care of her.

Ah, what was the expression? The evil you know...

And anyway, she was carrying Carlos's baby. She'd seen how desperately he wanted Kelsey's child. When he knew about the baby Vanessa carried, wouldn't he be devoted to her? To their child?

The sound of a car door slamming had her glancing out the window.

There'd been three men besides Mateo and Carlos. One was in the car. The engine roared to life, and he drove away. Another man climbed into the pickup with the trailer attached. He followed the car down the narrow road.

Interesting. The evacuation had already begun. There was one car left. Mateo, Carlos, Kelsey, and Vanessa would have to share it. The man with the red parka, who knew what had become of him? But if he returned... Would the five of them fit in the small car? And what about Eric? If they found him, would he be leaving with them, or would they leave his body here?

She turned away from the window, angry at herself. What difference did it make which car was there, what people were left? She had to focus, find a way to help, to show Carlos he needed her. Because now that Kelsey was back, Vanessa feared she'd be the one riding in the trunk.

She rubbed her belly again. Her hands were trembling when she gripped the gun she'd taken from Eric. She would do something. Somehow, she would find a way to help, to prove her worth, to secure her place at Carlos's side.

FORTY-FOUR

THE SNOW WAS FALLING FASTER NOW, MAKING it more difficult for Eric to avoid leaving footprints. But it wasn't the worry it had been before, since the men who'd come looking for him had tromped all over the place. His footprints would be indistinguishable from theirs.

After Kelsey disappeared into the house, Eric had watched, had seen the men loading the cars, then watched two of them drive away.

That left the guy Kelsey had ridden with on the snowmobile, the surfer dude, the girl who'd flagged him down, and Otero.

Four against one. Not the best odds.

He had no idea what he was going to do, but he had to do something.

He heard the snap of a twig, then the words, "Got 'cha, dude."

He spun, prepared to fight, but the man was yards away. Eric spied the handgun pointed at him and lifted his hands. "You got me."

Surfer Dude didn't look good. A huge gash on his forehead

was caked in dried blood. It was hard to tell in the dim light, but Eric imagined his face would be good and bruised tomorrow. Concrete verses face—concrete always won.

Served him right.

The guy motioned, not toward the house but toward the woods. "Start walking."

The woods? If Eric were taken to the house, he might have a chance to...to do something. But the woods? "Do you know I'm a cop?"

The guy blinked. "Uh, no. But, like, it doesn't matter now."

"Well, assaulting a police officer is bad news, but shooting one—"

"Look, I just do what I'm told." Gone was the bravado from earlier. The man's hands were shaking.

Bravado would have been easier to handle. Fear made people do crazy things.

"Doing what you're told," Eric said. "That'll hold up in court. You killed a cop because somebody told you to. Good plan. Inside, Carlos will no doubt murder my wife, too, when she doesn't give him the information he wants. An innocent woman who wanted nothing more than to escape him. And then when you guys all get caught—and I promise you, you *will* get caught—Otero is going to make you take the fall. He's done it before. Just about his whole organization went to prison when my wife testified against him, but not Otero. He's got a knack for ducking behind his underlings to avoid prosecution. You'll spend life in prison for this."

The man said nothing. Maybe something was seeping in.

"If you help me," Eric said, "I'll put in a good word for you."

Surfer Dude thought a minute, or maybe he only pretended to, because then he smiled. "Otero's got an extra fifty grand for me if I do this. I'll risk jail. Let's go."

"Ah." Eric kept his hands up, nodded as if he had inside

information. "You're betting on him, on a guy like Otero, paying you *extra* after you let me escape?" Eric forced a chuckle. "Dude, at this point, jail's the best you can hope for."

A muffled ding—an incoming text, Eric would guess. Surfer Dude glanced toward his jacket pocket but didn't reach for his phone. His eyes narrowed.

"He won't let you live," Eric said. "You don't help me, and you'll have ridden your last wave."

Surfer Dude ran a hand through his hair. It got caught on the stupid sunglasses, and they fell into the snow. He seemed to be thinking extra hard. Eric figured any minute he'd see smoke coming out of the guy's ears.

Then Surfer Dude shook his head. "Carlos is a good dude. We're tight. And when this is over, I'm outta here. Nobody'll ever connect me to this." He motioned again toward the woods. "I'd rather not have to drag your body out of sight, but I can shoot you here just as easily. You wanna live another couple of minutes, start walking."

Eric kept his hands lifted near his shoulders and turned toward the woods.

FORTY-FIVE

When she'd first seen Carlos in the doorway, Kelsey had only stared. The bright light behind him had cast him in silhouette, but the voice, the presence, were unmistakable.

She'd frozen, and not from the biting cold or the falling snow. More than nine years had passed since she'd seen Carlos. She'd let herself believe she would never see him again.

What a fool.

"Come, *mi dulce*." He'd beckoned her forward with his old nickname for her. "We have much to discuss."

Mateo climbed off the snowmobile and offered his hand. His voice was soft. "Don't make it harder than it has to be."

She took his hand, squeezed, and whispered, "Help me."

He responded just as quietly. "I tried, but you ignored my warning."

She slid off the snowmobile, and Mateo led her gently to the man in the doorway. They climbed the steps and stopped one level below Carlos. He towered over them. When he stepped back into the house and the light hit him, his features became clear.

Creases had set in around his eyes. His dark brown hair

hung almost to his shoulders. He looked as if he hadn't shaved in days. That didn't surprise her. When he was worried, he didn't bother with little things like shaving and eating. She'd always known to fear him most when his beard grew with his hunger. Because when Carlos worried, he hid it behind anger. And anger often came with pain.

A smile on his lips, but she didn't miss the worry hovering in his eyes. "You are just as beautiful as I remember." He held out his hand.

Mateo squeezed hers, and for a moment, it was almost as if she had a friend beside her. But Mateo had always been and would always be Carlos's man.

Mateo let go of her, and her hand hung between them awkwardly.

She didn't want to reach for Carlos. Didn't want to willingly walk to him. But Eric... She had to do what she could for him. Maybe Carlos would let her see him one last time.

She took Carlos's hand, swallowed a sob, and stepped into the house.

He led her down a short set of stairs. "We will have privacy down here."

She said nothing as they reached the bottom, turned down a short hallway, and walked through a door.

It was the room from TakeTwo's videos. A bed was pushed against the wall. There was a window above it.

Eric wasn't there.

Her heart sank. She'd had such hope.

Carlos led her to the bed. "Please, have a seat."

She did, and he stood in front of her. His grin was still wide. "Make yourself comfortable. I need to speak with Mateo."

He stepped into the hallway, leaving her alone. She strained to make out what the men were saying, but they were too quiet.

Apart from the staged bedroom, the rest of the space was concrete and metal. Camera equipment was pushed beneath the window against the far wall. Splinters of wood, pieces of a smashed chair, littered the floor. And...was that blood? Had Carlos lost his temper? Had Eric been the recipient of that anger?

She squeezed her eyes closed and prayed. If there was a God, they desperately needed him now.

The window behind her led to the front of the house. She scrambled across the bed, stood, and unlocked it. It had a second pane of glass, a storm window, and she struggled to lift it. The metal latch was stuck and freezing, and cold bit into her fingers. Finally the latch slid, and she tried to lift the window. It was jammed, but if she could just wiggle—

A distant gunshot exploded in the silence.

She jumped, fumbled with the window, frantic now.

Eric. Where was Eric?

Another gunshot.

Oh, God, oh, God, oh, God.

Silence in the hallway.

Footsteps on the stairs, then Mateo burst outside. He froze in the driveway, scanned the forest.

She dared not move with Mateo standing so close. Dared not think about what that gunshot had meant.

Mateo pulled out his phone.

A moment later, he returned to the house. The screen door slammed.

She slid the storm window up, struggled to make it stay latched. Finally, it caught.

Mateo's voice rose. She couldn't make out the words as she hefted herself up.

"Excellent." Carlos's response boomed in the quiet.

With her knee on the windowsill, she reached forward,

grabbed a bush outside the window. The leaves shifted and dropped snow on her arm.

Carlos continued. "You will take care of it, and then we'll go."

She heard the door open behind her. Tried to scramble out.

A hand gripped her foot and yanked. She fell onto the bed on her face.

He pulled until she was on the edge of the bed. He released her foot, and she twisted around to face him. Lifted her hands to defend herself.

Carlos crossed his arms.

What? No punishment? No backhand? No punch?

"If you try to escape again," he said, "I will not be as kind. But I understand this is not how you expected your evening to go."

Cold air blew in from the open window behind her.

Carlos's smile was just as cold. If anything, it was wider than it had been before. The worry was gone. "It was probably my fault you tried to escape. Rude of me to keep you waiting, *mi dulce*."

"I am not *your sweet*. Where is my husband?"

"Always with the temper. I see you haven't changed."

"Nor have you."

"I suppose not. You asked about Eric, no? He claimed he didn't know where our child was. I decided to believe him."

Her stomach retched. She thought of the gunshot she'd just heard.

Her body knew what her mind wouldn't face. Couldn't face.

Carlos nodded toward the windows. "Mateo's gone to dispose of him. I doubt anyone will ever find his body."

No.

The nausea rose. She swallowed it back.

"You're turning green." Carlos grabbed a small trash can

from the far side of the room. "Please, I'd prefer you didn't make a mess. We already have much to clean."

She took the can, vomited into it. Wiped her mouth with Mateo's jacket.

"Are you ill?" he asked. "You always threw up easily. Of course, you were..."

His voice trailed off. She looked up to see his eyes had narrowed.

"If you are pregnant now, I will kill you."

Pregnant? He was insane. But oh, how she wished she were carrying Eric's child, to have a piece of him with her to the end.

"Are you pregnant?" Carlos demanded.

She couldn't speak. Because Eric couldn't be dead. All she'd wanted was to see him one last time.

She'd lost her husband. She'd never see her son again now.

What did she have to live for?

Carlos gripped her arm and squeezed, face red, anger boiling. He yanked a pistol from his pocket and pressed it against her belly. His voice softened, but it had the force of a roar. "Are you pregnant?"

"No." She looked at his hand, which was white-knuckled against the pistol grip. "No."

He removed it, stepped back, lifted his eyebrows. "If you're lying, I'll know soon enough."

She focused on the concrete floor beneath her feet. If only she could melt into it, disappear. She'd do anything, anything, to not be here.

Carlos took the soiled trash can to the far side of the room. When he returned, he stood in front of her, the gun still in his hand. "Are you sick?"

"You just told me my husband is dead. I guess my stomach didn't like the news."

He seemed to accept that. Didn't seem to care. "Where is my child?"

She smiled, though she doubted it looked any more natural than it felt. "I have no idea. I gave her up for adoption."

His eyebrows lifted. "But I know that's not true. You were spotted, you see. A few years ago in Shreveport. My contact photographed you with a child. It was hard to tell, but it looked very much like a boy."

He'd seen her there? Thank God she'd moved on before Carlos had caught up with her. "In Shreveport?" She forced a laugh. "I was working as a nanny. The kid he saw belonged to a couple of doctors who'd hired me to take care of him."

Carlos shook his head. "You were always quick with the lies."

"Why would I keep your kid, Carlos? Did you think I could ever love a child of yours? My luck, she'd grow up to be a tyrant, just like her father."

"A tyrant?" His temper flashed in his eyes, and he lifted the hand that held the gun.

She winced, shrunk away from the blow she knew would come.

Carlos lowered his arm. "Ah, *mi dulce*, after all this time, must we fight?" He sat beside her on the bed. "I don't want to hurt you. I long for him, you know? I long for my son like I've never longed for anyone. I need to see my son."

"It was a girl."

He launched himself up, turned, and shouted, "I do not believe a word you say. It was a boy. It is a boy."

"It is not an 'it.'" She glared at him. "We're talking about a human being. Not property. Unfortunately, you don't know how to treat people as anything but property. And you will never get your hands on my child."

"Your child?" He crouched down, put his hands on either

side of her face, the steel of the gun barrel cold against her temple. "Our child."

If he knew the truth, he'd kill her.

She should tell him.

Tears burned her eyes, but what right did she have to cry? She'd caused all of this. She'd led these evil people to this town, to her husband. She'd led her husband to his death.

He released her face and stood. "*Mi dulce*, I've longed for you as well." His gaze softened, roved over her face, her body.

She leaned away from him. His anger, she was prepared for. But that look... She remembered that look. She wouldn't land in his bed, not again. She'd die first.

"All these years," he said, "all these years, and I still dream about you. I roll over in bed expecting to find you, always to find someone else. A warm body, *sí*. A beautiful body. But not yours." He kneeled in front of her. "I want you back. I want things to be the way they were before."

"You murdered my sister."

He waved his hand as if he were flicking away a fly. "That was a mistake. You will forgive me."

A command, not a request. The man was insane.

"You murdered my husband."

Now he glared. "You belong to me. You gave birth to my child. You spent months in my bed. That man had no claim on you."

"I love Eric. I will always love Eric."

"He is dead. You will love me."

"You can't command my heart like you would one of your thugs."

"*Mi dulce*, I forgive you for your betrayal. I survived, and my operation continues. You will not do it again. For years, I wanted nothing more than to make you pay for what you'd done." He stroked the end of the gun barrel gently down her cheek. "But now I realize... I want things to be as they were. I was never happier, I never felt more complete, than when you were by my side."

He placed his other hand on her thigh, slid it upward.

She shuddered as his touch blasted open the door to the well of rage inside her. Power thundered through her body. She throbbed with strength. She tore the gun from his hand and smashed it against the side of his head with crazy fury. He tumbled and landed on his back.

He struggled to his knees, his hand to his head. It came away bloody. He stared at it, looked up at her. His face a rictus of hatred, he balled his fists and started to rise. "I will smash every—"

She pulled the trigger. The shot boomed within the concrete walls. Carlos was thrown back and fell to the floor. He gripped his belly with one hand, then started to push himself off the floor with his other.

Kelsey stood, pulled the trigger again, but nothing happened.

Again.

Nothing.

She threw the gun, and it hit him in the face.

She had to get out. She couldn't get past him. She scrambled backward on the bed toward the window.

He stood, blood seeping between the fingers of the hand on his stomach. He reached out for her with the other—

A gunshot split the silence.

FORTY-SIX

Vanessa stood in the doorway, power like she'd never felt coursing through her.

A red stain spread across Carlos's back.

Still kneeling, he turned, faced her. His eyes were wide, his mouth open in shock.

The woman, Kelsey, had screamed, but the sound had died quickly. She scooted until her back was pressed against the wall.

"Don't move." Vanessa sounded as confident as she ever had. Felt that confident, too.

Kelsey lifted her hands.

Vanessa stepped closer, kept the gun pointed at Carlos. His eyes were wide. His hands were pressed against his stomach. Blood seeped through his fingers.

His mind seemed to catch up with him. "Put that gun away."

"You..." She laughed and sounded like a *ludak,* a crazy person, but she felt good. "I gave you everything. I was... I was..." She couldn't think of the word in English. "I was on your side. I was *odan.*" The word came to her. "Loyal. Like a wife to a husband. Like Mama to Tata, even when he sold me. And now I know you always were dreaming of her."

Kelsey leaned further away, eyes wide.

But Vanessa didn't care about her. Kelsey didn't matter. Vanessa didn't matter. None of them could matter as long as Carlos lived.

"I am carrying your *beba.*" With her free hand, she rubbed her belly, felt the warmth there. "And you want hers. She doesn't love you. She never cared for you. Always me, doing what you say, sleeping with you. And you think of her?"

"Vanessa, *mi dulce...*" He reached toward her.

But the words, *mi dulce...*

The same thing he'd called Kelsey.

He was a liar.

She fired again.

The bullet hit his chest this time, and Carlos slumped onto the concrete.

Whether he breathed or not, she did not care. She did not belong to him any longer. She was her own woman now.

She aimed the gun at Kelsey.

FORTY-SEVEN

KELSEY LIFTED HER HANDS HIGHER. "Please, don't."

The woman, Vanessa, Carlos had said, flicked her gaze to Carlos.

Kelsey looked, too. Wished she hadn't. Carlos was twitching, struggling for breath. Blood seeped from the wound on his back. It pooled on the concrete.

She forced her gaze back to Vanessa. "I'm a victim, just like you." Kelsey's voice was shaky. Eric was gone, but Daniel... She could see her son again. Be with him again. If only she could survive this. "I just wanted to be free of Carlos. You can understand that, right? I ran away."

The woman still said nothing. Her brow creased.

"I'm a victim," Kelsey said again. "Like you."

Carlos's breath rattled. Stilled. Rattled again.

"I am giving him an heir." Vanessa lifted her chin, scowled at Carlos. "I tried to prove to him that he needed me. Now I don't need him. I will take his money. I will have what he had. And I do not wish to fight you for it. My child will not be second to yours."

"But you don't understand." Kelsey took a deep breath. She

had to keep her words slow, steady, confident. "The child I gave birth to isn't Carlos's."

Vanessa narrowed her eyes. "You are lying. He said the child was his."

"I lied. If he'd known... You know how he is. I was pregnant, he would have killed me if he'd known the truth. He's jealous, passionate. I feared for my child, and I was trying to rescue my sister."

Vanessa tilted her head to the side. "Whose child is it then?"

She took a deep breath, spoke the truth, the words she'd never allowed herself to say. "He is my husband's son."

FORTY-EIGHT

He is my husband's son.

The words stopped Eric.

He leaned back against the house beside the open window. Daniel was his son?

Could it be true?

That kindhearted, beautiful boy...his son?

Eric couldn't think about it now. He had to focus. To save Kelsey. He looked through the window again. He could see Kelsey just below him, but the other woman was out of sight.

Eric slipped off Surfer Dude's red parka and the skullcap he'd found in the pocket and left them on the ground. The ruse had worked. He'd replied to the text Surfer Dude had received on his phone, then slipped into the other man's coat. Mateo—the older man Kelsey had ridden in with—had come to help dispose of Eric's body. Eric recognized him from the photos Garrison had shown them that day.

Eric had caught him off guard. Mateo was now unconscious, lying in the woods beside Surfer Dude's corpse. The police were on their way, but Eric couldn't wait for them.

He had to deal with the woman, Vanessa.

Killing Surfer Dude had been bad enough.

But to kill a woman, a woman carrying a child?

He didn't want to, but he would if he had to.

He crept up the front porch steps, through the front door, and down the stairs.

Both women were out of sight. He could only see the raised gun, his gun, which she'd taken off him earlier. It was aimed at his wife.

Eric lifted the weapon he'd taken from Surfer Dude and crept closer. He needed a better vantage point.

"It must have been worse for you," Kelsey said. "I was your age when I was taken, maybe older. How old were you?"

The gun wavered. The hand was trembling. "I was ten."

"Oh, honey." How could Kelsey direct that much compassion toward a woman aiming to kill her? "I cannot imagine the kind of life you've had. I remember what they did to us. The locked closets that were terrible, but at least in the closet you were safe. Alone."

"*Da.*" A pause. "Yes. Safe when they left you alone, but also hungry and scared and desperate."

"Those conflicting feelings that came when you heard the keys jingling outside the door, hoping they would free you, but knowing it would be worse when they did. For me, I heard the keys and worried for my baby sister. I could hear her screams, but I couldn't protect her." Her voice cracked. "I could do nothing to save her."

Eric felt Kelsey's anguish to his very toes.

The woman said nothing. But the gun lowered just a little.

Eric stood just beyond the door. From here, he could see Otero's body. The man might've still been alive, but he wasn't moving. Eric could see the front edge of the bed, and in the other direction, the woman's raised arm.

"It wasn't a closet for me," Vanessa said. "We were held in

one big room, together. We had each other, and we held onto each other, because to not meant to freeze, *da*? When the men came, it meant a bed, blankets, food. We hoped to be chosen, because as terrible as it was with the men, at least we wouldn't starve."

"Nobody had the right to treat us that way, Vanessa. We are worth more than that."

The gun dipped a little lower. Maybe if Kelsey could get her to leave voluntarily...

"You never have to feel like that again," Kelsey said. "What that man did to you..." Kelsey paused, and Eric imagined Kelsey pointing at Otero. "He deserved what he got. You shot him to protect me. Nobody will blame you for that. You can be free. You never need to fear him or people like him again. I've been free for over nine years. I made my own way. And I did it with Carlos looking for me. You... you can just walk away. You never again have to be treated like chattel."

"I do not know this word, chattel," Vanessa said.

Eric willed Vanessa to lower the gun completely. He feared how she would respond when the police arrived.

"Chattel means property," Kelsey said. "Humans should never be treated like property."

There was a long pause, like the woman was considering it. Then, the gun was raised, aimed properly again. "*Da*. But you will tell the police."

"You've done nothing wrong."

"What do you know? You know nothing of what I've done."

"You saved my life. You were held against your will. You'll be protected."

There was a long pause. The woman seemed to be thinking, considering.

Lower the gun. Just lower it.

The gun was lifted, its aim true. "I can't risk it."

Eric launched himself into the room, stepped in front of Kelsey, and aimed the gun at Vanessa.

The woman gasped.

Behind him, Kelsey said, "Oh, my God. Eric!"

Vanessa aimed at him.

A standoff.

"Nobody has to get hurt." He held the gun in his right hand, lifted his left like a stop sign. "I don't want to shoot you. And I sure don't want you to shoot me."

The woman's eyes were wide, terrified.

"The door is open. The car is out there. If you know where the keys are, grab them and go."

"You will follow."

"I don't have a car," Eric said. "But the police are on the way. If you want to escape, you need to go now."

Her gaze flicked to Otero.

"Does he have the keys?" Eric asked.

"I think, yes."

"Kelsey," Eric said gently. "Can you search his pockets, see if you can find the keys?"

He felt her move, but he didn't take his eyes off Vanessa.

The keys jingled, and he held out his left hand. "Hand them to me."

Kelsey did, and he held them out toward Vanessa.

A few feet separated them. He took a step forward.

She took a step back.

"You're going to have to trust me, Vanessa. I don't want to hurt you. And I am sure as heck not sorry you killed Otero. But if you run into those woods, chances are good you'll freeze to death before you ever find a way out. The baby you're carrying deserves better than that."

"You will hurt me."

"I won't. I swear." He stepped forward again, the keys resting in the palm of his hand like an offering. "I'm not like him. I don't want to hurt you."

She moved toward him. He shifted toward her.

She didn't lower her gun. He didn't lower his.

Finally, she reached out and snatched the keys.

She bolted out the door and up the stairs.

Eric grabbed Kelsey away from the window, pulled her behind him, and stood in the center of the room. His gaze jumped from the door to the window, waiting.

A moment later, a car started. Vanessa drove away.

FORTY-NINE

WAS IT REALLY OVER?

Kelsey stood behind Eric, waited for him to relax as the sound of the car disappeared in the distance.

He didn't move.

She touched his back. "Eric?"

He spun, wrapped her in an embrace.

She collapsed against him and wept.

"It's okay." He held her tight. "You're safe now. You're safe."

"They told me you were dead."

"I know." He stroked her hair, kissed her head. "I know. I thought, when I saw you..."

His words trailed off.

But he didn't need to explain, because she knew. The fear, the worry, the despair. To lose the one you loved was the worst torture in the world.

She wanted to apologize for all she'd put him through. But she could never make up for what she'd done to him. She'd taken his child, stolen his chance to know the most beautiful expression of their love.

Had he heard her confession? Did he know? She was afraid

to ask, but she had no right to keep the information from him another minute.

She pulled away, looked up to meet his eyes. "About Daniel—"

"Is it true? Is he mine?"

Tears burned her throat until she couldn't speak. She nodded.

He squeezed his eyes shut, but tears escaped anyway. He lifted his face to the ceiling.

"I'm sorry," she said. "I didn't know how to keep you both safe. If I'd come home, he would have found me years ago. I was afraid to put you in danger. Afraid to put Daniel in danger. I didn't know what to do except to hide. Can you ever forgive me?"

He pulled her close again.

She pressed her face into his soft sweater, felt his warmth seep through to her skin.

Sirens echoed in the distance.

"I'm sorry. I'm sorry." She didn't know what else to say. All she knew was that she loved him, and she loved her son, and she'd done all she knew to do to protect them both.

And ultimately, she'd put them both in danger.

Eric stepped away. He held her at arms' length and met her eyes. His were red-rimmed and filled with tears. "I'm not sure how to feel right now except just...just happy you're safe."

The sirens were suddenly cut off. They must have turned off the main road. They'd be here any moment.

"I stole him from you," Kelsey said in the silence. "I stole ten years from you."

"Not you, Kels." He pulled her a few feet away, turned her to face the corpse on the floor. Eric pointed at Carlos's body. "He stole that time from us. None of this was your fault."

How could Eric be this forgiving? She turned again to face

him. "I was trying to... I was trying to make it right. If I hadn't sprained my ankle, if I hadn't gotten caught at that house..."

"What?" His eyes narrowed. "What would have happened?"

"I was going to call the police, tell them the child was yours. I never planned on Daniel ending up in foster care. My plan... I thought... I was trying to make sure he'd end up with you."

"You were going to...?" His words trailed off as he processed what she'd said.

"I knew you could keep him safe, safer than I could. I thought, if you two were safe, then whatever happened to me..."

He crushed her to his chest, kissed her hair. "Thank God." His voice was thick with emotion. "Thank God for that sprained ankle." He backed up, his watery eyes narrowed. "But then why didn't you tell me about him sooner?"

"At first, I thought I would run away, make that call when I was gone so nobody would know Daniel was my son." Pain flashed in his eyes, pierced her to the soul. "I didn't want to leave you. But I needed you both to be safe. By the time I'd decided to stay... I should have told you Friday night. I just... I still wasn't sure what I should do. And then you found out Daniel was mine, and you were so angry. I was afraid you'd hate me even more when you knew the truth."

"I could never hate you." He pulled her close again.

Slamming doors. Voices outside the open door.

Eric called, "We're down here." Then he turned back to Kelsey. "It's over. Now, we can be a family."

FIFTY

VANESSA BARELY KNEW how to drive. She did not know how to drive in the snow.

After she'd left the house, she'd turned away from town, away from the policemen who were on their way. What would they do to her if they caught her? She'd killed a man. Killed him in cold blood. And she wasn't sorry.

Kelsey was right. Carlos did not have the right to treat her as he had. She was not...what was the word? Chattel. She was not merchandise to be bought and sold. And she would never be again.

Assuming she could escape in this storm.

Ahead, a man staggered into the road. His hands were lifted, waving, like he needed help.

She'd already been going slowly. She took her foot off the gas and let the car drift to a stop.

The man...it was Mateo.

She grabbed the gun, rolled down the passenger window, pointed.

He raised his hands higher. "Are you all right?"

"Carlos is dead. What happened to you?"

"Eric. It was a trap. He jumped me, knocked me out. When I got up, I was disoriented. And then I heard the sirens and ran."

They stared at each other.

He swallowed. "We need to go, or we'll both get caught."

"Why should I take you?"

He ducked his head like he always had with Carlos. "I'll be happy to drive, and I have a phone with a map. I can get us out of here."

She flicked her gaze to the road in front of her. Snow, hills, forest. She'd never find her way out.

Mateo's hands were still lifted. "And I have access to all of his accounts."

She had access, too. But Mateo didn't need to know that until he got her out of there.

Mateo's gaze darted everywhere. Desperate. "You and your little one will need money."

Your little one...? "How do you know about that?"

"I've seen how tired you are. I've seen how hungry you've been lately. I know you went to the doctor last week. It was only a guess."

He'd observed a lot more than Carlos had. Carlos had hardly paid her any attention, but Mateo? He noticed everything.

"I don't want to hurt you, Vanessa." His hands dropped to his sides. "I never did. I only wanted to keep you as far from this... this ugliness as possible."

She didn't believe that. On the other hand, she had the gun. "You're driving."

He ducked his head again and lifted his phone. "You will navigate. We'll work together."

FIFTY-ONE

Eric yawned, rubbed his eyes, and stared at the log cabin in the woods. The place that had been the lair of an evil man and become a place of threats and murder. Snow was still falling, covering everything in a coating of beauty. How could that be, after all the horror?

"You all right?" Brady asked.

"Heckuva day."

Brady smiled, but it faded fast. "I'm kind of ticked that you did all this without me. Most exciting thing to happen in town since..."

"Not that long ago," Eric said. "Just since Sam and Garrison—"

"Good point."

Eric turned his attention to the front door, where two officers carried a gurney with Carlos Otero's body down the porch steps. The men slid the body into the back of the coroner's van.

"Maybe we've had enough excitement in Nutfield for a while," Eric said.

Brady nodded. "You ready to tell me what happened?"

Eric turned to his friend, his chief, and nodded. He

explained the unbelievable events of the last few hours, at least the ones he knew.

"So you escaped, but you came back?"

"What choice did I have, Brady? They'd gone to get her."

"I understand. Go on."

"I was outside trying to figure out how to rescue Kelsey when Surfer Dude found me."

Brady's eyebrows lifted. "He found you? I just assumed you'd seen him. How'd you get away?"

He remembered the moment. The gun pointed at his back as he walked deeper into the woods, away from his wife and toward his own death. His own death—that, he could have handled, but knowing Kelsey was in Carlos's hands... No, he'd had no choice but to fight.

There'd been nothing special about the tree he'd chosen. He'd just gotten up his nerve, and when he walked by it, he ducked behind. Then he bolted behind another tree, then a bunch of shrubs. He'd kept low.

The man had been smart enough to keep his distance. Eric hadn't been able to reach him, to attack. But the distance worked against him now. He followed, shouted threats.

Eric ran.

The man chased him. And he was fast. And armed. Eric had figured he'd start firing, but Surfer Dude didn't waste his bullets or pause to aim.

Pure adrenaline pushed Eric forward. But the man never fell far enough behind, especially with Eric ducking behind trees, trying to stay out of his line of fire.

Eric dashed behind a tree, circled it, and attacked Surfer Dude head-on.

The man was shocked. He aimed and fired, but the bullet zoomed past Eric's head.

Eric tackled him, managed to get his hand on the weapon, and fought for control.

Surfer Dude hadn't been the quickest pup in the litter, but he was strong. And he fought dirty.

Eric could fight dirty, too. And he had more to fight for.

He got the man on his back, got his gun arm extended, but the gun flew a few feet away. Eric came down on the man's arm hard. It snapped.

The man screamed.

Eric lunged for the gun, but the man grabbed his foot with the hand on his good arm. Tackled him.

Eric yanked on his broken arm.

The man screamed again.

Eric pushed him off and grabbed the gun.

Turned.

The man lunged.

The memory was too close. Eric relived every moment as he told Brady.

"So you fired," Brady said.

"I fired. He went down."

"Okay." Brady looked toward the forest where Eric had directed a few cops as soon as they'd arrived. "And the other man, the one you said was unconscious?"

"Mateo. I texted him from Surfer Dude's phone. He'd asked for an update on the search, and I told him I was dead. I asked Mateo to come help me dispose of the body. When Mateo got there, I jumped him, knocked him unconscious with the gun, and left him there."

"Good thinking," Brady said.

"Good training. Except I had nothing to tie him up with, and I was focused on getting to Kelsey." Eric looked at the closed ambulance door. His wife was inside being examined, though she'd insisted she was unhurt.

Alive and safe and free of all of this at last.

He still couldn't believe it.

"And the woman," Brady said.

He looked back at his boss. "A victim. One of Carlos's...girls."

"She could have killed you. According to your wife, she shot Carlos."

Eric shrugged, stared into the forest. "Yeah. She could have killed Kelsey. But she didn't." What kind of life could that woman have now? A slave for half her life, a killer. A child on the way.

He'd leave that in God's hands. He had his own family to worry about now.

"We found my truck, by the way."

Eric turned back to his friend. "Oh, good."

"It was fine."

"And Rae's okay?" Eric asked again. He'd been horrified to hear how Carlos had lured Kelsey out of the house, horrified that Rae had been in danger. Donny was a cop. He'd signed up for it. But Rae had just gone along to keep Kelsey company.

"She's fine," Brady said. "Safe and relieved you guys are, too. She's already talking about writing a series of stories on human trafficking."

"Rae, the crusading journalist."

Brady smiled the way he always did when he talked about his wife. "Yup. At least she's willing to lead her crusades from the safety of Nutfield, New Hampshire."

"Right." Eric took in the scene—the ambulance, the coroner's van, emergency vehicles, and all their lights reflecting off the fresh snow. "Because Nutfield has proved to be so safe."

Brady's laugh filled the snowy night.

FIFTY-TWO

IT WAS OVER.

It was really over.

Kelsey looked at the man beside her in the Jeep. Her husband.

He glanced at her but spoke into the phone pressed to his ear. "Okay, thanks for letting me know. How about the other two?"

He paused, nodded. "Keep me updated."

He ended the call, tossed his cell into the console, and grabbed her hand.

"You can put the calls on Bluetooth," she said. "It's not like I don't know what's going on."

"It's police business, ma'am."

She smiled. "But you're going to tell me."

He focused on the road as they crossed the rickety bridge. They'd gotten a ride into town and retrieved Eric's Jeep. Now they were headed back to his house. The snow was still falling, but the snowplows had been busy, and the roads were passable. From the little she could see in the glare of Eric's headlights, snow had accumulated on every telephone wire and tree branch they passed.

The sight was breathtaking.

She turned back to her husband, another breathtaking sight. "Well," she said.

"They found the other two guys, the chubby one and the one who got you from the lake house."

"Where were they?"

"Halfway to Dover, probably driving too fast trying to get away. Their truck ran off the road and got stuck in the snow-bank. The cop drove by when they were taking the snowmobiles off the trailer."

"Good," she said. "So now it's just Mateo and the girl."

"Are you hoping they get caught?"

"Mateo, definitely. The girl?" She knew what that girl had gone through. "She was a victim."

"She was going to kill you."

"She could have let him kill me. She protected me."

"Not exactly what happened, Kels." Though he'd missed most of the action, he'd gotten to the window just a moment before the woman had shot Carlos. In cold blood. "She was mad that he wanted to replace her."

"You don't understand... She's been a slave since she was ten years old."

"I know."

"I would have done it. I would have killed him, if I could have." She turned to him. "Why didn't the gun work?"

"I'm guessing it jammed when you hit him with it." He glanced at her, one eyebrow quirked. "I'm gonna to do my best to stay on your good side."

Her little laugh felt good.

"I feel bad for her," Kelsey said.

Eric's huffed breath told her he didn't agree. "She was going to kill you."

The memory of the moment sent a shudder down her spine. "She was afraid. And angry. And now she has to live with it."

"True." Was Eric thinking of Carlos or the man whose life he'd taken that night? She took his hand. "You had no choice. It was you or him."

"I know. It's still hard."

When he didn't say more, she turned to the window to watch the landscape go by.

"Nate and Marisa will head back first thing in the morning."

She snapped her gaze back to his. "Daniel?"

"He'll be..." He paused, swallowed. "He'll be home tomorrow."

The tears she'd kept at bay for hours burned her eyes. She didn't know what to say. She lifted her husband's hand and kissed his knuckles.

They were silent for the rest of the drive.

When Eric parked in his driveway, she reached for her door handle.

"Don't even think about it."

She sighed for his benefit, but she couldn't help the smile.

Eric jogged around the car and opened her door. They held hands as they walked to the house. He unlocked the door, and she stepped inside. The light was on, but it was quiet.

"Where's Magic?"

"She's at Rae and Brady's. We'll get her tomorrow." He closed the door and stopped beside her. "You hungry?"

She shook her head.

"Thirsty?"

"Just tired."

He took her hand again, and they walked upstairs. "I can give you a fresh toothbrush, since we don't have your stuff."

"Okay."

"And a T-shirt to sleep in, if you want."

"Okay."

They reached the upstairs hallway. She looked at the guest room door, then back at him. "I think we've spent enough time apart, don't you?"

He squeezed her hand and smiled. "I was hoping you'd say that."

FIFTY-THREE

Eric had planned to let her sleep. They'd both been dog-tired after the events of the day. He'd figured he'd endure the sweet torture one more night, just hold her and let her rest. But Kelsey had had other plans. She'd slipped into his bed...their bed...and reached for him.

After nearly a decade, they still fit together perfectly.

Kelsey had drifted off to sleep, and he'd watched her, mesmerized.

He'd awoken to the sight of the magical snow-covered world outside his bedroom window. The clouds had moved on, leaving the sky the brightest blue.

Daniel would be coming home soon.

Anticipation had him in the kitchen, puttering around. He made coffee, toasted a slice of bread, then another. He wiped the counters a couple of times. Swept the floors. Stared out the window.

Now, it was nearly ten a.m. Kelsey hadn't stirred, and he hated to do it, but he needed to wake her. He carried a cup of Irish Breakfast tea to his bedroom. Their bedroom. He set the tea on her nightstand and sat beside her. She was curled up, her long hair covering her beautiful face. He brushed it away, gently kissed her on the temple. "Kelsey, my love. Time to wake up."

She opened her eyes, blinked, and smiled. "Hey."

"I brought you some tea."

She glanced at the cup, then back at him. "Is everything OK?"

"It's perfect. Your son...our son..." He swallowed the emotion, smiled. "He'll be here soon."

Her eyes widened. "How soon?"

"'Bout thirty minutes."

"Oh, oh, oh!" She glanced at the clock. "Oh, my word. How did I sleep this late?"

He chuckled. "I guess I wore you out last night."

She blushed, laughed, and smacked him playfully. "I guess you did." She nudged his thigh resting on the bed. "I have to get up. I must be a mess! I don't want him to see me like this."

He didn't move, just leaned back and gave her a long look. Her hair was tousled. She wore nothing but a smile. "You look perfect."

She smacked him again. "For you, maybe. Probably not for Daniel."

"Good point." He stood, took her hand, and helped her out of the bed. Then he took another look at her and wanted to toss her right back in it.

"Don't even think about it," she said.

"Too late." He should have woken her an hour earlier. He nodded toward the master bath. "Go ahead. You'll find everything you need. I'll be downstairs."

And he should have left her then, but he couldn't resist watching her. She passed him on the way to the bathroom, and his gut tightened with longing. He forced breath into his lungs. It was going to be a long day.

Brady and Rae showed up a few minutes later with Magic,

who ran around the house like she'd been gone for a month, sniffing everything and kangaroo-hopping in her joy.

Rae and Brady laughed at the sight. "How is it we've never been here?" Rae asked.

Eric shrugged. "I guess I'm not very hospitable."

"Thought Southern country boys were big into hospitality," Brady said.

Eric just rolled his eyes.

Brady handed over Kelsey's backpack, and Eric ran upstairs and left it on his bed for her. At least she'd have something to change into.

He returned downstairs. "Y'all want some coffee?"

"If you don't mind," Brady said. "Thought I'd give you an update."

Eric grabbed some mugs. "What happened?"

"We found Mateo. Someone called in a tip that he was on a bus. Cops were there to meet him when he arrived in Boston."

Eric handed Rae a cup of coffee and poured one for Brady. They sat at the barstools, and he leaned against the counter.

His phone dinged. He read the text from Marisa. *Running late. Roads are worse than we thought. Another thirty minutes at least.*

Thirty minutes until he'd see his son again. His son. He still couldn't process it. What would Daniel think about all of this? He had no idea. But however Daniel took it at first, he knew it would work out, because they were meant to be a family. And the God who'd been with them the night before—been with them through all of this—would work that out, too.

"Everything OK?" Rae asked.

Eric looked up from his phone. "Yeah. They're running late." He focused on Brady. "Interesting. I wonder how Mateo got to Manchester."

"Good question," Brady said. "We'll ask him when he gets to

Nutfield. The FBI will be here to question him. With Carlos dead, I figure the guy has no reason not to tell them everything about Carlos's human trafficking ring. We should be able to dismantle the whole thing."

Eric thought about the stories Kelsey had told him, the girls still held against their will. He prayed they'd be freed and returned to their families. Prayed they'd find peace from the scars they'd carry with them forever.

"How about the girl?" Eric asked

"No sign of her yet."

Kelsey came downstairs. "Y'all talking about Vanessa?"

Eric stared while she walked through his living room and stopped at the end of his counter. Her hair was wet and combed out. She had on no makeup and wore jeans and a sweatshirt and was utterly gorgeous.

Brady held out a napkin to him. "Dude, you're drooling."

Kelsey blushed.

Eric smacked Brady's hand away and tried not to blush himself. Sheesh, he was like a lovesick teenager.

"What's going on?" Kelsey asked.

They caught her up on what had happened. Rae and Kelsey talked about the night before, which made his stomach hurt to hear. She'd run out of the cabin—and into the hands of her enemies—to protect his friends.

Could he love this woman more? He wrapped Kelsey into his arms and kissed the top of her head. "You were very brave."

She circled her arms around his middle but didn't say a word.

The doorbell rang.

She stepped back, eyes wide. "Is that him?"

"Probably not. Marisa just texted, and they're running late."

Her shoulders drooped. "Oh."

"He'll be here soon. It's the snow."

Brady opened Eric's door like he owned the place. Not that Eric minded. He sure didn't mind having a house full of friends —and his wife to boot.

"Come on in," Brady said. "They're in the kitchen."

A minute later, Sam and Garrison came around the corner. Sam immediately hugged Kelsey, then turned to him. "I just had to see you two." She looked between them, tears in her eyes. "Make sure you were okay."

"We're good." Eric wanted to say more, but emotion clogged his throat.

"We're perfect," Kelsey said.

Brady peered at the white box Garrison set on the countertop. "What'd you bring?"

"We stopped at McNeal's," Garrison said. "Figured you guys might want some breakfast."

Plates came out of the cabinets. More coffee was poured, and the six of them crowded around Eric's small counter and enjoyed the most delicious breakfast Eric had ever eaten.

And then the doorbell rang again.

Kelsey looked at Eric, eyes wide. He took her hand, and together they walked to the front door. He turned the knob, pulled it open, and stepped back.

"Mama!"

The boy barreled through the door and into his mother's arms. Kelsey fell to her knees and held him tight, tears streaming down her cheeks. Eric couldn't see Daniel's face, but the boy's shoulders shook with sobs.

Eric wiped his own eyes as emotions he barely had names for overflowed.

Nate, Marisa, and Ana stood on the front stoop. Marisa was crying, too. Everybody was crying. Eric had never seen so many tears in all his years. But he wasn't complaining. He'd take tears of joy any day.

Finally, Kelsey stood and urged Daniel away from the door.

Eric beckoned Nate and his family inside. He'd appreciated them for taking care of the stranger he'd found in his woods. Now, he knew they'd been taking care of his own son.

He hadn't told them that yet. Hadn't even told Brady. Until Daniel knew, the rest of the world could wait.

Daniel hadn't even noticed Eric. But he saw Magic and hugged the dog's neck. Kelsey came back to the doorway. She looked at Marisa, seemed unable to speak. Marisa just held out her arms, and the women held each other. Kelsey turned to Nate, hugged him, too. "Thank you."

"You're very welcome," Nate said.

Eric turned to see the rest of his friends in their coats and gloves. Brady said, "We'll leave you guys alone. I'll call you with updates, but I don't expect to see you at work this week."

Eric nodded. All the things he should say to this group of people who'd welcomed him, made him feel at home, and protected his wife. But he couldn't seem to put any of that into words right now.

Brady clasped him on the shoulder. "We'll talk soon."

He and Kelsey said good-bye to their friends. When the door closed behind them, he turned to find her right beside him. She took his hand, and together they walked into the living room, where Daniel was watching them, Magic curled up beside him

It was time for Daniel to meet his father.

FIFTY-FOUR

DANIEL WAS HIDING in the woods.

The trees were all green now, and the birds chirped something fierce overhead. Squirrels hopped from branch to branch, shaking the leaves above him.

Magic bolted from the yard and barked at the squirrels.

"Shh," Daniel whispered. Dumb thing was gonna give him away.

He still couldn't believe things had turned out like they had. One morning, he'd been scared he'd never see his mama again. The next morning, Mr. Nate and Miss Marisa had delivered him to her—at Mr. Eric's house.

And then, it got really good.

"Gotcha!"

Before Daniel could run, Daddy swooped him out of his hiding place.

"Man, you always find me!" Daniel said.

Daddy set him down on the dirt. "You complaining, little man?"

"Nah, 'cause you can't catch me!" He bolted toward the yard,

Magic on his heels. Daddy was right behind, laughing too hard to catch up.

"You two better quit," Mama called. "Company'll be here in a minute."

Daniel made it to the yard about a half a second before his daddy did.

"Hand me the platter." Daddy went right to the back steps and kissed Mama, who was standing in the doorway. "I'll start grilling before the guys get here and tell me I'm doing it wrong."

"I guarantee you're doing it wrong."

He and Daddy turned to see Chief Brady coming around the house, his hand around Miss Rae's back. She was practically waddling now, carrying that baby in her belly. He couldn't believe anybody could get that big. And how was that baby ever gonna get out?

He'd have to ask. Daddy knew everything.

Johnny was toddling toward the swing set and squealing. Daniel figured he'd spend half the day pushing the kid, but he didn't mind. Real men were nice to women and kids. That's what Daddy always said.

He grabbed Johnny, tickled him, and slid him into the toddler swing.

Mr. Garrison and Miss Sam came around the side of the house, too. Aiden was right behind them.

"Hey, sport!" Aiden joined Daniel at the swing set. "You got sucked into Johnny-duty."

"I don't mind." Daniel liked Aiden. He didn't get to see him much, because Aiden didn't live with his father. He lived in some apartment with a bunch of other guys. Daniel'd heard Mr. Garrison call it a sober living house. No idea what that meant, but Aiden seemed happy, so he figured it must be a cool place to live.

Miss Marisa and Ana rounded the corner, followed by Nate, who called, "Hey, Daniel."

He waved to him and Miss Marisa while Ana ran over and climbed onto the swing. "Push me, too!"

Caro followed them into the yard holding hands with her boyfriend, Finn, who was also Nate's brother. Daniel wasn't related to any of these folks, except Mama and Daddy, of course. His friend Caleb back in Oklahoma had a big family, and Daniel had always been jealous of all those people he got to hang out with all the time. Daniel had a big family, too. Some lived in Georgia, and some lived in Texas. He'd gone to visit Daddy's family a few months before, met all his cousins. They were nice, but he didn't know them very well.

Caleb's cousins had all lived right there in town, and some of them were jerks, and Caleb had to be nice to them anyway, 'cause they were blood.

But these kids here at Daniel's house, they were like cousins, and the grown-ups were like aunts and uncles. This was even better, because he and his folks got to choose these people. They went to church together, they had cookouts on holidays together, they celebrated birthdays together. And sometimes, they just got together for the fun of it, like today. Just because they were friends.

Across the yard, the women all squealed and looked at Miss Sam's hand.

Maybe she'd found a cool bug or something.

Daddy smacked Mr. Garrison on the back. "Better hurry before she changes her mind."

"What's going on?" Daniel asked.

Aiden stared at the grown ups, shook his head. "Dad and Sam are getting married."

Caro said, "Hey, that's great." She looked at Aiden, eyes narrowed. "Or, is it?"

Aiden smiled. "It's great. It's awesome."

"Push me higher!" Ana screamed.

Johnny joined in. "Higher, higher!"

Daniel pushed the boy as the sound of laughter and the scent of grilling burgers filled the air.

The lady at church said something about streets of gold in heaven. He wasn't sure about that. No, Daniel figured heaven would be just like this.

AN EXCERPT FROM NO MORE LIES

A HIDDEN TRUTH NOVELLA

Just when they thought they were safe.

Caro stretched. "I'm getting some punch. Anybody need anything?"

Sam stood to follow the girl.

Rae said, "Sam, you're the bride. What do you need?"

Marisa started to follow, but Sam waved her off. "I know where everything is. You girls relax. I just want to get some more water."

Marisa shrugged and focused on Rae. "She's the guest of honor. It's not like we can tell her no."

Rae blew on her fingernails. "She doesn't hear the word no." She spoke louder and turned toward the kitchen. "Because the bride's as stubborn as a mule."

From the kitchen, all they heard was a giggle.

"Sam's like a starry-eyed teenager," Kelsey said. "I don't think she's quit smiling since Garrison proposed."

Sam was so happy, and who could blame her? She was

about to marry the man of her dreams. Marisa knew just how she felt.

The front door banged open, and a man burst into the house, his handgun pointed straight at the women.

Somebody gasped. Nobody screamed. The room was strangely, surreally silent.

The man's gaze slid from one woman until the next until it landed on Rae. "*Finalement*. I found you."

Rae blinked twice, shook her head, and forced a smile. "Geoffrey. You look just like Julien."

This story is not available in stores. It's a gift just for you. Visit my website at RobinPatchen.com/NoMoreLies to download the ebook for free.

DEAR READER

Thank you for spending your limited money and time on *INNOCENT LIES*. If you liked it, would you leave me a review on Amazon, Goodreads, and your favorite retailer? And then tell a friend about my books. You'll be doing me a big favor.

The little boy, Daniel, looks and behaves a lot like my son Jacob. Except Jacob was a bit more ornery at nine years old. Of course, I never abandoned him in the woods in a strange state. In fact, when I wrote that first scene, I cried for that fictional little boy, imagining how my son would have felt.

Attitudes have changed about human trafficking in the last decade. Organizations have popped up nationwide to fight this growing problem. Pray about getting involved—with your time, your talents, and your financial resources. The enslaved girls and boys need our help.

If you haven't yet, check out the first book in this series, *CONVENIENT LIES* (sign up for my newsletter, and I'll send you a free copy). It tells the story of Rae, Brady, and their adorable little Johnny. Then move on to *TWISTED LIES*, which tells Nate and Marisa's story, and *GENEROUS LIES*, which tells Sam and Garrison's story.

Right now, I'm offering a free novella, No More Lies, a Hidden Truth novella, to my newsletter list. If you'd like to download that or get information about new releases, you can sign up for my newsletter, where I announce contests and giveaways and sometimes, offer free books. I promise not to sell or share your email with anybody, and I promise not to send you stuff every day.

If you're not interested in getting my emails but you would like to know about my latest releases, follow me on Amazon or BookBub. They'll alert you when I have a new book coming out.

I'd love to hear from you. Keep in touch on Facebook to hear what's going on with me and to share what's going on with you. And check out RobinPatchen.com to find out about my other books and follow my progress as I write.

Thank you for reading! Nothing makes this author happier than to share her stories.

In Christ,

Robin Patchen

ALSO BY ROBIN PATCHEN

Chasing Amanda

Finding Amanda

A Package Deal (part of the Matched Online anthology)

Hidden Truth series

Convenient Lies

Twisted Lies

Generous Lies

Innocent Lies

Copyright © 2018 by Robin Patchen

All rights reserved.

No part of this book may be reproduced in any form or by any electronic or mechanical means, including information storage and retrieval systems, without written permission from the author, except for the use of brief quotations in a book review.

Scripture references are from the King James Version of the Bible.